Annja felt her eyes widen as she listened to the woman's warning

"Be always alert to the difference between righteousness and self-righteousness."

Annja smiled tentatively. "I've been told that while saving the world is my job description, I need to learn to prioritize."

"That's true, but only part of the truth," Tsipporah stated. She leaned forward and caught Annja's hands in hers. "Listen to me on this. Hear me. Demons do their deadliest work through our virtues. And that is why Mark Peter Stern is a very dangerous man, my dear. Not because he's a bad man, but because he's so good—and so invincibly convinced of it. Such a man is capable of anything. For the good, of course."

Annja felt a sinking sensation in her stomach. "What you're really warning me against," she said quietly, "is myself."

Titles in this series:

Destiny
Solomon's Jar

ROGUE Angel

Alex Archer

SOLOMON'S JAR

A GOLD EAGLE BOOK FROM
W✪RLDWIDE®

TORONTO • NEW YORK • LONDON
AMSTERDAM • PARIS • SYDNEY • HAMBURG
STOCKHOLM • ATHENS • TOKYO • MILAN
MADRID • WARSAW • BUDAPEST • AUCKLAND

For Shelley Thomson for kind consultation.

First edition September 2006

ISBN-13: 978-0-373-62120-0
ISBN-10:   0-373-62120-5

SOLOMON'S JAR

Special thanks and acknowledgment to
Victor Milan for his contribution to this work.

The
LEGEND

...THE ENGLISH COMMANDER TOOK
JOAN'S SWORD AND RAISED IT HIGH.

The broadsword, plain and unadorned,
gleamed in the firelight. He put the tip against
the ground and his foot at the center of the blade.
The broadsword shattered, fragments falling
into the mud. The crowd surged forward,
peasant and soldier, and snatched the shards
from the trampled mud. The commander tossed
the hilt deep into the crowd.
Smoke almost obscured Joan, but she continued
praying till the end, until finally the flames climbed
her body and she sagged against the restraints.

Joan of Arc died that fateful day in France,
but her legend and sword are reborn....

1

On long tanned legs Annja Creed ran through the hard-wood forest. Rays from the sun hanging precariously above the great mountains slanted like pale gold lances at random between the boles. They caressed her sweaty face like velvet gloves as she ran through them.

Despite sweating in the heat, she breathed normally, dodging thicker stands of brush, crashing through the thinner ones. Late-season insects trilled around her and in sporadic spectral clouds tried to fly up her nose and into her mouth. The birds chattered and called to one another in the trees. The woods smelled of green growth and mostly dried decayed vegetation, not at all the way she imagined a true rain forest might smell, lower down in the Amazon basin proper. Up in the watershed of the

Amazon's tributary the Río Marañón, in eastern Peru, the early autumn was drier and cooler, the growth far less dense.

Her heart raced as much as any person's might have after running at high speed for over two miles, up and down steep ridges. It had little to do with the exertion, though.

She ran for her life.

DAYLIGHT CAME LATE and evening early to the small Peruvian village of Chiriqui. The sun had rolled well past the zenith. Though shadows weren't yet very long, it wasn't far from vanishing behind the tree-furred ridge to the west when the blast of a diesel engine ripped the calm air.

Beyond the ridge loomed the mighty peaks of the Andes themselves, looking close enough to topple and crush the little village into its dusty hillside, their blue tinge hinting how far away they really stood. The hills were mostly covered in patchy grass, dry as the hot Southern Hemisphere summer ended. Stands of hardwood forest rose on some of the heights, interspersed with tough scrub.

Chickens flapped their wings in annoyance and fled squawking as a big blue Dodge Ram 2500, battered and sun faded, rolled into the small plaza in the midst of the collection of a couple of dozen huts. A tethered spider

monkey shrilled obscenities and ran up a pole supporting a thatch awning as the vehicle clipped the edge of
a kiosk and spilled colorful fruits bouncing across the
tan hard-packed dirt. The owner remonstrated loudly as
the vehicle stopped in a cloud of exhaust and dust.

Men began bailing out of the truck's extended bed.
Men dressed in green-and-dust-colored camouflage who
carried unmistakable broken-nosed Kalashnikovs and
grenades clipped on their vests like green mango clusters.

They were gringos, unmistakably, who towered over
the small brown villagers. The vehicle sported a powerful Soviet-era PKS machine gun mounted on a roll bar
right behind the cab.

The people of Chiriqui knew better than to call attention to themselves when such visitors came to town.

"Gather 'round," the apparent leader commanded in
clear but *norteamericano*-accented Spanish. He wore a
short-sleeved camo blouse, a similarly patterned base-
ball cap atop his crewcut red head, and carried a black
semiautomatic pistol in an open-top holster tied down
his right thigh like a movie gunslinger.

Unlike people familiar with such things only from
watching television from the comforts of their dens, the
villagers knew well the difference between semi and
full automatic.

The villagers stared, more as if their worst night-
mares were coming true than from any lack of compre-

hension. Because, of course, that was exactly what was happening. The gringo soldiers with their hard faces grinning mean white grins spread out in pairs with rifles at the ready to enforce their leader's command.

IN THE RELATIVE COOL of her hut Annja Creed sat straining to read by the light coming in by dribs and drabs through gaps in the hardwood-plank wall. A bare bulb hung by a frayed cord perilously low over her head at the table on which she had spread the ancient book. It was unlit. The people of the village of Chiriqui had already done more than enough for her; she had firmly but with effusive thanks refused their offers to burn up more of their scarce, precious fuel to run the generator to provide artificial illumination. She could smell hot earth outside, the thatch, the sun-dried and splitting planks of the walls. And most of all the familiar musty odor of an ancient volume.

"...herb has most salubrious effects," she read, "particularly with regards to ye falling sickness, the effects of which fit it serves to ameliorate most expeditiously..."

That was how she would have translated it into English, anyway. The Jesuit Brother João da Concepção's seventeenth-century Portuguese gave her no problems; modern Portuguese had changed less in the intervening centuries than most languages. Even other Romance languages, which if translated literally tended to sound archaic and formal even at street level to English ears.

She knew her Romance languages. She knew the majors, Spanish, French, Italian and, of course, Portuguese. Plus she was rudely conversant in some of the minors, such as Catalan. Of the whole group she knew little of Romanian. She read and wrote Latin superbly; it had formed the core of her language study since she had learned it in the Catholic orphanage in New Orleans.

What gave her fits was Brother João's crabgrass handwriting. The ink had faded to a sort of faint burgundy hue on the water-warped pages of the ancient journal. In some places water spots or mold obscured the text entirely. In others the words faded entirely from visibility as of their own accord.

"This would probably be easier if I went outside in the direct sun," she said aloud. She had a tendency to talk to herself. It was one of several reasons—that she knew of—that the villagers called her *la gringa loca*, the Crazy White Lady. That she spoke Spanish and was willing to share her medical supplies or give impromptu English lessons to the local kids—or their elders— helped keep the inflection friendly when they said it, so all was well.

As for going out in the sun, she'd had about enough of it in the weeks she'd spent tramping the hills looking for the tome. It wasn't as hot there as it was down lower in the Selva, the great jungle of the Upper Amazon. But to compensate, the high-altitude sun was more intense, with less air to block the UV rays that punished her fair skin. And it was hot enough. Even in the shade of the hut she had to keep constantly on her guard to prevent sweat from running the line of her chestnut hair, tied back with a russet bandanna, and dripping off her nose onto the priceless pages.

"Anyway," she said, aloud again, "I'm just being impatient. I could just wait till I'm back at the hotel."

Having searched a month to find the book, she was eager to confirm its contents. However, she was still a day or two from any kind of reliably illuminated, not to mention air-conditioned, surroundings; she was meeting a farmer from up in the hills about sunset. He had agreed to give her a lift into the nearest town of consequence in his venerable pickup.

Annja's impatience was rewarded. It seemed that the hints she'd been pursuing had been correct. The long-dead friar had cataloged a wealth of herbs of the Upper Amazon and watershed, along with a remarkable accounting of their observable effects on various maladies so systematic that it prefigured the scientific method. She wondered if an early stint in China, with its extensive *materia medica* assembled over millennia, and its own tradition of systematic observation and trial and error, had influenced him.

Excitement thrilled through her veins as she carefully paged through the book, reading passages, looking at the pictures Brother João had drawn in almost obsessive detail. She knew nothing about botany, and even the mid-seventeenth century was straying beyond her actual scope of formal training, which was medieval and Renaissance Europe. But since she had taken on this new life, she'd found herself constantly expanding her horizons.

She was barely conscious of the outlaw-motorcycle rumble and snarl of the diesel truck pulling into the plaza. None of the villagers possessed a motor vehicle, but a few, mostly pickup trucks, wandered through Chiriqui almost every day.

"Senorita," a childish voice said, low and urgent behind her. She turned.

"What is it, Luis?" she asked the tiny figure who stood in the door, a tattered T-shirt hanging halfway down his bare brown legs. His eyes were great anthracite disks of concern beneath his thatch of untamed black hair.

"You must go," he said.

He looks so innocent, she thought, not overly concerned despite his apparent urgency. She knew how kids tended to dramatize.

"Why?" she asked.

His eyes grew bigger and his voice more grave. "Bad men come," he said.

From outside came the sudden, unmistakable clatter of automatic gunfire.

THE VILLAGERS CROWDED into the square and stared as one at the man who lay writhing on the slope across the stream, guts and pelvis pulped by a burst of steel-jacketed rifle bullets. The stink of burned propellant and lubricant stung the air.

"My, my," the intruders' leader said, wagging his head reprovingly. "You people are slow learners. Don't you know by now that when we come around you don't run, because you'll only die tired?"

For a moment there was no sound but the pinging of the truck as it cooled and the groans of the mortally injured man. "Don Pepe, front and center," the redheaded man in the ball cap commanded.

A burly black trooper rudely thrust an old man with a full head of white hair forward. Don Pepe was skinny and stooped, in his formerly purple-and-white-striped shirt, faded by sun and repeated washings to dusty gray, his stained khaki shorts and rubber sandals. Big dark splotches of sweat spread outward beneath the pits of his scrawny arms.

Don Pepe staggered a few steps. Then he straightened and approached the intruder with dignity.

"Why are you doing this?" he asked. "We paid our taxes. Both to the government and to Don Francisco."

"Don Francisco is the main *traficante* in the region," Luis said. He stood beside Annja as she crouched in the shade of an awning behind a blue plastic barrel used to collect rainwater. "These are his enforcers."

Annja made gestures to silence Luis. The boy seemed unfazed by the throes of the man who'd been shot. Annja knew him as a villager who'd lived here his whole life; he was probably at least a semidistant cousin of the boy. *This isn't the first man he's seen shot*, she realized with a jolt. Maybe not even by these men.

She felt a flare of righteous fury. She suppressed a strong desire to rush in. The mercenaries were too many and too well-armed, and she knew well what her failure would cost her friends.

The tall man, his skin sunburned an uncomfortable pink, wagged a finger. "Ah, but that's not why we're here. You're harboring a spy—a journalist."

Don Pepe raised his head and stared the man in the eye. He did not speak.

"Not going to deny it, huh?"

"Tell him, Pepe!" a middle-aged woman screamed. "She's no journalist! She's an archaeologist."

A Latino soldier drove the steel-shod butt of his Kalashnikov into her belly. She staggered back and sat down hard in the dust, clutching herself and gasping for breath.

Annja went tense.

"Anybody else care to speak out of turn?" The redhaired man surveyed the crowd. The villagers shifted their weight and glared sullenly. But they said no more.

"Didn't think so. Now, Don Pepe, here. He's a man of the world. Aren't you, Pep? He knows all this archaeology noise is just a bunch of bullshit. Right?"

The old man shook his head. "It is true. She is no journalist."

The mercenary shrugged. "Doesn't matter. A spy's a spy. You know better than to shelter outsiders. So do yourselves a favor and give her up."

Don Pepe shook his white head. "No."

The other cocked his head to one side. "What's that, old man? I don't think I heard you correctly."

"I will not. We will not. She has done you no harm. She has come among us as a friend. She—"

The vicious crack of a 9 mm handgun cut him off. Don Pepe's head whipped back, but not before red blood and dirty white clots flew out the back of his ruptured skull. He fell.

The red-haired man tipped the barrel of his Beretta service side arm skyward. A tiny wisp of bluish smoke curled from the blue-black muzzle.

"So much for old Don Pepe. Anybody else care to step forward as a spokesperson—preferably somebody smart enough not to contradict me?" The echoes of the gunshot reverberated on and on, from the far hillside where the first man still lay dying in agony, from all around.

Behind the rain barrel, Annja backed away. "Where do you go?" Luis asked in alarm.

"To give them what they want," she said grimly.

"You can't! They'll kill—"

But she was gone.

LOOKS TO ME as if there's gonna be a village massacre here, boys," the redhead told his men in English. "Those atrocity-loving leftist guerrillas. So sad."

"Even if they give the bitch up, boss?" a hatchet-faced trooper asked.

"Do you even need to ask? Examples need to be made here. Remember, we got to be back in time to secure the airfield by 1900. Got an extraspecial shipment headed out tonight on the Freedom Bird."

Then, returning to Spanish, the leader announced, "All right, people. Listen up, here. You have ten seconds to give up the spy. Or else the nice lady sitting there gets it in the belly. Understand?"

THE TROOPER WHO STOOD in the Ram's bed behind the mounted machine gun had blond hair shorn to a silver plush and ears that stuck straight out from the sides of his head beneath his crumpled camouflage boonie hat like open car doors. He couldn't possibly have been as young as he looked. Not and be old enough to have had the military training and the seasoning these men showed. Annja was still new to the game, still finding out—as she was to her horror today—just what it entailed. But she knew it took time to become a killer.

Her rage, her sense of mission, quieted the roiling in her gut. And the adrenaline song of fear in the pulse in her ears.

The boyish gunner had his attention focused wholly on the villagers.

So stealthily did Annja creep up in the dust behind the truck that he would have had a hard time hearing her even if he had been listening. But there was no way he would miss the shift in balance as she climbed up in the bed, no matter how carefully she moved.

So instead she simply crouched, then leaped like a panther, over the tailgate and in behind him. The corrugated soles of her ankle-high hiking boots still made little noise as she landed. The truck's rocking alerted him. He started to turn.

She caught him around the throat with one arm, his head with the other. He reached for the combat knife hanging from his belt. But the sleeper hold she put on him cut off blood flow to the brain and put him out almost instantly.

Annja held him for an endless half minute, just to be sure. Heart pounding, she feared one of the intruders would look around, or one of the villagers would spy her and give her away, deliberately or through simple reflex surprise. But the mercs and their captives had eyes only for one another, as the shadows of evening stole across the village.

Slowly she lowered the unconscious man to the bed.

The machine gun was fed by a belt from a box attached to its receiver. Annja stood up straight behind the weapon, grabbed the pistol grip, swung the butt around to her shoulder and boldly announced her presence.

"Here I am!"

"WHAT HAVE we here?" the leader of the intruders asked sarcastically, putting his hands on his hips. "You here to do the right thing and give yourself up, save these good people a lot of suffering and dying?"

Annja swiveled the barrel so it aimed straight at the freckled bridge of his nose. "Not a chance," she said. "Throw down your weapons and walk out of here, and it's you who'll be saving yourselves."

"I think not," he said. "I think I'll just start executing one of these little people every count of ten, say, until you decide to surrender." He raised his Beretta and aimed it at the head of a man who stood nearby.

Annja pulled the trigger.

Nothing happened.

Safety, she thought, with a gut slam of shock. She knew pistols and rifles fairly well. But next to nothing about machine guns.

She spun away as a trooper behind the leader

whipped his AKM to his camo-clad shoulder and triggered a burst. The bullets cracked over her head. She dived over the tailgate as a grenade thumped in the bed.

The explosion drove the big Ram down hard on its suspension. As it flexed back up, the fuel tank went up with a loud whomp, sending an orange ball rolling into the sky, trailing a pillar of black smoke.

A figure reared up from the truck bed, all orange, waving wings of flame. Demonic screams issued from it.

"Billy!" shouted the trooper who'd thrown the grenade.

Frowning slightly, the leader raised a straight right arm, sighted down his handgun and squeezed off a single shot. The flame-shrouded head snapped back. The shrieking ceased. The figure settled back into its pyre.

"Spread out. Find the bitch," the redhead said coldly.

"What about these people?" asked the tall black trooper.

"The hell with them. I want her dead!"

THROUGH GATHERING EVENING, Annja ran.

Not so much for fear of her own life. To her own surprise she felt little concern for that. Rather, for her mission. The thought that her mentor might have labored half a millennium to find the sword, and to find a new champion, only to have his labors made futile by such men as these made her blood boil.

Her footfalls thudded in her ears, above the buzz of swarming insects and the swishing and piping cries of the birds that swooped between the trees in pursuit of them. She had no idea how many men hunted her through the hills. They seemed to operate in teams. Three times they had spotted her and opened fire with their false-flag Russian weapons. Fortunately her reflexes—or distance—had prevented her being tagged.

That and her knowledge of the terrain. She had spent the better part of a month tramping these hills, looking for buried treasure: the cache where Brother João had hidden his voluminous journal from the planters and the troops who hunted him to steal his secrets. She had found it not two days before beneath a cairn of stones half-buried in a hillside, using clues left by the friar after he made his escape to Goa, India.

She knew Chiriqui's intimate environs far better than her pursuers were likely to. And they didn't seem inclined to slow themselves down by dragging along a local to serve as a guide. Besides, she could see they were manifestly arrogant to the point of blindness, accustomed to believing themselves so superior to anyone else that they'd never think of dragooning help.

She paused in the shelter of an erosion-cut bank, trying to control her breathing with a yoga exercise. The sun had gone from sight, although the sky remained light, stained with peach toward the west. The hollows and low places were filled with a sort of lavender gloom that was almost tangible.

A deep ravine gashed the land just over the next ridge. Using such cover as scrub and rock outcrops offered, she climbed the slope, senses stretched tight as a guyline. She paused in the deep shade of the broad-leaved trees at the crest. A hill across from her still hid the sun. Below her the ravine was a slash in gloom crossed by a pale blur—a rope-and-plank footbridge common in the erstwhile Incan empire.

She drew a deep breath. Almost out of here, she thought. She walked down the slope.

A nasty crack sounded beside her left ear. She felt something sting her cheek. By uncomprehending reflex she turned to look back up the hill.

A yellow star appeared in the brush at the foot of the trees, not far from the point where she'd left them. It flickered. She heard more cracking sounds.

She turned and raced for the bridge. The short, steep slope gave no cover. The bridge gave less. But the only chance she saw was to make it across and lose herself in the night and far hills. Her pursuers might have night-vision equipment but she'd just have to chance it.

She zigged right and zagged left, running flat out. The grayed, splintery-dry planks were bouncing beneath her feet with a peculiar muted timbre as she darted out onto the bridge.

It had not occurred to her to wonder why these hardmen, who seemed to know their business had gotten a clear, close shot at her back—and missed.

But then a pair of men rose up from the bushes clustered on the far side and walked onto the bridge to meet her. Men in mottled brown-and-khaki camouflage. Each carried a rifle with an unmistakable Kalashnikov banana magazine slanted in patrol position before his waist.

Feeling sick, she grabbed the wooly guide rope with one hand and turned. Another pair of men strolled almost casually down the hill behind her, likewise holding their weapons muzzle down. Their crumpled boonie hats were pulled low, making their faces shadows.

"Might as well give it up here, miss," a man called from the bridge's far end in a New England accent. "Only way out is down. And it's a long step."

"What do you think you're doing?" a nervous voice asked from behind her.

"What do you think?" the New Englander called out with a nasty sneer. "The first white woman we see in weeks, and she's a babe with legs up to *here*. You want to let that go to waste?"

"Plenty of time to waste her later," the big merc added. "Sorry, lady. Nothing personal. Life's just a bitch sometimes, ain't she?"

Annja let her head hang forward with a loose strand of hair hanging before it like a banner from a defeated army. Her shoulders slumped. She sat back against the guide rope heedless of the way it swayed over emptiness.

"That's more like it, honey," the trooper said. "You've got a good sense of the inevitable."

He was close now. Holding his weapon warily in a gloved right hand, he reached for her with his left.

Her face hidden, she frowned in sudden concentration. She reached with her will into a pocket in space, into a different place, always near her but always infinitely far away.

Suddenly a sword was in her hand, a huge broadsword with an unadorned cross hilt. She swept it whistling before her.

The hand reaching for her pulled back. Blood shot out from the arm, more black than red in the twilight. It sprayed hot across her face.

The mercenary staggered back, shouting more in astonishment than pain. That would come later.

But he had no later.

Annja dropped to the planks, catching herself with her hands, her right still wrapped around the sword's hilt, ignoring the agonizing pressure on her knuckles. She could see the stream meandering more than three hundred feet below, visible between wide-spaced planks as a pale ribbon through shadow.

Gunfire rapped from the bridge's far end. The flash and vertical flare-spike from the muzzle brake lit the canyon like a spastic bonfire. The bridge bounced and boomed as men raced toward Annja.

She jumped to her feet. She looked at them for a heartbeat. The man in front faltered, allowing the one behind to blunder into him.

"A *sword?*" he asked, momentarily stunned.

His eyes read Annja's intent. He flung out a desperate hand. "No!"

The sword went up and down. Left and right. The guide ropes parted with ax-blow sounds, turning into muted twangs. Turning her upper torso sideways, Annja seized the hilt with both hands and slashed through both foot ropes with a single stroke.

The bridge parted. Its sundered halves fell into the ravine. So did all the men on it.

The merc in back on the west side might have managed to get a grip and conceivably climb to safety. But his partner panicked, turned and ran right into him as the boards fell away beneath his boots. The two fell in a screaming tangle of arms and legs and weapons.

Annja let the sword slip back into its space as she fell. She felt no fear, only thrill-ride exaltation. She had escaped. That was victory. Her right hand shot out and caught a plank. Splinters gouged her palm. She gripped with all her strength regardless.

The slam into the sheer bank broke her nose. But it

did not break her grip. She hung on while bells and fire-crackers went off behind her eyes.

Then, blood streaming over her lips and dripping from her chin, she began straining her eyes to pick out the best climb down to the safety of the streambed.

2

"Say, lady," a voice called through the rain. "Hey, pretty lady. Hey, there."

Annja paused. She was walking home from the little Puerto Rican bodega around the corner from her loft with a small bag of groceries. She wore a light jacket, a calf-length skirt in dark maroon and soft fawn-colored boots that came up almost to meet it, leaving just two fingers of skin bare. A long baguette of French bread stuck up from the brown paper sack, shielded from the patchy downpour by a black umbrella. She liked to get small amounts of groceries during the brief intervals she spent at home, to force herself to get out at least once a day. Otherwise she'd spend all her time cooped up with her artifacts and monographs, turning into a mushroom. Or so she feared.

She looked into the doorway framed by grimy gray stones from which the words had issued. The speaker looked anything but threatening.

Don't make too many assumptions, she warned herself.

A small man lay sprawled in the arched doorway with his legs before him like a rag doll's. He looked emaciated within a shabby overcoat, knit cap and a pair of ragged pants, smeared with patches of grime, that came up well above grubby, sockless ankles and well-holed deck shoes. All might have possessed color at one point. Now all, including his grime-coated skin and stubble beard, had gone to shades of gray

The closest thing to color he displayed was the yellowish brown of his teeth and the slightly lighter but similar shade of the whites of his mouse-colored eyes.

In a quick assessment, she reckoned she could take him. It was part of the calculus of life as a New Yorker. And even more of the life she had taken on.

"What can I do for you?" she asked.

"Need some change," the man muttered in a voice as colorless as his skin. "Got some change for me?"

"You're right," she said. "You do need change. But I can't give it to you."

The man cawed bitter laughter. "Shit, lady. I need a drink not a sermon." Spittle sprayed from his gray lips, fortunately falling well short of her.

"At least you're honest," she said. "I do want to help you."

The impatient traffic hissed through the rain behind her. "But if I give you money, am I helping to keep you here? Is that really kindness or compassion?"

He had cocked his head and was staring at her fixedly. She realized he was contemplating trying to threaten her or outright rush her: a nice middle-class twentysomething white girl with more education than sense.

I've got victim written all over me, she realized.

She had already stopped talking. Instead she turned and lowered her head to bear squarely on his face and hardened her eyes. She would not summon the sword unless he displayed a weapon. And maybe not then; even before her transformation she had known how to take care of herself and been surprisingly good at it.

But if he actually tried to coerce her she would react with force as ungentle as it was unarmed. She had always hated victimizers. Now as her life's destiny had begun to unfold she found herself growing almost pathological in her hatred for them.

Something in her manner melted his resolve, which had never so much as gelled. The readying tension flowed out of him. His head dropped and he muttered into a filthy scrap of muffler wrapped around his neck.

Annja realized he wasn't a victimizer, not really. Just another opportunist who had realized on the teetering brink of too late that the opportunity he thought he saw was the eager smile of the abyss. He was weak rather than committed to anything. Even evil.

In a way she found that sadder.

She struggled with her groceries, her hand fumbling in her pocket, then handed him the first bill she found. "In the end, I find myself fresh out of answers," she said. "So I guess I'll take the easiest course." And wonder who's really the weak opportunist, she thought.

He snatched it away with crack-nailed fingers swathed in what might have been the shredded gray remnants of woolen gloves, or bandages. The movement sent a wave of his smell rushing over her like a blast of tear gas. Eyes watering, trying not to choke audibly, she turned and walked away.

"Hey, what's this?" he screamed after her. "A lousy buck? Tight-ass bitch! Don't care about anybody except yourself."

HER LOFT HAD a window seat. She liked to half recline on it as she studied or read her e-mails. It gave her a cozy feeling, surrounded by her shelves of books and the artifacts, the potsherds, bone fragments and chipped flint blades, that seemed to accrue on every horizontal surface. Today the clouds masked the time of day and veils of rain periodically hid and revealed the distant harbor. Rain ran long quavering fingers down the sooted, fly-spotted glass.

She sipped coffee well dosed with cream and sugar. The way she'd loved it as a child at the Café du Monde. Which, of course, wasn't there anymore.

As active as she had always been, she had never had much need to watch her diet. And now that her activity levels had increased, her main problem was keeping *up* weight.

She frowned slightly as she finished downloading headers from her favorite newsgroups, alt.archaeology and its companion, alt.archaeology.esoterica. There enthusiasts, nuts, grad students and professional archaeologists, mostly anonymous, would splash happily together in the marshy outskirts of her chosen discipline.

She quickly surveyed the headers in alt.archaeology. To her annoyance a number were obvious spam. While she was in South America she hadn't been able to keep the filters up to date. She resented having to spend the time and effort to do so, but it was like weeding a garden: either you did it regularly or gave in altogether to the forces of entropy.

Part of living in the modern world, she told herself, as she added a few new exclusions. It helps to keep me appreciative of the Middle Ages. Not that she was naive or romantic enough to wish away little things such as air-conditioning and antibiotics, she thought with a laugh.

The spam du jour was real estate. Before that it had been small-cap stocks, and before that, the heyday of male enhancements. She had filtered all of them out. She manually deleted all the new spam she could identify as such, and also the vast majority of legitimate headers that failed to spark her interest.

The usual controversies were being trotted out, she saw: the coastal-migration theory of the human settlement of South America. The authenticity of the Vinland map. Nothing of terrific appeal to her. As usual the flames raged hot and furious.

She switched to alt.archaeology.esoterica. Though it dealt with the far fringes and beyond of archaeology—or what was accepted—the discourse was actually less vitriolic than the regular archaeology group. If only just.

There was the usual debate about pre-Columbian visits to the Americas from Europe and Asia, and a thread about the building of the Great Pyramid that people kept poking at sporadically like a hollow tooth. She opened a message at random:

> I give you your Caral pyramids, built even before the Egyptian pyramids. But if there was contact between Peru and Egypt, why didn't the Caral people learn about ceramics, as well as megalithic civil engineering?

The next header down was something new and different. It caught her eye. "Solomon's Jar?"

She downloaded the thread and read.

I have come into possession of an antique brass jar, which I believe may be the jar in which King Solomon is said to have bound the demons after he used them to build his temple in Jerusalem. Can you tell me, please, how to authenticate? Also how much it might be worth?

The poster was shown as trees@schatwinkel.com.nl. Annja knew the suffix .nl meant the address was in the Netherlands.

The last question could have been asking what the worth of such a discovery would be to science. Somehow she doubted that was how it was meant. The responses—many—were the usual flames and derision such naive questions from obvious nonprofessionals engendered. About half of them were from the reflex skeptics who derided the idiocy of believing in demons, in a jar in which they were bound, and for that matter that any such person as King Solomon ever existed. The others were from believers of one degree or another abusing the debunkers.

"Hmm," she said aloud. Annja closed the cover of her notebook computer.

THE SWORD IN HER HAND, she flowed through the ritual motions.

Though it was a gray day outside, she left the overhead light off. She enjoyed a companionable semidarkness; unless she was reading or examining an artifact, she didn't care much for intense light.

Annja had changed into a gray sports bra and a matching pair of terry trunks that clung to her long, lithe form. Her feet were bare on the hardwood floor of her exercise space, which was separated from her living area by a fifteenth-century north German carved altar screen representing the Annunciation. Her steps echoed. Though it cost her dearly, she lived in that most enduring of Hollywood clichés, a New York loft apartment.

Still, it was worthwhile. She needed room both to keep her specimens and books, and to *move*. To work out.

It wasn't as if she was dependent on grants anymore. She had some royalties from her book. Although it was temporarily in abeyance she also had money in the bank from her work on the cable-television series, *Chasing History's Monsters*, from which she was taking an indefinite sabbatical as she sorted out the details of her new life. When she'd gotten back from South America she had found her answering machine jammed with pleas from the show's boy-wonder producer, Doug Morrell, to come back immediately if not sooner....

The sword made soft swishing sounds in the air. She

turned, holding it blade up in her right hand. She had the first two fingers of her left hand extended and pressed against the inside of her right forearm.

The ritual had nothing to do with the sword as such, nor her mission—so far as she understood either. So far as she knew. Which, she had to admit, wasn't far.

SHE HAD MET ROUX, the ageless man of mystery when the earth literally opened at her feet and swallowed her up.

It happened on a mountain in France, while hunting the legend of the Beast of Gévaudan for *Chasing History's Monsters*. Shortly thereafter she had fallen into a sinkhole that opened beneath her feet during an earthquake. In the caves where she landed she had found the skeleton of the beast herself, as well as the man who killed it—and a medallion that proved to be the final, missing piece of the sword of Joan of Arc, which had been broken by the English when she was burned as a witch at Rouen in the fifteenth century.

Roux, it turned out, had been there. He had been Joan's mentor.

The old man had stolen the medallion from Annja in a restaurant. She had tracked him down to his mansion near Paris with the help of billionaire industrialist Garin Braden, who claimed to have been Roux's apprentice—half a millennium before. And there, by some means of which she still had not the slightest comprehension, she had *healed* the ancient blade—made it whole again out of fragments by no more than the touch of her hand.

It had caused Roux to proclaim her the spiritual descendant of the martyred Joan, and her fated successor as champion of the good. It had also inspired Garin to try to kill her. Or at least to break the sword, fearing that its restoration would break the spell—Roux named it a curse—that had kept both men alive and unaging for centuries.

She was still sorting this all out in her mind, trying to integrate a lot of fundamentally dissonant facts.

Unexplained things happened. She knew that. That the parents she could not remember had died and left her in an orphanage in New Orleans had rubbed her nose in that truth at a very early age.

Earthquakes happened. The earth opened. But that didn't stop it all from being a little too coincidental—providential, one might say.

The fact she just happened to be dropped more or less on top of the final piece needed to restore the sword was just too neat for rational explanation. Thinking about that—she did that a lot these days, trying to find her bearings—made her wonder about what she had been accustomed to thinking of as "rational." Because in this case truth and rational explanation were divergent. They had wandered far down very different pathways indeed.

IN THE WEEKS since taking the sword as her own burden to bear, Annja had worked assiduously to learn to use the mystic weapon. Roux had her start conventional fencing, mostly for conditioning. Even with her impressive physical abilities, she needed training. And that training hurt, for she was using her muscles in unaccustomed ways and taxing them to their utmost.

But Roux expressed contempt for fighting with what he called "car aerials," although he admitted the épée approximated a useful weapon in size and balance, and that the cut-and-thrust of the saber mimicked actual combat, however faintly. He spurned the modern mythology of point-fighting as the be-all and end-all of sword combat.

So she went beyond modern, conventional fencing. She studied sixteenth- and seventeenth-century sword manuals by masters such as Vadi and Meyer—even published a paper on them. She sought out live-steel masters of reconstructed sword techniques from the Middle Ages and Renaissance and learned from them.

What she was doing now, though, was a form meant to be performed with a two-edged sword. It was convenient to do, kept her body fluid and mobile and perfected her balance. It helped familiarize her with the sword—and it with her. The form also helped to soothe her mind and spirit. That was something she put a premium on these days, even as she found it increasingly difficult to do so.

She especially liked the symbolism of the left hand,

the empty hand. It was traditionally held with first two fingers extended, the latter two folded into the palm with the thumb across them: what was called the spirit sword.

She found it appropriate, somehow. And the slow motions were easy on her nose. It was still tender from having been broken when she did the face-plant against the cliff in Peru.

AFTER SHE HAD GONE for a run in the rain, then come back and spent twenty minutes stretching, she showered and occupied herself fixing dinner. Then she watched part of the DVD set that had arrived in the mail while she was away, the first season of *Ally McBeal*. She didn't really watch much television, and hated waiting from one episode to the next of a show. She much preferred being able to watch as many episodes as she cared to at a sitting. Besides, she'd always harbored a sneaking prejudice for artifacts of the past…even the very recent past.

Leaving the television turned on for a little bit of light and motion, but no sound, she settled herself back on the window seat to see what had developed in her newsgroups.

As the colored shadows played disregarded across her face, and outside the great light went down and the little lights came on in fairy profusion, she went back to alt.archaeology.esoterica. The post about Solomon's Jar had elicited a new slew of comments. She scanned the headers.

The majority remained abusive. As usual, she found that once the comments nested more than a couple of removes from the main thread they had little or nothing to do with the ostensible topic. So she concentrated on comments on the original post, and immediate replies to them.

One username caught her eye: seeker23@demon.-co.uk, a British domain. She had seen the name before. Often. He was a quixotic defender of the borderlands of respectability, of the realm of the possible—who nonetheless spoke knowingly in the jargon of archaeology. And never once in screaming caps. Seeker23 even knew that *it's* isn't a possessive, a rare attainment anywhere on the Net.

She downloaded the comments he—or she, but the tone caused her to sense the poster was masculine—had posted. Mostly they were calm pleas for open minds. But one uncharacteristic sally made her sit up and open her eyes.

There are even rumors that the crew of a Greek fishing trawler who found the supposed jar were mysteriously slaughtered on board afterward. Such a massacre did take place, in Corfu a couple of months ago. It's possible, always, that was merely coincidence. But I hope Trees is exercising due caution.

That brought him a positive flame tsunami, of course. Annja paid no attention. She could have recited most of the contents of the negative responses aloud without ever reading them anyway.

She minimized her newsreader window and fired up Firefox. A Google search of news items brought a number of hits from the wire services. Six Slain In Fishing-Boat Massacre, she read. The crewmen had been found hacked to death as the boat lay tied at the dock in its home port on the island of Corfu.

Annja closed her computer and stared out the window. The rain had started up again. The hard little lights across the East River seemed somehow muted, as well as blurred by chill tentacles of rain that stretched across the windowpane, that ran down the glass like the fingertips of dying men....

Shuddering at the sound of unheard screams, the nape of her neck tingling, she opened the computer up again and went to a travel site to check flight times and prices to the Netherlands.

3

A string of Balinese brass bells tinkled musically to announce her as Annja pushed her way into the little shop in Amsterdam.

Inside was warm, dark and fusty after the late North Sea afternoon with its high, pallid sky and brisk spring breezes off the IJ estuary. She closed the door as gently as she could, not wanting more racket from the string of tiny bells, while contradictorily saying "Hello?" at normal conversational volume.

Great, she told herself. I try to sneak in while announcing myself out loud. She sighed. She had a lot left to get used to, it seemed.

No one answered. She looked around.

The bronze plaque outside had described the establishment as Trees's Schatwinkel. What trees had to do with it she wasn't sure; the somewhat skinny lime trees on the street hadn't struck her as anything to name a shop after. Her first impression was that it was like her own home, but more so. The walls were lined with shelves of books, some glassed in as if to indicate rarer and more expensive volumes. The muted glow, which became more apparent as her eyes accustomed themselves to indoors, came from lights on the sculpted and painted metal ceiling. They were turned to spill illumination down the bookcases, and a few discreetly spotlit displays. Tables of artifacts were crowded between the bookshelves, along with some glassed-in cases.

The street sounds were muted to a near subliminal murmur. The tiny shop had the sort of reflective quiet she always associated with such places, along with museums and cathedrals. Its smell struck her as unusual, though. Along with the usual dust and mildew one encountered in such places, however scrupulously kept up, and the smell of old paper and leather and paint, her nostrils detected incense and a particular if unidentifiable sweetish smell. There was something else that underlay it all, but she couldn't yet define it.

Along with the books the store was crammed with a variety of artifacts, from age-blackened icons hung in the niches between bookcases to various coins in glass display cases. In one case near Annja lay an exquisite wheel-lock pistol with an ebony stock intricately inlaid in silver; beside it lay a scrap of Egyptian papyrus inscribed with faded hieroglyphs. Annja couldn't read them; they were too far out of her own scope.

A quick survey told her most if not all of the merchandise on display had likely come from private collections—including the rather nice trilobite fossil resting on its own pedestal to the left of the cash register. None of it, at a guess, was extremely valuable, in part because of clouded provenance.

Perhaps more importantly, none of the artifacts looked to her like illicit antiquities. It was basically a curio shop, and the items for sale would range in price alongside high-end souvenirs or contemporary artworks in the modest little galleries that catered to tourists in the Old Town district of the city's center.

But then, she thought, if they are trafficking in illegal antiquities, they'd hardly have them out front in the display cases.

She was surprised that no one had emerged to the sound of the bells or her own cautious greeting. Perhaps the Dutch were unusually law-abiding, although she'd seen her share of panhandlers and tough, drawn street people working the canals and narrow streets. Still, she guessed the proprietors knew their own business.

In the back of the shop a door opened onto what was presumably a storeroom. A dingy yellow light spilled out into the small main shop. No doubt the clerk or proprietor was back there somewhere, most likely in the bathroom. In the meantime, Annja walked up to the cash register and looked around.

She saw nothing out of the ordinary. There were small items like chocolates wrapped in brightly colored foil for sale in baskets on the counter, and on the wall behind hung what she guessed were licenses and permits of various sorts, along with a number of small framed lithographs from various time periods. Half-tucked under a rubber mat meant to keep metallic objects from marring the glass countertop a business card caught her eye.

She pulled it out with the tip of a finger. It was slightly yellowish off-white, like old ivory. One end was printed in dark green, with a stylized tree showing through in the color of the paper. In the same dark green was embossed The White Tree and below it, Metaphysical Inquiries and a UK address complete with phone number and e-mail.

She slipped it back where it had been.

She looked around. Still no sign of life in the place. Perhaps the staff had slipped out back into the alley for a smoke to abide by the stringent EU antismoking laws.

Annja slipped behind the counter. She wasn't sure what she was looking for; she only hoped she'd know if she found it.

Unconsciously she realized her nose was wrinkling. There was an unmistakably off smell mingling with all the others. The air was still and definitely beginning to cloy.

A phone with a digital display sat beside the register. The command buttons were unsurprisingly labeled in Dutch. They looked fairly conventional. She hit a sequence of keys she hoped would bring up the last number to have called the shop. A numeral string obediently appeared. Annja was surprised to see a New York area code.

Little bells rang as the front door suddenly swung open.

A young man entered the shop. For a moment the bright light from outside gave the impression he was surrounded by a nimbus of light. Then he stepped in and shut the door, and the illusion was gone.

He looked to be about Annja's height, five foot ten. Slim, he wore a white shirt with an open collar and the sleeves rolled up to midforearm and blue jeans. His hair was dark and curly and hung down around his ears. When he stepped forward with a smile she saw his complexion was pale, with very pink cheeks. His eyes were penetrant blue.

"Do you work here?" he asked in English as he came up to the counter. His accent was British.

"Oh, ah, no. I'm sorry. I was just making a phone call," Annja replied.

It was a clumsy evasion. She saw suspicion flicker in his eyes. They narrowed, and his smile slipped.

"Where's the proprietor?" he asked.

"I don't know, actually," she said. "I came in and there was nobody here."

"So you just went around behind the cash register?" His tone was challenging.

She shrugged. "I just got into town. I needed to call my hotel."

He leaned forward to peer over the counter. "You're wearing a cell phone at your waist."

Annja smiled sheepishly. "Battery's dead. Isn't that the way it always goes?"

"You came to an antiquities shop before you even checked into your hotel?"

"I'm really very fascinated by antiquities. It's like a hobby." She patted the backpack she was still wearing. "I travel light, anyway."

He scowled as he looked at the backpack. For a moment she thought he would demand she open it to prove she hadn't filled it with purloined goods.

"Oh, really," he said. "American, aren't you?"

"Yes. You can always tell, huh?" Maybe if I play stupid enough he'll get exasperated and go away, she thought. She felt a bit of a pang at the thought; it was too bad they were getting off on the wrong foot like this.

"What sort of antiquities, then?" he asked. "Americans aren't usually interested in the past."

"I guess I'm the exception that proves the rule. I like antiquities of all kinds."

"Like this figurine here?" he asked, tapping a finger on the glass above a four-inch tall statue of a bearded warrior with a conical helmet and staring eyes. "Viking, wouldn't you say?"

"Oh, no," she said. "Eleventh-century Friesian."

He looked at her. Uh-oh, she thought. I let my stupid slip, there.

"You do know your antiquities, don't you?" he murmured. "Have you really no idea where the owner of the shop is?"

She shook her head. "Like I said, I just came in—"

He held up a hand. "I know. To use the phone. Well, don't you *wonder* why no one's come out to ask what we're about, then?"

"They're out to lunch?"

He looked at her levelly for a moment. She could tell he was dying to remark that they weren't the only ones. She seemed to have recouped her airhead bona fides.

"I think I'll just have a look in the back room," he said.

"I'm not sure that's a good idea," she said, moving out from behind the counter. He glanced at her, more with curiosity than anything else. She realized she didn't have a very good pretext for preventing him. Indeed, she wasn't even sure what her reason was. But she didn't want him looking in the back room.

His slightly snubbed nose wrinkled. "Do you smell something odd?"

"Yes," she said. "A little bit…stale, I guess. Maybe a rat died in the baseboards."

"If you don't mind I'll have a look in the back, make sure nothing's wrong," he said, and stepped past her.

He froze in the entryway. "Oh, my God," he said.

THE PROPRIETOR HAD BEEN stout, middle-aged and female. She wore a skirt and practical shoes with white ankle socks. And that was about all Annja could tell. Because her face was a crumpled pudding of blood, her upper garment was soaked and her hair was dyed and soggy with the stuff. Blood was splashed in bright sprays and swatches on the cardboard boxes and crates to either side of the body. It was congealing in pools on the scuffed linoleum floor. There were even suspicious stains on the bare lightbulb hanging from the ceiling overhead.

The smell was blatant now that she knew what it was. It was a smell most archaeologists were quite unfamiliar with: they had few occasions to deal with fresh death. Annja knew it all too well. But the incense and other odors had masked it.

She pushed past the young man to kneel by the body. She touched a bit of blue-white neck between blood rivulets. The skin was cool and gummy, and there was no pulse, confirming what the smell, and the visual evidence, had told her already.

Something lay by Annja's left shoe. She looked down. It was a small oblong box with gaudy colors and unfamiliar writing. "Clove cigarettes!" she exclaimed. Some of the other kids at the orphanage had tried smoking them, to hide the vice from the nuns. It never worked. Nothing ever fooled the nuns. "That's what that spice smell was."

"Don't touch anything!" the young man said.

"I won't," she said, standing. The tips of her fingers felt strange where they had touched the dead skin, and she felt an urge to wash them. Maybe you never get used to this sort of thing, she thought.

"Shouldn't we call the authorities?" he asked. He was shaking.

"Not from here," she said, "unless you feel like answering a lot of questions for some very skeptical police officers. There's nothing we can do for her now."

"But we have to do something!"

"Really?" She cocked a brow at him. There didn't seem any point in keeping up the bubble-head act any longer.

With a musical ripple of sound the front door opened once again.

The young man went tense. Annja looked past him as three men entered the shop. The first was on the small side, at least a couple of inches shorter than she was, wearing a tan suit over a shirt with an open collar. He was trim and moved with unusual assurance and economy. His hair was cropped short and seemed to be light and receding. With him standing in the darker outer room it was impossible to tell more.

The two who came in behind him towered over him. One was lean, dark haired and unshaved, wearing a shiny suit coat over, of all things, a white T-shirt with horizontal blue stripes. The other was more like a granite slab. His suit fit as if he went to a tailor who specialized in circus chimps.

Annja's life experience had taught her enough to make the two big guys as cheap goons immediately. The smaller man was a different order of being entirely, she knew at once. Not any nicer, perhaps. But he wouldn't come cheap. Not at all.

"Excuse me," he said, coming forward. His English was excellent but strongly Russian accented. "Are you Trees, by any chance?"

Then he stopped. Intuition-flash told her he recognized the smell before he saw the body in its graceless supine sprawl on the linoleum.

He rapped out a command to his men. Annja didn't understand much Russian. But she didn't need to.

There was no mistaking the intent of the two henchmen as they advanced toward her and the youthful Englishman.

4

Annja kicked the moving block of concrete in the baggy crotch of his suit pants as he reached out a golem arm for her. Sometimes the old ways were best.

It was an easy move to block, as she knew perfectly well. But that old devil perception played the huge Russian false. Her appearance took him in—both their appearances, as middle-class young Westerners, students most likely, culturally conditioned to thoroughgoing helplessness in the face of threats of violence. He wasn't expecting the attractive young woman with the green-and-brown backpack to plant a boot in the old and dear.

The air exploded out of his huge chow-dog face and he staggered, bending over to clutch at his violated parts. The very hair in his ears seemed to stand up in anguish.

His leaner, darker partner cruised past him. His body language told Annja he'd sized her up as a basically helpless woman who'd gotten lucky. He wasn't going to mess with an open-handed bitch-slap, but he did feel confident enough to launch a fist in a looping haymaker.

Annja spun away from the blow, clockwise and kept turning into a spinning back kick that caught the man in his wide-open right rib cage. With a loud crack of bones snapping he was catapulted sideways into a pile of crates. All fell over with satisfactory crashing and banging.

The big goon, cursing in a strangled voice—she was fairly sure that's what he was doing, but *all* Russian sounded to her like swearing—reached inside his revival-tent-sized suit coat. She knew what that gesture meant.

Turning away, she snagged the ingenue young Englishman by the wrist with one hand. He resisted like a little boy trying to avoid a bath. It did him as much good. She caught a corner-eye flash of his sky-blue eyes going wide as he found himself towed irresistibly after the young woman.

She heard the dapper little Russian shout something. It may have been a command not to shoot, or the big guy, who wasn't having his best day at the moment, fumbled his piece getting it into action. Whichever way the shattering noise and searing pain as bullets sleeted into her back didn't happen.

It was a straight dash to the back door of the shop. Because Annja was moving faster, the young man came gangling after her in a sort of high-speed prolonged stumble, devoting more effort to not falling on his face than anything else. In racing flat-out for the door, she placed his body between potential gunfire and hers. It was not an ideal way to protect the innocent, but compromises sometimes had to be made.

As she approached the door she gave the Englishman's wrist a final yank to keep up his forward momentum. Then she jumped into the air, half-turning to deliver a flying side kick. She turned her hips so that her leg shot out straight behind her as if in a back kick. Under normal circumstances, especially with the momentum of a brisk sprint, she knew it would be perhaps the hardest blow a human body could deliver.

Annja felt the door resist. She feared it may have been bricked over on the outside. Or perhaps it was simply rusted in place by long disuse. For an instant of compressed perception she feared her shin bone would give way before the door did.

Then with a squeal of tormented metal and wood both jamb and hinges gave. The whole door exploded out into the alley in a whirlwind of dust and splinters. It landed with a thud and bounced. Annja belly flopped on top of it. Last of all came the young man, sprawling on top of her. The breath left her body in an ungraceful grunt.

At last the anticipated gunfire ripped the air. A snarling burst of fully automatic fire sounded high-pitched and rang in her ears. A handful of bullets cracked over their heads to splatter against a whitewashed brick wall opposite, and ricocheted with nasty whining moans down the alley. Clutching at random for a grip on the young man, she rolled the two of them violently to the right, to get them clear of the doorway's fatal funnel.

She had by chance seized an upper arm. Somewhat to her surprise it had a refreshingly wiry tone to it, despite his peaches-and-cream complexion and somewhat soft impression. She jumped upright, hauling him bodily to his feet with her.

"What on earth are you?" he started to say.

"Later," she said. Grabbing his wrist again like a mother with a recalcitrant child, she ran for the traffic crossing the alley mouth as another burst crashed through the doorway.

"UNCULTURED IDIOT!" Valeriy Korolin snarled, slapping the big man's sparsely furred head. "How often have I told you not to use that stupid Stechkin? No one can hit anything with a full-auto pistol. Why don't you use a Glock like a normal human being?"

"But it shoots real fast," the man replied.

"Augh! Can you miss fast enough to catch up? Anyway, I told you to grab them, not shoot them. How did you ever get out of the Panjsher alive?"

"My colonel always used to ask me that, too," the big man replied.

"Well, catch them, dammit! You too, Arkasha!"

The lean man with the striped T-shirt beneath his sports jacket rubbed a stubbled jaw. Several other men had come in through the front door. "How, Captain?" Arkasha asked.

"The old-fashioned way. Run after them, very fast. Chase them down. Lay hard hands on them. Bring them to me. Alive!"

The two men stood staring at him. "You are still here, why?" he asked, his voice low, sinuous and dangerous.

They fled.

ANNJA AND HER COMPANION had almost reached the end of the alley when another pair of burly men came running into it.

By this time the Englishman was running on his own. Annja wasn't sure whether he was actually following her or simply fleeing in the same direction. Either way served her purpose.

One of the Russians reached to grab her. In a move far more reminiscent of rough flag-football games at the orphanage than her extensive martial-arts training, Annja stiff-armed him. He flew back into his comrade, who in turn slammed back against the green brick corner above the gray stone footing of the building.

Annja risked a lightning glance toward the front door of the shop. Several more overt hardmen milled near the brass plaque of the curiosity shop.

"What in bloody hell is going on?" demanded her accidental companion, stumbling as he stared at the fallen pair. She towed him remorselessly into traffic. Somehow, amid squealing brakes and bleating horns, they made the other side.

"Russian *mafiya* convention, looks like," she said.

"And who are you?"

"Probably your best chance at living to see sunset. Come on."

From the corner of her eye she saw the man she had stiff-armed. He lay on his back, jerking feebly. More to the point, she saw his partner, still half-leaning against the wall, dive inside his own *Miami Vice* pastel sports coat with one hand. She yanked the Englishman around the corner as a burst of gunfire rattled off the pizzeria at the near end of the block, miraculously missing the plate-glass window. A flyer hit the sidewalk and ricocheted off into the high white sky with a lost-soul whine.

The tourists, locals and vendors on the street showed little reaction as Annja and her companion raced away. Either they think it's fireworks, or there's a lot more street violence in Amsterdam than I knew about, she thought.

In a moment they were among a thicker crowd. She

slowed. The young man slowed with her. He was breathing hard and seemed aggrieved to see she was not.

"What are you?" he asked. "Some kind of CIA cowgirl?"

She laughed. "That's the last thing I am. I'm just a tourist with an interest in antiquities. You?"

"The same." She noticed he wasn't any more eager to volunteer his name than she was. It was far down on her list of priorities. "What now?" he asked.

She looked back. Several men shouldered purposefully along the street behind them. At least one had his hand ominously inside his coat. "We need to lose them," she said.

In front of them a bridge crossed one of the innumerable canals lacing Amsterdam. She had no idea which one; the street signs would have meant little to her even if she had been able to read Dutch. It was as much as she could do to know they were inside the Singelgracht, the canal that had once encircled the medieval city, and innermost of the major concentric canals radiating from the arm of the North Sea called the IJ.

Glancing right, she saw the street widen where the space between two parallel canals had been paved over. A crowd of people were gathered there. She heard tinny distorted techno music and voices expanded and garbled by loudspeakers.

"This way," she said. "We might lose them in the crush."

Her companion glanced back the way they had come.

His color had risen high in his cheeks. He was really very pretty, she couldn't help noticing, although still very masculine. His was an appearance that put her in mind of the poets Shelley and Lord Byron—though without showing any signs of the latter's brooding and somewhat sinister nature. She had let his arm go by now. He continued to follow, probably because he had no idea what else to do.

He thinks I do, she thought. Silly rabbit.

"They're gaining," he grumbled. She looked back as if rubbernecking in approved tourist fashion. He was right. She could pick out at least half a dozen men, distinguished from the crowd not so much by their attire, which ranged from eighties casual to ill-tailored modern professional, as by their unidirectional purpose. They were like steel marbles rolling through custard, although they did restrain themselves from jostling the burghers and tourists too briskly and drawing further attention to themselves.

"Even they won't shoot in a crowd scene like this," she said, mostly because they hadn't. Not unless they're sure of their targets, she chose not to say. Why they had been shooting she found more than a bit mysterious. But she didn't plan on asking them.

Not unless she managed to get one alone for a brief and personal conversation.

The crowd on the wide paved common in front

seemed to be protesting something. But the crowd looked like a group of hippies. As she and her reluctant escort worked their way among the protesters she could see the fronts of their signs. She couldn't read them. They were all in Dutch. They seemed emphatic. They were also very… illuminated, to borrow a term from medieval manuscripts: embellished with fancy borders and scripts, sometimes to the effect she wouldn't have been able to read them had they been written in English.

There was a platform erected up front, near the end of the commons. A skinny speaker with a rainbow afro that might have been a wig exhorted the crowd in Dutch, vying with the thumping blast of music that was so distorted she suspected it was being piped through an amp from somebody's iPod. Near the front, an eight-foot-tall black-and-white bipedal cow cavorted, waving its forehooves as if to emphasize the speaker's impassioned rhetoric.

"Excuse me," she said, inadvertently jostling a large man with a peace-sign bandanna and an almost white beard.

"Certainly," he said with a smile. His English was crisp despite his accent. That was something she'd noticed about the people of Amsterdam: most of them spoke English, and most were unfailingly polite. Even when protesting, it appeared.

"What are you demonstrating about?" she asked. Glancing back, she saw several of the Russians standing on the edge of the protest, looking around as if uncertain what to do. If they dived into this crowd the way they had driven through the pedestrians, however crowded together, they would attract way too much attention from the Dutch police standing around looking politely bored in their khaki uniform shirts and dark trousers. "Animal rights?"

"No," the man said. "I am sorry. We demonstrate here for higher government subsidies to artists. We are all artists here."

"And craftpersons!" said the woman who stood on the other side of him, a smallish intense woman with a great cloud of kinky white-streaked ginger hair and a severe face.

"Ah, yes," he said.

"But what about the person in the cow suit?" Annja asked.

"That's Thijs," her informant explained.

"Why a cow suit?"

He shrugged. "He does soft sculpture of animals. Last time he was a giraffe. It was truly something to see."

"Sorry I missed it," she said. "Thanks."

The latter was spoken as she moved on with as much purpose as she could muster without calling attention to herself. The Russians had split up and were working their way around both edges of the herd of subsidy seekers.

"What was that all about?" her companion demanded

to know. Taken apparently by surprise when she started walking, he had darted a few yards to catch up, fortunately drawing little attention.

"Camouflage," Annja said. "Also curiosity. I'm a stranger in town."

She kept her face turned vaguely in the direction of the podium, where a mime had taken the stage and was mugging and making inexplicable circular motions in the air with gloved palms toward the crowd, to the evident annoyance of the speaker.

"Mimes," her companion said in distaste. "I hate mimes."

She flashed him a smile. "There's something else we have in common."

She kept her eyes moving briskly side to side. Trusting her peripheral vision to alert her if any *mafiya* goons overtook them on the crowd's fringe, she mainly scouted for their next escape route.

Ahead to the left, one of the ubiquitous tour boats, low slung with a glass top, had pulled in just short of the commons' end. The tourists were filing off up a brief stairway of stained white stone to street level. She got the impression this was a shopping stop; there seemed to be no ticket kiosk at the small stone pier.

From nowhere a hand gripped her bicep. Hard.

5

"A word with you in private, miss," a heavy voice said in her ear, in English with a Russian accent you could have knocked off in chunks with a chisel.

"Oh, I'm sorry," Annja said. "You say you're ill?"

She turned her hips clockwise, at the same time rolling her shoulder. It put the whole weight of her body at the gap between his thumb and gripping fingers. Even had he been anticipating the action, which clearly he hadn't, it was unlikely he could have kept his grip.

As soon as her arm came free she rotated back to face him. He was another tall and rangy sort in a weird, faintly pink sports jacket and dark blue shirt. His breath smelled of lavender pastilles, of all things. He smiled, but it was reminiscent of a shark's.

"Ill?" he said, trying to not too obviously snatch her arm again. "I don't have any idea—"

She twisted again, this time even harder. Her left hand, knotted into a fist, drove the knuckle of her forefinger into the Russian's right kidney with the force of a riot baton.

The air rushed out of him. The color drained out of his fair face, leaving him green beneath his indifferently barbered blond bangs. His knees buckled. She caught his right arm as people turned to stare.

"The poor man," she said to them. "I think he's got appendicitis."

Some warning sense within her tingled. She felt a hand grab her right shoulder even as she readied herself.

She spun back as if startled. Quicker than the eye could follow, she hoped, her right elbow stabbed into the solar plexus of the beefy man who had seized her. His blue-green eyes, slightly slanted, bugged out as he doubled over.

"Oh!" she exclaimed. "You poor man. Perhaps there's a food-poisoning epidemic?" She turned, peeled his loosening hand the rest of the way off her shoulder, twisted it in a discreet come-along and, with pressure on the elbow, drove him face first to the cobblestones. He hit hard—but to all the nearby onlookers, themselves conditioned heavily against violence, it looked like nothing so much as if he had collapsed on his own, and his weight had proven too much for a girl, even a tall, athletic one, to control.

"We'll go get help," she told the circle of pale surprised faces turned toward her. "Come on, Eric."

The protesters crowded in on the fallen pair. The man Annja had kidney punched sat on his knees, moaning. The other lay with a trickle of blood running down his stubbled slab cheek; he had either broken a tooth or bitten his tongue, and was in all events stunned. As the artists and craftspersons all pushed together, jostling and trying to outshout each other with knowledgeable-sounding advice, Annja grabbed the Englishman's wrists and they were off again, running ahead and to the left.

"Eric?" he demanded. He wasn't hanging back this time.

"Improvising!" she said.

She turned her head enough for her peripheral vision to register that at least two men pursued them along the left-hand edge of the crowd. The commotion she had caused with the pair she had dropped was serving as a strange attractor for much of the crowd now. Everybody else seemed to be looking that way, even the disgruntled orator and the mime.

"What are we going to do now?" the Englishman asked as they darted free of the crowd, heading for the stone steps, now vacated by the tour boat passengers, who had wandered off down a side street toward one of the local attractions.

"Commandeer a ride," she said.

"Commandeer? You mean steal?" He sounded outraged.

"Whatever. Would you rather get to know the *mafiya* up close and personal?"

Heavy footsteps drummed the pavement behind her. A large flock of pigeons took off in a panicky flight from the top of the canal wall.

"You go negotiate passage for us," Annja said, propelling him down the steps with a hand between the shoulders. The boat driver, a young man with dark blond hair hanging lank from beneath a billed cap, looked up, his mouth agape beneath the gold ring in his nose.

She turned. Two new Russians slowed to a heavy-breathing stop three yards away and began walking toward her with broad grins.

"You gave us a good run, miss," said the taller of the two, walking straight toward her. He had a gold incisor and a startling Aussie accent overlaying the Russian. "Now the show's over."

She punched him. Hard. She threw a good, straight right, putting her hips into it, driving with her legs, putting all the force she was capable of up the bones of her arm and through the last three knuckles of her fist into his face. She felt cartilage squash and blood squirt, as if she'd punched a fruit. The man sat down hard and fluids began to flow.

His partner was all over her from her right side, trying for a bear hug. She reached up, grabbed a handful of padded shoulder and, putting her right hip hard into his groin, cartwheeled him right over her shoulder. It could easily have been a death stroke, but she wasn't ready for that. Rather she pulled him in so that instead of smashing the back of his skull to pulp on the stone of the pier he slammed down on the top of his back. The air exploded out of him, and she thought she felt his shoulder pop free of the socket. What a shame, she thought with a grin.

The other guy was rubbing his face, trying to clear his eyes of tears and the scarlet sparks that the pain from his nose were doubtless still shooting through his forebrain. Her own nose panged in sympathy. She leaped down the six feet to the landing, flexing her legs to take the shock.

Her companion stood arguing with the tour boat pilot. Both turned to gape at her. She hopped onto the boat, said, "Sorry," to the young boatman and pushed him straight over the gunwales. He landed in the water, limbs flailing, and threw up a giant wave of stinking green water.

"Let's go," she said, revving the engine and grabbing the tiller.

The Brit stood still staring openmouthed at her. She got the boat's prow turned upstream, away from the pursuit, and accelerated. He windmilled his own arms. She had to grab the front of his shirt to keep him from flying over the stern.

She dragged him to a seated position. From behind a ripple of gunfire crashed as one of their pursuers opened up from the concrete railing. Bullets sent miniature geysers spouting white behind the churn of their propeller. Then they were through the round arch of the next bridge down.

Her companion was staring at her with eyes and hair wild. His shirttail had been pulled out of his jeans. His hands were plucking and pushing at it as if to tuck it in again, but he didn't seem to have good command over them.

"Are you quite sure you're not some covert government agent?" he shouted at her.

"Yep."

"You're daft!"

"Pretty much," Annja replied laughing.

Something cracked right above their heads.

THE SOUND WAS MORE like something breaking than a pop. It *was* something breaking, Annja knew instantly: the sound barrier. Someone had fired a high-velocity round at them.

She reached out, grabbed her companion by the shoulder and pitched him facedown to the deck before he could react. Then she looked back.

The Russians were living up to their reputation for dogged determination. Three of them had hijacked a canal boat of their own and were speeding in their quarry's wake. Two of them were standing up, risking a nasty high-speed spill into the murky waters of the canal, firing handguns at them.

She turned her eyes forward just in time to swerve through an archway of another bridge rather than accordion themselves on a piling. With her free hand Annja grabbed the young man by the collar and hauled him to a seated position. Ahead she could see the masts of sailboats and a long, low, rust-colored barge cruising slowly past the canal mouth.

She felt a sharp pang of yearning for her sword. She was aware, all too aware, it couldn't help her here. She couldn't slice bullets out of the air with it, and anyway, the middle of a densely populated city was not the place to pluck a sword from thin air and start waving it around. She knew that through her wit and will alone she would prevail or fail.

"What now?" the young man asked.

Good question. The last bridge was coming up fast. The Russians were closing, though still a good hundred yards back. Annja undid her belt, yanked it off, leaned over, did something fast and purposeful. Then she threw both arms around him.

"Take a deep breath," she said.

THE RUSSIANS DUCKED low as their boat flashed beneath the final bridge. Ahead of them their quarry wallowed and then began to turn right in the slow but heavy crosscurrent.

"We got them!" one of the men crouching in the bow shouted triumphantly.

His comrade, less intrepid, had gone all the way to his knees. "Wait!" he shouted over the whine of their engine. "Where did they go?"

The smaller boat rolled as it cruised out into the IJ. The standing man toppled and barely prevented himself from going into the estuary.

"It's empty!" he shouted.

The water flattened around them in a sudden downdraft. Above them they heard the sound of a helicopter rotor.

And from the quay behind they heard the distinctive, angry voice of their leader.

BOBBING TO THE SURFACE in the dark shadow of the archway, the young man shook his head like an angry terrier.

"You're daft!" he exclaimed. "You're mad. Barking bloody mad!"

Treading water beside him Annja looked out into the IJ. The pursuing boat had cut its engine and was drifting sideways as its impromptu crew put their hands in the air. A harbor patrol helicopter hovered above them.

"It worked, though," she told him.

She swam back to the upstream side of the bridge and climbed onto the small concrete pier. She reached out a hand to help her companion from the water. He shook her off angrily and sprang out. He was fairly fit, she realized—agile. Plus he'd mostly kept up with her, although unlike her he was breathing hard.

He followed her into a side street. "We've got to go to the authorities," he told her.

She shrugged. "Your call. It might take you longer than you like to answer to their satisfaction the questions they're going to ask. And our friends, there—" she bobbed her head back toward the canal, clearly indicating their erstwhile *mafiya* pursuers "—are known for having tentacles deep into police forces all over the world."

"But there are surveillance cameras everywhere!" he exclaimed, waving his hand toward one mounted on a metal post beneath a lantern with a crown surmounting it. It seemed to stare at them like an idiot eye.

"They've got them all over your country, too," she said, "and street crime's skyrocketing there."

He made an inarticulate noise compounded of frustration, disgust and reaction. He held up his hands before his dripping, anger-pink face and shook them. "Don't," he said, "follow me. We're done. Understand?"

"Have it your way," she said. She resisted the temptation to call, "You're welcome" after him as he stomped off down a side street. Instead she began looking around.

Something tells me, she thought, I need to get out of Holland fast.

THE LITTLE BOXY rental car was parked with its snub snout almost touching one of the three-foot metal stanchions that studded most of the sidewalks to protect pedestrians from vehicles and also to keep the drivers off the sidewalks. Valeriy Korolin stood before it, arms akimbo, glaring into the estuary with the tails of his sports coat flapping in a brisk breeze that smelled of fish, stale saltwater and diesel fumes.

"Now look what you fools have done," he said. "What possessed you to shoot at them? This is Amsterdam, not Tbilisi."

"But Captain," said one of the two men who'd piled from the car with him. "They killed the shopkeeper."

"Fool! Did you see any blood on them?"

"Well, no—"

Around them sirens blared. "Did you fail to notice," the captain said, voice razor edged with sarcasm, "that the interior of the storeroom looked as if someone had set off a grenade in a can of red paint? Haven't you ever beaten anybody to death before, Gena?"

"Well, yes, comrade Captain. But—"

"It's not 'comrade' anymore, you buffoon. And quit calling me Captain!"

"This is the police!" a polite but brisk electronically amplified voice called out.

The car had been surrounded by Amsterdam police cars, white with red-and-blue hashmarks on their sides. Either presuming that anybody making such a commotion in Amsterdam must be a Yankee, or simply playing it safe since most Netherlanders and most tourists understood some English, the officer spoke that tongue. "Put your hands behind your heads."

"All right, all right," Korolin called. He turned to face the nervous pair of cops approaching behind drawn handguns. They held their weapons as if expecting they might suddenly turn and bite them, like vipers. "I am Colonel Sergei Arbatov, of the Russian Federal Security Bureau's Anti-Terrorism Task Force. You will find my identification in my right inside coat pocket. Please permit me to speak to your superior at once!"

6

Still breathing easily after a brisk two-mile ride, mostly uphill, Annja swung off the bicycle before the gateway to the manor house. Red brick gateposts rose from pale granite bases. The gate had a black wrought-iron arch across it with a tree worked in the center and painted white. The gates themselves stood open. A brass plaque, on the near upright, kept polished to a bright yellow, read Ravenwood Manor—The White Tree Lodge.

The sun hung low over green hills to the west. The clouds, strung across the sky like clots of cream, had toward the horizon begun to take on evening tints of cream and gold below, pale blue and dove-gray above. The hills were fairly sharp for England, though their outlines were softened by grass and copses of trees. They stretched west from the ancient Cinque Ports town of Hythe, bounding the fabled Romney Marsh. The Kentish Channel coast had become heavily encrusted with urbanization, especially since the building of the underwater chunnel from Featherstone, and the green countryside of Kent as a whole had been reduced by the encroachment of suburbs and bedroom towns from London.

The hill rose in a gentle slope toward a big white house on the crest. An immaculately tended crushed-shell drive curved subtly up through an equally compulsively manicured lawn, as uniformly green as a carpet. Annja saw no formal garden around the three-story Georgian house. Rather it stood amid a stand of trees, big ashes and vast, spreading oaks with massive, bent, cracked-bark trunks, themselves probably older than the nearly three centuries the house had stood. They masked several outbuildings, at least one of substantial size, which stood behind the great house on the back slope.

She took a drink of water from the bottle clipped to the bicycle frame. Then she swung a long, lithe leg over the seat and started pedaling up the hill. She felt no fatigue, only a bit warm, and that from exertion in the thin high-latitude sun more than ambient temperature, which had been on the cool side since she'd set out. Annja's rented bike was an ancient but well-repaired blue machine with a white fender on the front tire and no top strut on the frame, what was often called a "girl's bicycle" back home.

She wore khaki pants with some subtle cargo pockets, a cream-colored shirt with the sleeves unbuttoned and rolled up her tanned forearms. It was practical yet not disrespectfully slovenly to the people she meant to talk to.

It was an excellent disguise, she thought. She'd masqueraded as herself.

Crushed shell crackled beneath her tires as she rode up the sloped drive. She studied the house and its environs as she reflected on what her research had unearthed. A moldering stone wall encircled the structures behind it. The largest took shape as a half-ruined slump of stone, its walls almost obscured by ivy. It was an ancient abbey, built, according to legend, on a sacred site immeasurably more ancient, sacked and burned some said by Henry VIII's looters, and others by Cromwell's iron-clad iconoclasts. The manor itself had been destroyed during the English Civil War. When, decades later, a new noble master had built the current manor house atop the hill the ruin was left in place as a sort of garden ornament.

Not that the derelict abbey had remained unused. Legends spoke of unholy rituals—or orgies outright, depending on point of view—conducted between the once consecrated walls by the well-connected members of the scandalous Hellfire Club from nearby London. And the current proprietors likewise conducted rituals within its precincts. Annja had read all about it on their Web site.

The house was built of local limestone, with a sloping roof of gray slate. Though carefully pruned shrubberies huddled against its foundations like green sheep, its walls were kept clear of climbing vegetation, giving the manor an austere but not quite stark look.

Annja leaned her bike against the concrete footing. As she did she felt a curious chill, as if the sun had fallen behind a cloud on its way to the horizon. At the same time her nostrils wrinkled to a faint but unmistakable stink of decay. It was as if a breeze had blown over a recently opened grave. Just a random smell from the old graveyard out back, she told herself, though she had felt no actual motion of the air.

She put it from her mind and walked between stone lions weathered almost to outsized pug dogs to ring the bell. A medium-sized man with dark receding hair, middle-aged and trim in a butler's garb, greeted her. He accepted a business card embossed with the name of Amy Corbett, archaeological researcher and the name of a private North American institute—one that actually existed and would vouch for her identity thanks to *Chasing History's Monsters*.

The butler escorted her into a foyer. A spray of hothouse flowers in a white porcelain vase painted with climbing roses sat on an antique table on one side and a silver-framed oval mirror on the other. Bidding her to wait in tones more superior than deferential, he bowed and disappeared into the house's interior. Annja used the mirror to check herself and tucked a few vagrant wisps of hair back into the severely professional bun she'd tied at the back of her head.

"Ms. Corbett?" a cultured voice said. A cultured young masculine voice.

She turned. A painstakingly well-groomed young man stood there, her height or a little taller, her age or a little older, with round pink cheeks creased by a smile and dark hair slicked back sleek as a seal's fur. The pinkness of his cheeks reminded her of her nameless companion of her adventure in Amsterdam, but the resemblance ended there. He lacked the ivory whiteness of skin that had given such contrast to that young Englishman's complexion, to say nothing of a demeanor light-years from the mildly but boyishly disheveled affect the lad who fled with her through streets and canals had displayed. And though his smile seemed genuine, as most heterosexual males' tended to be when looking at her up close, his politeness was buffed to a polish so high and hard she couldn't see the character behind.

"I'm Reginald Smythe-George," he said. "So pleased to meet you. Please come with me."

He bowed slightly and gestured to a hallway opening

to her left. He wore a dark suit whose exact shade she could not distinguish in the foyer's half light, subtly pinstriped, with a stand-up collar and four-in-hand tie. She had little knowledge of fashion much past the sixteenth century, but his outfit suggested late Victorian to her—or Carnaby Street in the sixties. He also wore a large silver medallion bearing an image of the tree that was on the front gate.

"Of the noted occultist family?" she asked. She started walking the indicated path.

He slid past smoothly, to open a white-painted door before her. "Indeed," he said. "I'm surprised you know of us. So many in your profession tend to…look down upon my distinguished forebears."

"I try to keep an open mind," she said. "Scientific objectivity is a powerful tool. But like fire, it's a capricious master."

He raised an eyebrow. "Indeed? You possess rare insight for one with so much of your career before you."

Points for a diplomatic way of calling me young, she thought, given his own age. She smiled a middle-candlepower smile at him—it never hurt to keep things cordial, without lighting any fires she might need an extinguisher to put out later—and entered a white sitting room. Or what she suspected might be a sitting room.

It had chairs and tables, in any event. A low fire crackled in a white marble fireplace. Something else practically screamed for her attention. She fixed it upon the young man's sleek, smiling visage.

"Sir Martin will see you shortly," her escort said, and went through the next door, which he quietly but firmly closed behind him.

She took stock of her surroundings. The room fell just short of sterile. It was painted and decorated in a variety of shades: off-white, ivory, cream, bone. The chairs were upholstered in a leather that was almost pale beige. Some touches of color decorated the room, largely hues of gold, including the ormolu clock on the mantel, the frame of a large painting and the painting itself, depicting a pure white tree standing amid a green sun-shot forest.

There was one more touch of yellow metal. It was the thing that had caught her attention on entering the room. A plain container of shiny brass, like a globe with a tall narrow funnel stuck in the top and curling thin handles, perhaps a foot high.

A jar.

It looked like an antique Mediterranean jar might look, dredged from the sea bottom, if the sea-salt deposits and verdigris were cleaned off. It was a procedure no responsible archaeologist could condone, for risk of damaging the artifact. But a collector might not be so scrupulous. Nor might someone with other than strictly scientific ends in mind.

She took it from the mantel to examine it. If cleaning it didn't hurt it, picking it up won't do much, she thought—except leave fingerprints she could readily wipe away. Provided it's even an ancient artifact in the first place.

It felt surprisingly heavy in her hand. She was far from expert on biblical-era artifacts. But within her limited scope of knowledge she could discern no reason it might not have dated from Old Testament times. The wide mouth was open.

It was, she saw, inscribed with symbols. The marks were thin, shallow, spidery; invisible from a few feet away. The symbols were unfamiliar to her: lines, curved, straight and angled; circles; odd compound geometric shapes.

Something about the vessel felt strange. Then she realized the strangeness wasn't a result of something the jar possessed, but what it lacked.

If King Solomon had had a jar, and had once bound demons in it, this was not that jar. She felt certain such a use would leave it charged in a way that even after millennia its very touch would send a thrill like electricity through her body. This object was inert as a hammer.

She turned it over. The lower curve was curiously dented. In the indentation she thought she could see small flecks of dried brownish residue. She smelled a faint, cloying stench.

Then once more she felt a chill, and seemed to smell an opened grave.

A footfall from outside the door alerted her someone was coming. She quickly replaced the jar and turned.

Reginald Smythe-George opened the door, entered with a quick smile for Annja, and stood aside. A tower-tall and spectrally thin man entered at stately stilting pace behind.

"Sir Martin," the young factotum said, "may I present Ms. Amy Corbett? Ms. Corbett, Sir Martin Camdessus Highsmith, *Adeptus Primus* of the White Tree Lodge."

She stepped forward, extending a hand. Sir Martin took it in a firm, dry grip and shook, once. His hair was white and looked as if each individual strand had been arranged by hand just before he entered. His face was a collection of knobs and flanges that looked almost harsh. He wore an immaculately tailored suit with the same color scheme as the room itself—jacket, trousers, shirt and old-time silk cravat all in shades of white and near-white.

The only discordant element in the whole image was his eyebrows. They were fierce white projections, untamable as flames, above eyes of a blue so pale they were almost a shade of white themselves.

"Pleased to make your acquaintance, Ms. Corbett," the master of the house said in a baritone voice that might have been toned by a tuning fork. "Please be seated."

He waited until she sat in one of the lesser chairs, then took what she had rightly guessed was his accustomed place in a cream-colored wingback.

"This is a very beautiful house, Sir Martin," she said. "Is it your family's?"

"Thank you. And no, Ms. Corbett. My esteemed ancestors frittered away the family fortune before the Great War—our estates were sold for taxes between the wars. This house is provided to the lodge through arrangement with the National Trust."

He cocked his head at her. "You are an archaeological researcher, then?" he asked.

She smiled and nodded. "Writing an article for *Archaeology Today* magazine. On spec, I'm afraid. With, ah, an interest in the history of the Western Hermetic tradition," she said.

"Indeed? I imagined it was the archaeological heritage of the site that drew you here."

"To be sure, that adds interest, Sir Martin. As I understand, the manor is built on the site of one of the earliest Anglo-Saxon hill forts and the attached abbey at what is supposed to be the juncture of several ley lines."

"You've done your homework, then," he said, nodding approvingly. "But what I think you will find most vital—and key to our whole endeavor here—are Neolithic artifacts discovered on the grounds that demonstrate that this site has been recognized as holy throughout the entirety of its human occupation."

His eyes had begun to shine.

"I'm afraid my primary knowledge is focused on the

Middle Ages forward," she said, "although I was aware of Neolithic and Bronze Age discoveries."

"*Bronze* Age," he said as if mentioning something the dog did on the rug.

She raised an eyebrow at him. "My knowledge is incomplete and purely academic," she said, "but I thought it was cold iron that conflicted with magic."

"Iron. Bronze. This to them!" He dismissed all metals with a wave of a long, well-formed hand. "They are pollution in and of themselves."

"Do they not occur in nature, Sir Martin?"

"Of course. It is when they are plundered from the bosom of the good earth and elaborated in profane ceremonies that they become taints, poisoning the human spirit and poisoning all life."

"I had understood that Wiccans—"

"We see again that *knowledge* is not the same as *understanding*, Ms. Corbett. Therein lies one of the tangled roots of the modern malaise, prizing mere information while understanding nothing, or next to it!"

"I think I agree, Sir Martin, but I'm not sure I see your point," Annja said.

"If you will forgive my rudeness in contradicting you, you don't understand our lodge at all if you believe we are part of Wicca. To be sure some of their rituals have merit, and a certain naive power, for all that they were largely created from whole cloth in the nineteenth century."

"But it was my understanding—forgive me, my impression—that the lodge practiced a traditional Western form of nature worship."

"That much is certainly true. But that does not make us Wiccans, dear lady."

He leaned forward, and his passion seemed to glow from his eyes and radiate from his prominent teeth, which were themselves a shade of off-white, she couldn't help noticing.

"Leave aside the truth or falsity of the ancient worship of the Great Mother and the horned god," he said. "We subscribe to the *true* old religion," Sir Martin proclaimed.

"Don't the Wiccans make similar claims?" Annja asked.

He dismissed the notion with a wave of his hand. "I mean the religion of the dawn men. From before the druids, before the pyramids, before the great crime of agriculture. Ours is the primal religious ecstasy expressed by the cave painters of Lascaux. Our worship is devoted to the earth's very self—we do not profane and diminish the earth by personalizing it as a mere human. Especially now, when humans have covered much of the beautiful face of the planet with their concrete canker sores, and the waters with their muck and ooze."

He sat upright again with a half-rueful smile. "You must forgive my vehemence," he said.

"You certainly have the courage of your convictions, Sir Martin."

"Thank you, my dear. You are most kind."

"So the lodge believes that our modern technological civilization is a mistake?" she asked.

"A desecration," he said.

Then his near white eyes slid past her. She turned her head but slightly. Far enough for her peripheral vision to register the direction of his gaze. He was looking straight at the brass jar on the mantel.

He knows, she realized. Might as well be hanged for a sheep as for a lamb, she thought. She drew in a deep breath. Then she plunged in head first.

"Given your institute's focus on prehistoric native beliefs," she said, "I admit I find its interest in a relic such as the alleged jar in which King Solomon bound the demons to be quite curious."

He looked directly at her for a moment. It seemed that his expression hardened, and that his eyes went from silver to steel.

"So," he said—softly, as to himself. "The margin of error is small, so small, in this terrible modern world of ours. As you observed, Ms. Corbett, I am passionate in my convictions. Sometimes my passions overwhelm me. Especially when my dearest expectations are raised, only to be cruelly dashed."

He stood. "As to my interest—our interest—the

earth's interest in the jar of Solomon, it would be pure waste to tell you now. No point, really."

Either his disdain for modern technology did not forbid him from carrying some kind of wireless communicator hidden on his person, or he possessed strong psychic powers. Annja did not discount the latter possibility as readily as she might have a year earlier. The door opened suddenly and two men, dressed in rough, soil-stained workman's garb that seemed itself to belong to an earlier century, stepped in.

"Mal, Dave," Sir Martin said. One newcomer was short and broad, with dark hair on his balding head and sticking from his prominent ears. The other was a huge, near shapeless mound of muscle. He was an albino with skin as chalky as the famous cliffs nearby and hair whiter than anything else in the white room. Both wore silver lodge medallions. The squat dark man carried a double-barreled shotgun under one arm.

"My Purdey, Dave?" Sir Martin inquired.

The squat man shrugged. "It'll do the job, won't it, Squire?"

"Ms. Corbett is leaving us," Sir Martin said. "Permanently, I fear. Reginald, I fear we need to clean up after my…indiscretions. See to it, won't you, there's a good lad?"

"Of course, Sir Martin," Reginald said coolly.

"Please take our guest into the back garden, kill her

and bury her in the churchyard where none will be the wiser. And for nature's sake, do it quietly!"

THE HUGE ALBINO, Mal, picked up a shovel leaned against the moss-grown stone wall as they passed beneath a gateway arch at the back of the great white house. Annja didn't know whether it was intended to kill her or inter her. Probably both she guessed. The White Tree Lodge did not seem to disdain modern concepts of efficiency. She wondered, idly, how they justified their reliance on the techniques and technologies they so despised.

The derelict abbey reared to the right. Ivy practically encrusted the limestone walls, which had fallen in at the top. A passageway led between rosebushes just beginning to bud with spring. Beyond lay another arched gateway. Through it the granite-and-limestone headstones of the churchyard were visible, jumbled gray-and-white shapes in the thickening twilight.

"We really don't have to play it this way, gentlemen," Annja said when there were walls all around. Flying things fluttered about, shadows tracing oddly irregular paths, bats or swallows she could not tell. The sun no longer shone here this day. It felt as if it never had.

"Coo," said the short, squat Dave. "I fancy hearing what the bird has to offer. What about you, Mal?"

The albino grunted.

"Not a bit of it, lads," Reginald Smythe-George called out, coming along seven yards or so behind as if pulling rear guard. Maybe he didn't want to risk getting his expensive trousers splattered, Annja thought. "This is lodge business. No time for frivolity," he said.

"What's the point of belonging to a fertility cult," Dave groused, "if you can't enjoy a few rites o' fertility—if you know what I mean?"

Mal smiled.

"So this is the way it has to be?" Annja asked. She walked toward the churchyard with head down and shoulders slumped.

"That's right," Dave said, "and a damned dirty shame it is. But there it is. Just take it easy, now, and it'll go easy, if you know what I mean."

"Sure," she said, and spun.

Mal's bulk and slow, shambling motion conspired to suggest slow-wittedness. But there was nothing slow about his response. No sooner had Annja begun to turn than he raised the shovel in both hands. Even as she came around to face him the blade descended to split her head.

But her right hand was no longer empty. She hacked across her body right to left with the sword. She felt two moments of resistance.

Blood hosed her from the stumps of two thick, severed arms.

Mal's mouth opened and closed. His tongue looked

red as blood in contrast to his colorless face. Or perhaps he had bitten it in shock. He made gobbling sounds, quick and bubbling with desperation as he stared at his massive wounds.

"Bloody hell!" Dave exclaimed. He brought up the Purdey.

Annja was on him. A backhand slash severed both barrels of the priceless double shotgun with a belling sound. Reflex made the man yank the now-sawn-off shotgun skyward. Reflex clenched his finger on both triggers. The barrels gouted pumpkin-sized flames into the dove-gray evening air.

Dave roared in surprise and pain as the unexpected recoil broke his trigger finger and possibly his wrist. He had not been gripping the gun properly when Annja amputated two-thirds of its barrel. The giant muzzle flames blossoming so close to his face had ignited the front of his curly hair.

His cry was cut short as Annja took the sword in both hands and raced past him to his right, swinging horizontally as she passed him.

He froze. Blood gushed from his mouth and jetted from his chest. He fell to flagstones half-buried in the turf.

A flash snapped her eyes forward. Simultaneously Annja heard a *pop*, not particularly loud. Then another. Something plucked like fingers at a lock of her dark hair hanging by her left cheek.

Young Reginald Smythe-George had a tiny black pistol in his hand and was shooting at her from twenty feet away.

Her instructors had always told her to run away from a knife but charge a gun. Of course, they might not have been so cautious about the knives had they known she had a very large knife indeed, carried in the otherwhere where an act of will could bring it to her hand at need. But the advice for firearms remained sound. Fast as she was, she couldn't outrun bullets. Nor even appreciably dodge them.

She *could* try to dazzle the shooter with footwork, throw off his aim—which was lousy anyway—and perhaps even startle him too much to shoot. She ran two light steps toward him and threw herself into a cartwheel, neat as a high-school cheerleader.

She heard no shots, felt no slap or sting of impact. Her hair flying loose about her shoulders, she landed on her feet and flowed instantly into a lunge.

The sword entered Reginald's chest right between the wings of his natty coat.

For a moment they posed there, eyes locked on eyes. Smythe-George's were very surprised. He tried to say something, but it came out as a large slurp of blood that ran down his chin and made his wine-colored necktie darker. Then his eyes rolled back and he slumped over as life left him.

Annja turned her hips away as his knees gave way beneath him, pulling the blade from his body. Then she flicked her wrist, clearing the mystical blade and dewing the broad leaves of the ivy on the passage wall with blood.

"You gave me no choice," she said.

With a push of her will she put the sword away. She looked around. The western sky looked as if the blood she'd shed had stained it. The manor showed no light nor sign of life. If anyone had witnessed her reversal of circumstance, they were keeping mum about it.

Gathering herself, she climbed to the top of the six-foot side wall. Then she dropped down to the lawn outside. She hoped to have cycled most of the way back to the bike shop before Sir Martin thought to miss his lackeys.

7

Roux pushed his sunglasses halfway down his nose to look at Annja as she walked toward him along the Riviera beach. She wore a green tube top with a hint of blue, shorts in an explosion of colors, red, yellow, blue, white. With her lithe shape and panther poise, she could. Silver-framed sunglasses hid her eyes behind dark lenses. Her hair blew free in the brisk Mediterranean morning breeze.

"You certainly took your time," the old man said querulously.

He had a metal-and-yellow-plastic-mesh chaise longue unfolded on the sand beneath a green-and-white parasol. He wore a Panama hat with a red-and-black band, a bush jacket, Bermuda shorts and sandals. He sipped a tall iced drink through a straw.

Annja sat next to him on a towel he had spread out beside him in anticipation of her arrival. She drew her long legs up under her chin, and gazed out to sea, where the surreally long low shape of a supertanker made its way west toward the Straits of Gibraltar.

"I thought I was here on time."

"I don't mean today, girl. I mean, what in the name of merciful God took you so long to think to come and visit me? You've left half of Europe in an uproar in your wake. You're more like a hurricane than a force of good."

A pair of adolescent girls emerged from the surf wearing nothing but bikini bottoms. They ran past, giggling in the self-consciousness of their scandalous near nudity. Annja shook her head.

"You disapprove?" Roux asked.

"I'm thinking about the sunburn." She shuddered.

"What about you?"

"What about me?"

"Will you remain covered?"

"Of course. I don't need that kind of sunburn." She tipped down her own shades and studied him. "Are you being a dirty old man?"

"Who knows? Perhaps I would disapprove."

They sat a moment in silence. Above them the sky was clear but for a few faint brush-strokes of cloud and a contrail making its way south across the sea. Gulls swarmed above the water like white scraps of paper borne on the breeze. The beach smelled of hot sand, salt water, seafood somewhat past its sell-by date, semirandom petroleum fractions. Roux smelled of sunscreen with aloe vera and coconut oil, old man's sweat and faintly of alcohol.

"What about Peru?" she asked.

"The manuscript has been duly sold to an Asian consortium that will ensure its discoveries are brought to the world at reasonable price, not coopted by either greedy governments or the Western pharmaceutical cartel." He sipped and smiled. "We realized a tidy sum on this transaction. Altogether a good thing; we certainly have expenses to defray."

"What about the people?" she asked impatiently.

"No further harm came to them." He shrugged. "For the most part drug barons cannot afford to act the way their counterparts do in the movies. They sacrifice too much of their support among the populace that way. They start to act like outlaws."

"What about those mercenaries? What happens to them?"

"Nothing."

"Nothing?" Annja was outraged.

"Nothing. Their operation is very highly connected in the United States."

Annja shook her head in disgust.

"You must learn to accept what is beyond your

power to change, child," Roux said. "You cannot save the world."

"I thought that was my mission."

"Perhaps. But you must learn to prioritize. Nothing is more certain than that you cannot save it all at once."

At that she turned a frowning face out to sea. A few sails stood up above the water like white fins. The supertanker had almost dissolved into the haze. The seagulls cried like lost souls.

"Tell me," Roux said at length.

So she did. She held back nothing, from the first hint on the Usenet of the discovery of Solomon's Jar; to her adventures in Amsterdam and subsequent escape from the Netherlands into Germany posing as the relief driver for a friendly, and well-bribed, Belgian lesbian trucker; to her visit to Ravenwood Manor.

At the last Roux grunted. "Does the expression, 'leading with your chin' suggest anything to you?"

She tipped down her shades and grinned at him. "Apparently a course of action."

He nodded and looked at the water. His expression was dark. "I have lost one champion already," he said. "I don't want to mislay another and spend the next half millennium looking for *her* replacement. Try to learn a modicum of caution, if you please."

"It's on the to-do list. You know what puzzles me?" Annja asked, quickly changing the subject.

"Of course not. I make no pretense at clairvoyance," Roux said, perturbed.

"It's not important at all, but it keeps niggling at my attention. Who or what was 'trees'?" Annja asked.

"Terry."

"Huh?"

"Don't say 'huh,' young lady. It indicates muddy and undisciplined thinking," Roux scolded.

Fleetingly Annja wondered just how much her predecessor had personified lucid and disciplined thinking. Not much, from Annja's reading of history. She chose to say nothing because it was a tender subject for Roux and she had no desire to hurt him with flippancy. Also, because he took gloomy satisfaction in lecturing her about her forerunner and her unpleasant demise, and it always made Annja acutely uncomfortable to hear the facts surrounding Joan of Arc's destruction.

"I beg your pardon," Annja said precisely and formally.

"That's better. 'Trees' is short for 'Theresia,' which is cognate to your English 'Theresa.' Trees's Schatwinkel means, Terry's Treasure Shop," Roux stated.

"Oh. I didn't know you spoke Dutch."

"You'd be surprised what oddments one picks up in a few short centuries, my dear."

He sipped his drink down until his straw slurped noisily in the ice at the bottom of his plastic cup. "So, has the true jar been found? What do you say?"

Annja frowned. "I don't know if we have sufficient evidence to say one way or another."

"Evidence? Bah!" Roux produced a theatrically Gallic sniff. "You moderns, with your veneration of rationality."

"Not everybody feels that way," she said.

"You refer to the Paleolithic dreams of your friends in Kent? Those who would cast away all modernity and return us to squinting at graffiti scrawled on the walls of caves by smoky firelight are as superstitious as those who cannot imagine life before text messaging! What you fail to realize is that rational thought is a *tool*. It suits some uses and not others. It is no less—and certainly no more."

She smiled at him. "I presume you had a point?"

"Of course! Use your intuition. You knew at once that the jar you found on Highsmith's mantel was false. What do you feel about the real Solomon's Jar?"

She expected to have to scrunch her face up and squint and concentrate. Instead she found herself answering, "It has been found," without her own conscious volition.

Roux nodded his white-bearded chin. "Indeed."

"You knew?"

"Of course. Otherwise, why would the crew of the fishing trawler who found it be murdered? A random maniac would be too coincidental, *non?* And the fact that six men were butchered in a manner which inevitably must have proven as noisy as it was messy implies strongly the existence either of confederates or supernatural strength and speed."

She cocked a brow at him. "You think demons were involved?"

"Perhaps. Not in the way you think." He shook his head. "No. Those men were murdered, most likely, by other men possessed of ample evidence that the true jar of Solomon had been found."

"Now you're using reason," Annja said.

"Of course. Did I not say it was a handy tool indeed—when appropriately used?"

He stood and began to fold his parasol. "I must be on my way. There's a world poker tour tournament commencing in Monte Carlo this evening, and I don't want to be late to put down my entry fee. I believe I've spotted a tell in Phil Ivey on the television."

"I'll never know how you square gambling with your service of the good."

"It's not important that you do so," he said. "Keep in mind that there are many paths to righteousness. And unrighteousness, as well. Your view of good will not always concur with that of others who may serve it as fully and diligently as you do yourself. That's another reason not to go looking for wrongs to right or, more precisely, not to go looking for witches to burn. You may find you have destroyed another great warrior for the cause."

Annja winced. She knew he would not use that particular metaphor lightly. He of all people.

"We will ourselves not always see eye to eye, my child," he told her, his voice gentler now. He folded up the chaise. "We may yet find ourselves at cross purposes, or even open opposition. And yet still fighting with true hearts for the same great cause."

"So you admit to working for good? I thought you were indifferent. Or undecided, maybe."

He ignored her. "The path of good is not supposed to be easy. That is the allure of the path of evil. Few who wreak great harm do so with any intention of working evil in the world. Most often their intent is exactly the opposite. And most who do lesser evils do so because it is the simplest and most expedient thing to do."

"So what's my next move?" Annja asked.

"Must I tell you everything?" Roux said dismissively.

"Well, if you aren't willing to forgo the pleasure of picking my performance apart after the fact—"

He sighed. "Don't imagine your powers shield you more than they do."

"I don't, by and large," she said. "Otherwise I wouldn't have run away so fast."

"I worry."

She reached up and briefly squeezed his hand. The flesh was resilient, like any strong hand. Yet somehow she thought to feel in its dry grasp the strength of ages.

"Thank you," she said.

"As for whence to proceed from here," he said, "you are the archaeologist. But I would be so bold as to suggest the source. I bid you good day."

He tipped his hat and walked off along the beach. His stride belied his years—the age he appeared, and vastly more his real age.

Seventeen hours later she was on an El Al Boeing 737 touching down outside Tel Aviv.

8

There was a riot going on at the Temple Mount.

Jerusalem was above all else a city of contradictions. Contrasts, between cultures, between faiths, between old and new, what had been celebrated or lamented into the ground centuries before were on studied display like trinkets in a tourist-trap window. The quaint biblical streets of the Old City, narrow and winding, were appropriately inconvenient. Mostly Annja found the place hot, dusty and tense. And that was before the riot.

Walking past a pair of Israeli soldiers standing in front of a coffee shop, their bulky battledress casting grotesque late-afternoon shadows down one of the broader streets, Annja found herself wondering why the

Holy City didn't make more of an impression on her. Although biblical archaeology wasn't her field, the fabled jar of King Solomon would have held at least academic interest for her, if not more.

Perhaps it was the depressing present. From the evident hostility among rival Christian creeds and sects, to the division between Arab and Israeli, to the less known but virulent differences among the Israeli people themselves, the city that should have been a haven of spiritual peace was a hotbed of worldly strife.

Annja had little plan at the moment. She was fairly sure the jar wasn't where legend had it, the demons King Solomon had subsequently bound within it had built him a mighty temple. Yet Roux had suggested she seek the source for knowledge.

The disturbance—maybe she had been premature in characterizing it as a *riot,* but she could feel something coming on, like a thunderhead rising from just beyond the horizon—was packed into the plaza where the Moroccan quarter had once stood, hard up against the retaining wall built by King Herod to aggrandize the temple, and also to keep the sides of Mount Moriah from slumping into what was even then a substantial urban concentration. Its gray stone face, knobbled like a collection of knees, age pitted and sprouting random tufts of brush like hair on moles, was turned all orange and gold by the setting sun. The crowd's sullen mutter washed against it and broke back like storm surf. Cutting through the white noise came the stridency of an electronically amplified voice whose words Annja could not make out.

She had passed through the forty-foot stone walls Süleyman the Magnificent had surrounded the Old City with in the sixteenth century at the New Gate and made her way through the Christian quarter. She wore what she considered standard adventure tourist drag: white cotton blouse with long sleeves rolled up, khaki cargo pants with many invaluable pockets, sunglasses and Red Wing low-top hiking shoes, unfashionable but likewise indestructible. The clothes were of good quality and were far from being glamorous or provocative. Annja knew conservative religious elements, of all three major faiths with spiritual interests vested in the country, had a record of hassling or even attacking female tourists whose dress they considered scandalous. Her ensemble was designed to make her unremarkable, as inconspicuous as her height and willowy build and looks allowed. She had a bulky pack that could serve as a daypack or masquerade as a big utilitarian purse slung over one shoulder. A digital camera rode around her neck on a strap.

As she approached the Western Wall, she noticed that the tourists and idlers and even businesspeople suddenly began to thin from the streets like townsfolk in advance of a gunfight in a Western movie. She started seeing more Galil-toting soldiers, then riot police standing between the mob and the Wailing Wall itself. The riot squad wore dark blue helmets and bulky synthetic body armor that looked startlingly like the armor of the Roman legionnaires.

Then she spotted that most infallible sign of trouble brewing, more certain than circling vultures. Vans from the international news services were parked around the edge of the big plaza, with satellite antennae sprouting from their roofs.

She didn't read Hebrew, so many of the signs being waved by the protesters, most of whom wore yarmulkes, meant nothing to her. But there were plenty of signs written in English to clarify the situation.

This particular disturbance, she gathered, was being pitched by West Bank settlers resisting government attempts to remove them from their claims outside the country's acknowledged boundaries. Some of the anti-government sentiments were astonishingly vitriolic, making her wonder what the signs she could not read might say. As she drew near she heard the cries of the protesters as they hurled insults at the riot cops and the soldiers who formed a loose cordon along the outside of the crowd.

The demonstrators were also throwing physical items that looked like bits of stone pried from the ancient walls and streets of Jerusalem itself. That tightened her brow and mouth and narrowed her eyes. She had to remind herself that more important issues lay at stake here than the preservation of random antiquities. But it ran altogether contrary to her archaeologist's instincts to think that anything could be more important.

Annja moved around outside the cordon of glumly businesslike soldiers. She still wasn't sure what she was doing here, what it was she expected to see. She felt an increasing sense of urgency, though. She was meant to be here; that much she knew.

The electronically amplified individual voice emanated from a podium erected hard by the wall itself. A tall man in a business suit with a yarmulke perched on an expensive-looking dark blond coiffure and some kind of cincture around his neck in lieu of a tie, urged the protesters to peace, love and moderation, in what Annja belatedly realized was English. Distortion and the setting's strangeness had conspired to prevent her from recognizing the calming words.

She frowned. She wasn't an avid follower of popular culture—at least, not more modern than five hundred years old or so. Still, she had the itching impression of having seen that rather handsome face, perhaps on the cover of a celebrity magazine on a table in a dentist's waiting room. She felt as if she *ought* to know who he was.

To her amazement the police and soldiers stoically

endured the stones pelting off their helmets and riot shields as if they were raindrops. Occasionally a demonstrator would turn and try to loft a rock up over the top of the wall toward the black dome of al-Aqsa Mosque, peeking over the wall's top. None of them had the range.

Some protesters turned their ire on a passing businessman—an Arab she guessed from his appearance and hunched, harried posture, though he wore a shabby tan Western-style suit. For a moment he just pulled his head farther down between his shoulders and tried to weather the abuse. Then something stung; he straightened, turned, spit something.

Instantly a pair of soldiers pounced on him and slammed him to the irregular gray flagstones with the metal butts of their rifles.

The mob surged outward, flowing around the other soldiers like water between tree boles. Whether they were themselves trying to attack other, largely Arab, passersby or simply started like a flock of pigeons by a sudden eruption of the violence that charged the air like electricity before lightning, Annja couldn't tell. The soldiers grabbed futilely at the protesters, or pushed them with their assault rifles. The mob largely ignored them, thrusting them rudely aside and flowing past, until a trooper managed to catch a handful of somebody's shirt.

Motivated, Annja guessed, by little more than the policeman's predator pounce reflex, the riot phalanx charged. They hit the mob from behind like a mobile wall. She noticed they used Roman techniques, too: jabbing with their short-sword-sized batons, then clubbing in lieu of hacking with the *gladii*.

Tentacles of the mob blew forth like debris from an explosion. One group blasted straight at her. It consisted mostly of unshaved young men who, in her flash impression, seemed more like middle-class kids dressing down than the proletarian types their work shirts and dungarees suggested. They spotted her and veered toward her, screeching in a combination of rage and triumph. Whether they took her for a possibly unsympathetic journalist or just felt like venting their feelings in some good old-fashioned foreigner bashing she couldn't tell. It didn't much matter. Annja turned and darted into the maze of narrow streets and alleys that veined the Old City.

Their cries pursued her. With the pedestrian traffic and obstructions littering her path she couldn't move very quickly. Indeed, because her pursuers had fewer compunctions about shoving people out of the way or simply running over them, they quickly gained on her.

When an age-bent man with a black hat, frock coat and snowy beard and earlocks opened a half-sprung screen door directly in her path, Annja's pursuers caught up. As she reared and stopped, without space even to dodge for fear of bowling the old man over, a hand roughly seized her right shoulder from behind.

It was almost a relief to be able to act rather than flee. As the man who held her pulled she did not resist, but rather clapped her left hand over his and turned the way he urged her. At the same time she peeled the hand off and twisted it painfully down against itself, then turned it to lock the man's elbow. Before he knew it her attacker was doubled over and immobilized.

Three more men closed in on her from behind. The lead attacker, who was skinny with a bluish white complexion emphasized by his white shirt and the blue-black hair spilling out from beneath his yarmulke, had arms spread as if to catch her in a bear hug. Sensing her first foe was controlled for the moment, Annja fired a high front snap kick straight at the point of the young man's chin. He was wide open and the kick came as quickly as a boxer's jab. His teeth clacked together, his eyes rolled up and he toppled, stunned, against a crumbling wall.

The first assailant was struggling and complaining in energetic Hebrew. Still keeping his wrist twisted and her forearm pressed against his arm Annja brought a knee up into his midsection. The breath burst from him. He doubled over even tighter.

The two still standing had fanned out left and right. They also wore white shirts, black pants and pasty complexions; one sported thick glasses. I'm beating up a bunch of nerds, she thought.

"We can call this off anytime," she told them.

They rolled their eyes wildly at each other. The one she'd kicked sat rubbing his jaw and weeping.

The two still on their feet issued inarticulate screams and charged. The one to Annja's left hugged the wall. She spun the man she was still holding and launched him into the man with a thrusting side kick. They went down in a tangle of limbs.

The last assailant closed, flailing punches. Annja ducked down behind raised forearms, fending off the flurry of swipes with motions of her elbows. The young man breathed like a bellows; his spittle sprayed Annja's face.

"Enough," she said. She quit blocking with her right, allowing a clumsy blow to glance off her lowered forehead. The hand she'd freed seized the front of the youth's shirt and yanked him toward her. She met him with a head butt to the bridge of the nose.

She heard cartilage crunch. She pushed the man away. He stumbled back several paces, sat down and stared at her. Blood cascaded from his broken nose and streamed into his lower jaw, which hung slack with astonishment. He gagged as he became aware of the taste of his own blood. Then he covered his face with both hands and began to wail.

Annja shook her head. She wasn't sure what had motivated the young men to attack her.

A furious shout brought her head up and around. Men crowded into sight around a dogleg in the claustrophobic lane behind her. Those she could see well enough in the thickening gray shadows and velvet gloom wore yarmulkes and protesters' armbands.

That ended their similarities to the quartet of fervent young students who lay moaning and disheveled in the gutter at Annja's feet. These men wore the same workmen's clothes. But these looked used. They were more filled out, too, especially in the area of chest, shoulders, and biceps—and bellies. Their hands were strong and work roughened. They gripped the tools of clubs and staffs and a length of metal pipe or two as if used to wielding hard things.

Burly as they were, they came fast. Annja turned and fled.

She vaulted a pile of crates. She paused long enough to scatter the pile across the narrow passage between stone walls irregular and grimed with not particularly graceful age. A couple of the lead pursuers duly tripped over them and sprawled hard on the cobblestones in sprays of splinters and curses in English and Hebrew. At least she assumed the Hebrew was cursing.

They swore louder as their mates trampled right over them, dogged in pursuit. Others smashed the crates to jagged slats.

Annja had long legs and a runner's wind. She should

have left the mob in her dust with ease; though the deep-tanned look of some of them indicated they had the kind of endurance to labor all day in the hot Holy Land sun, that sort of thing didn't translate well into running either fast or far.

But with random loose stones underfoot, various cornices or piles of goods intruding in the inadequate right of way, and the constant intrusion of passersby who simply couldn't get out of the way fast enough, she could run little if any faster than her pursuers. Glancing over her shoulder, she saw one of them stiff-arm an elderly man face-first into a wall.

Anger kindled within her, a smolder fanning rapidly to a blaze. She longed to invoke the sword and dispense some well-earned justice. A dozen armed and burly men pursuing a single woman was not some semiharmless emotional venting but a lynch mob. Why they were after her she didn't know, but they obviously didn't intend to sit her down for an earnest discussion of internal Israeli politics if they caught her. She knew she had every right to take their lives if they raised their weapons against her. She formed her hand as if grasping a simple hilt, began to summon her will….

Annja stopped herself. She ducked left down an alley, tripped over the supporting slanting stanchion of a shabby gray-and-black-striped awning, fell, rolled and was up again barely slowed, her trousers streaked with dust and alley grime. Her leading pursuers went down with furious yells, tearing at the cloth that wrapped them up and barking their shins on the planks.

I can't, she grimly realized. The bruises she had given the angry students were one thing. In the current political climate if she left bodies bleeding in the ancient dust all hell would break loose.

Yet her mission was too vital to be brought to an end in an alley by a band of thugs, whatever their motivation. Roux had warned her to be cautious. Even after half a millennium the terrible death of his first protégée was like an incurable wound within him.

Maybe I can handle them unarmed she thought. She did have advantages, not least of which was that none of her pursuers could possibly suspect just how effective she could be at close combat, with or without a weapon in her hand. But for all her speed, strength and well-honed fighting skills, and even for the fact that such a number of them would inevitably get in one another's way, particularly in such tight confines, she well knew it would only take one lucky hit to put her down.

She started left down another alley. A knot of beefy men appeared at the far end like a cork stuffed in a bottle. They held clubs, too. "There's the bitch!" one shouted in pure New Jersey English.

Where did these thugs come from? she wondered.

With a shock like a belly punch she realized this was no random outburst of violence. This attack was *directed*.

At her.

Annja turned and bolted out of the alley. A man loomed up to her right, both hands holding a length of white-painted pipe above a face beet-red from sun and blood pressure. She side kicked him in the midst of his well-filled work shirt. Air blew out of him in a furious shout, but his belly saved him from any serious harm. He did fly back into the faces of his nearest comrades, buying her a few shavings of a second to run again.

The street turned right before her. She darted around.

And found herself staring at the cracked khaki stucco of a blind wall.

She was trapped.

9

Annja looked up. A lot of the one-story buildings in the Old City had fairly low rooftops given that a millennium or two's accretion had raised the level of the streets. She could climb such. But it was hopeless. The three walls that hemmed her all rose at least two stories. A battered sheet-metal drain pipe ran down from the rooftop to her right. At least one of the clamps holding it in place had come entirely free of the crumbling wall, and the rest were being held in place only by paint or rust or habit for all she knew. Even if she could scramble up the pipe in time, there seemed no way it would ever support her weight. Muscle mass was dense. Especially hers.

Behind her she heard men's voices braying in unmistakable triumph. The thunder of pursuing boots dwindled. The thugs behind her had slowed to a walk.

They know I'm trapped, she thought. They're savoring the moment.

She eyed the rickety pipe again. If I can catch it high enough up… She braced herself to spring.

A doorway she hadn't even seen suddenly opened to her left. "This way, dearie," a voice hissed in English from the darkness within.

"Who are you?" Annja asked.

"Witness to your demise if you don't move *now*."

A voice called loudly from out of sight around the corner. The words weren't clear, but their import was.

Annja dodged through the door. It shut quietly behind, sealing off the last gray light of dusk.

For a moment it seemed she stood in hot, claustrophobic blackness. She felt panic thrill within her.

"Easy, dearie," the voice said. "Just breathe deeply. You're safe now—safe as you are anywhere, anyway. The door's locked. Also it's not so easy to see from outside, as you might have noticed."

Annja became aware of an orange glow rising before her. It became a brass oil lamp, reflecting the orange light of its own flame, being brought up to the level of her face. She sensed a shadowy form behind it, heard breathing.

"Come with me." The voice was American. It was that of a woman of mature years, she realized.

The lantern swung around. Butter-colored light glowed in the coarse weave of a hood covering the mysterious woman's head as she led off down a corridor. A moving arc of light traveled with them, revealing rough stone walls and a low ceiling. The passageway led down a ramp, sufficiently smooth from use to be slightly slippery, then up a set of steps.

Up and down the shrouded figure led her, right and left. Sometimes they passed open doorways, dark oblongs that signaled their presence by making the lamp-flame waver and brushing cool across Annja's cheek. Once or twice they came upon a side chamber illuminated from within, once by candles on tables and set in niches by the wall, a second by a low-wattage lamp beneath a heavy shade. In both, silent, dark figures huddled, reading or contemplating, Annja could not be sure.

Such directional sense as she may have possessed had long been destroyed by apparently random windings, and incipient strangeness, by the time her guide pushed open a door of age-blackened wood and led her into a small side chamber.

"Sit yourself down," the woman said from inside her cowl. She gestured toward a rude round wooden table flanked by two stools in the center of the room. It reminded Annja of nothing so much as a monk's cell.

When Annja hesitated the woman set the lamp down on one side of the table and said, "We have relatively little time here. Relatively, because it would take a lifetime or so to tell you all you need to know. And I'd have to learn most of it first. So let's get started with what I can give you, all right?"

She pushed the hood back. Big dark eyes gazed at Annja from a strong-featured, leanly handsome face. A mane of heavy dark hair, maybe black, and marked with a showy silver-white blaze above the right side of the forehead, framed it.

"I'm Tsipporah," the woman said. "I'm a student of kabbalah. I'll be your guide for this portion of your journey, so you might as well make yourself comfortable. And you are…?" She stuck out a hand.

"I'm Annja Creed. Pleased to meet you." She shook the offered hand, then blinked. "You acted as if you knew me."

"I know *what* you are," Tsipporah said. "It practically blazes from you. Be wary, child, because anyone you come across with any degree of real insight can spot you instantly. But my own understanding doesn't quite extend to names and personalities. Mostly I'm a keen spotter of the blindingly obvious. And while you might want to stand, I'm going to take a load off, if you don't mind."

Tsipporah sat. A beat later Annja emulated her. The room was almost claustrophobic, with pale-stuccoed walls and a low ceiling of dark planks. From the cool and earthy smell Annja knew she was underground. She realized the chamber must have been a first floor at some point, or perhaps higher. The street level had risen much farther over the years than she'd first appreciated.

"Excuse my ignorance of Jewish tradition," Annja said, "but I thought only men could study kabbalah. Or are you—?"

"One of the goofy followers of young Mark Peter up there?" The woman laughed. Picking up the lamp, she put the flame to a cigarette she'd produced from somewhere and puffed it alight. "I'm surprised you recognized him."

"It's hard to miss Mark Peter Stern in the media these days," Annja said. "Although it took hearing the name to jog it into my memory. He's the flavor-of-the-month guru for all kinds of celebrities, isn't he?" She shook her head. "Even somebody with as little interest in popular culture as I have can scarcely miss him. His face looks out at you from every other magazine cover in airport newsstands, as well as being all over television and the Internet."

Tsipporah nodded. "There are two traditional rules about studying kabbalah. One, that you must be at least forty years old. The other that you be a man. Neither was ordained by the Creator. One arises from sound sense, the other from fear. The first is wise—and as you probably gather, Stern certainly failed to honor it. He qualifies now, though you'd hardly know it to look at him. Meanwhile, I'm hardly the first to violate the latter prohibition, nor am I likely to be the last.

"But on to business. Time's an illusion, but it's a fleet one. You seek the jar, don't you?"

Annja hesitated. Roux had warned her almost compulsively about security—as if keeping secrets was anything alien to a kid raised in an orphanage by nuns. Yet Tsipporah seemed to know a lot about her already. Annja got no sense of evil or menace from the older woman—not that she regarded her danger sense as anywhere near infallible. And anyway, she thought, if she knows enough about me to even ask the question, what do I really give up by answering honestly?

"Yes," she said after processing her thoughts.

"All right." Tsipporah smiled as if her guest had passed a test. "Then you might benefit from the straight scoop, don't you think?"

Annja frowned. "With all due respect," she said, trying to match tone to content, "why are you helping me? I'm a foreigner and a total stranger."

"No stranger than anybody else in this town," the older woman said. "And as you probably guessed from my accent, I'm not exactly a local myself."

"New Jersey?" Annja guessed.

"Right the first time. You seem to have a bit of an accent in your own speech. Well hidden, but it's there." She cocked her head to one side. With her triangular chin and big dark eyes it made her look like a shrewd bird. "New Orleans?"

Annja nodded. "I didn't think any trace remained."

"I told you I'm very observant," Tsipporah said. "Anyway, about those demons. The story says that Solomon bound them and used them to build his temple overnight. Maybe it didn't happen literally that way. But take my word for it—there are demons out there. You probably have some idea about that already, although you still probably can't fully bring yourself to believe. King Solomon bound them to serve him. And serve him they did, in whatever particulars."

Annja felt her heartbeat pick up. The woman was reading her all too well, so far. "I don't want to…overstep any religious boundaries. But I thought Solomon was considered a holy man in Judaism, as well as Christianity."

Tsipporah held one hand out flat, palm down, and rocked it side to side. "You want to know why a righteous man would have traffic with demons, right?"

"Right."

"The short answer is because he could. Summoning and binding demons to your will is more of a gray area, morally and theologically speaking. It isn't intrinsically unrighteous."

"But aren't demons evil?" Annja asked.

"Absolutely. In ways I doubt you can begin to fathom.

Although with a little time I suspect you'll know far more about them than you want, dearie."

"Then why isn't it evil to deal with them?"

"We're talking about binding and using them, not the other way around. Of course, there's always the risk of role reversal—gives the whole thing a certain spice. You might think of them, in the proper hands, as tools, morally neutral when under control. For our purposes, I think you can safely take it that King Solomon was indeed a righteous man. And an extremely powerful magician."

Annja shook her head. "Forgive me. It's a little hard to get my mind around the concept of magic and evil. Demonology, anyway. In a conventional, I guess, religious conception."

"Oh, it *is* evil—to conventionally religious eyes. Remember your illustrious predecessor was condemned for witchcraft. And she never even practiced."

Annja caught her breath. "How do you know about that?"

"Joan of Arc? Doesn't every schoolchild—"

"That she was my predecessor. How did you know?"

"I know the signs. I travel the *sephiroth*—the spheres, you might call them. Sometimes I have visions. Sometimes I just have hunches. Sometimes I'm just a batty old lady who ought to take up a different hobby, like knitting."

Annja laughed. She couldn't help liking this peculiar woman, with her mixture of brashness and what seemed genuine humility. "I have a hard time seeing you knitting."

"Don't sell it short, sweetie. Keeps the fingers nimble and arthritis at bay." Tsipporah blew smoke at an angle up into the air. "To get back to my story, from which I so inconsiderately distracted myself, whatever the demons did for Solomon, when they were done with it—or he was done with them—he bound them in a brass jar. He then sealed it with lead, inscribing in it the sign of the five-pointed star—"

"Not six?" Annja interrupted.

"Nope. The good old pentagram."

"But I thought the six-pointed star was the shape of Solomon's seal, as well as the shield of David."

"That bit of confusion seems to have cropped up late in the nineteenth century. Probably for political and nationalistic reasons more than anything else—to kind of add throw weight to the six-pointed star as the symbol for Judaism. Good King Solomon sealed the demons in with lead, with the pentagram, and threw the jar into the Red Sea."

"The Red Sea? But supposedly the jar was just recently fished out of the Mediterranean."

Tsipporah wagged a finger back and forth before her. "Tch, tch. You're getting ahead of me. Legend says somebody fished the jar out of the Red Sea a long, long time ago. Treasure hunters, of all things, eager to use the demons to uncover riches."

"How'd that turn out?"

The other woman shrugged. "Don't know, truth to tell. Might not've turned out badly, if the people who uncorked the demons didn't get greedy and try to control them all, which is a very poor idea if you don't happen to be, say, King Solomon. Then again, anybody who'd let loose seventy-odd powerful demons on the world to get their hands on treasure is probably too greedy by definition, no? Anyway, I've never seen a good accounting for exactly what came next, not that I trusted, nor have I got any kind of insight into it. The key thing is, what with one thing and another, the jar, now emptied of demons but not power, got chucked into the Mediterranean. Where, in the fullness of time, it was discovered by some Greek fishermen who later came to very sticky ends."

Annja leaned forward. Her pulse spiked again. "So it's true? The real jar has been found?"

"What are we doing here, sweetie? You tell me. I'm not going to tell you to trust me. You do know never, ever to trust anybody who tells you to, right?"

Annja smirked.

"Good—thought so. But look at the circumstances. Here you are. Here I am. How did we happen to come together, anyway?" Tsipporah asked.

Annja looked at her for a moment. "All right," she asked, "how?"

"I don't know, exactly. I just know why. We were supposed to." She stubbed out her cigarette in a little flat tin that looked to Annja like a tuna can she'd picked up from the floor beneath the table. She immediately lit another.

Annja frowned slightly but resolved not to be a smoking prude. Lots of people smoked here anyway. Almost everybody, in fact.

"I might have hired those big, strapping men to chase you here," Tsipporah said through the smoke, "even if they are a bit sweaty for my tastes. But then how would I know those things I do about you? I didn't know your name before you came here. Didn't really know what you looked like, beyond some fairly broad outlines. But I knew you were good. And that you seek the jar."

Tsipporah smiled. "Put another way, it's destiny, sweetie. Get used to it. You'll find yourself being in the right place at the right time a lot. Or the wrong place at the worst possible time. All a matter of perspective."

"So what do you get out of this, anyway, Tsipporah?" Annja asked.

The older woman tipped her head back, let smoke trail toward the ceiling, laughed. "If more people re-membered to ask that question the world would be a happier place. Let's just say that I regard myself, in my own small and studious way, as a servant of good."

"Does that mean God?" Annja asked

Tsipporah smiled a crooked smile. "The Creator is served in many ways, some of which would curl your hair. We all serve the Creator, dear. The worst no less than the best. Let's just say that you and I both choose to serve the good and leave off splitting those particular hairs. Fair?"

After a moment Annja nodded. "Fair." She didn't sound any more convinced than she felt.

"Let's also just say I enjoy a vicarious thrill as much as the next person," Tsipporah said. "You're embroiled in a mission that has three parts. It's of the mind, of the spirit and of the body. Let's just say I'm not up to the run-and-jump part these days. In fact, being a kabbalist is about as bookish a pastime as there is. Sedentary, you know. So I get a kick out of being involved, at whatever remove, in your adventures."

Annja smiled. It seemed to her a little silly that anyone else might envy her the indecision and inconvenience and the not infrequent terror that went with her new life.

"Speaking of kabbalists—I know that's kind of a clumsy segue—but that reminds me about Mark Stern. What's he doing up there, anyway, with his megaphone by the wall?"

"He's associated with the settlers' movement. The

government wants to close down some of the settlements in occupied territory. Some of the residents object pretty vehemently." Tsipporah sighed. "There's a good reason I decided to immerse myself in the study of the Tree of Life, and put such worldly political concerns behind me."

With a sudden flash of insight, Annja said, "You were a political activist?"

"What else?' The older woman drew on her cigarette. "I'm still a devoted Marxist, of course."

"I didn't know they believed in kabbalah."

"Groucho's my favorite," Tsipporah went on laughing. "You probably figured that out already. Never really cared for Harpo, though."

10

"Mark Peter Stern positions himself as a voice of peace and reason between the government and the settlers," Tsipporah said. "Me, I'm not so sure."

"How good a kabbalist is he?" Annja asked.

Tsipporah compressed her lips to a line and sat back in her chair with her chin sunk toward her sternum. "Kabbalah is infinite," she said at last, "and to know who's *really* wise in its ways would therefore take infinite understanding, it seems to me. Not something I pretend to, egotistical as I am in my dotage. And then again, there are plenty of pious Jews rather more than Gentiles, I expect, who'd tell you there *is* no such thing as a good kabbalist."

She looked up sharply. "So I reckon what you

really want me to tell you is how good a *man* Mark Stern is. Right?"

"All right. You caught me. But don't expect me to buy any of that 'dotage' nonsense from you," Annja said.

"Allow me my little conceits. One of the worst consequences of a culture that overvalues youth is that eventually it comes to overvalue age. Big mistake—experience is a wonderful teacher, but she has some real schmucks for pupils. Also making a big deal of my age gives me license to spew random drive-by aphorisms like that. Anyway, before I disappoint you with my pop-psych assessment of the man, why do you ask?"

"Aside from the fact he happened to be in the same place at the same time as we were, functionally?"

"Right. There's no such thing as coincidence. But that doesn't imply everything is about us," Tsipporah said.

"I found a number for the Malkuth Foundation's New York offices on the caller ID of a murdered woman's phone," Annja said, "in a shop that may have had possession of the jar."

Tsipporah sat upright. "Tell me."

Annja did. She felt no more than the slightest tug of reluctance. She sensed no taint of evil in this woman or in this place. And even if she was wrong, it seemed unlikely she was telling her mysterious hostess anything she couldn't find out by some means of her own. *Or maybe I'm just rationalizing again*, she thought wryly.

"Hoo." Tsipporah let her breath slip out between pursed lips when Annja concluded. "That is quite the story. I'm caught up in more of an adventure than I even realized."

"I've been wondering, though," Annja said. "The jar on Highsmith's mantel. Was that the real jar?"

"What does your heart tell you?" Tsipporah asked.

Annja shook her head. "It told me it wasn't."

"In cases like this that's probably as good a test as any. A person in your position could feel the presence of power like that. Trust yourself."

"Not always as easy as it sounds," Annja said.

"Whoever promised you easy?".

"Something about the jar that was there puzzles me," Annja said. "Of course, I'm not sure it has any significance."

"Tell me," Tsipporah said. "Gratify my curiosity, if nothing else."

"It was covered with symbols. Small, crabbed, hard to read—at first I thought they were just scratch marks."

"What kind of symbols?"

"I'm not sure. I've never really seen anything like them before. Convoluted. The closest thing I can compare them to is symbols on an electronic-circuit diagram."

"Sigils," Tsipporah said.

"What are those?"

"Personal symbols for each demon that had been confined within the jar. Like seals—a king's signet ring, that sort of thing." She looked thoughtful in the wavering orange light. "That's highly significant. It may not have been the real jar—I'm sure it wasn't—but it sounds like an awfully good copy."

"Why would anybody make a copy of Solomon's Jar? For that matter, why would anybody want an empty jar badly enough to kill over it?" Annja asked, still unsure of what to believe.

"Because it has power. By use of the proper magics the demons might be forced to enter it again. Or it might be used to compel demons to obedience." She dipped her head briefly to the side. "It might even be destroyed—this being the preferred outcome of the demons themselves, I expect."

"Tsipporah," Annja said, "what are demons, anyway?"

"Bad. Powerful forces. Pretty much as advertised."

"Look, if there are demons, why don't we see them more?"

"I could give you the canned, expected answers about all the nasty things people do to each other," Tsipporah said, "except most of those are just that: we do them to each other. No demons need apply. A demon can get you to do nasty things. Things you'd never do on your own—that's what possession's all about. They can even boot you out of your own body for good and take over. That's what the Catholic Church calls *obsession*. But the bad urges that give rise to the bad things we do, demons don't cause them. They make use of them. They don't start the fire. But they do spray gas on it."

She took a hit from her cigarette. "And that's the reason you don't see them walking down the street. Under normal circumstances, at least. For various reasons—partly constraints imposed by the nature of reality, partly preference—they do the vast amount of their work indirectly. Influencing our thoughts and emotions. Their actions are almost exclusively in the realm of the psychological. Although to dismiss them as purely psychological phenomena is a very bad mistake indeed."

For a moment they sat in silence. The lamp flame flickered low. Annja realized she'd lost count of how many cigarettes Tsipporah had gone through. She was too caught up in what the older woman was telling her to be much bothered by the smoke, though it did make her throat scratchy.

"So what about Stern?" she asked at length. "Is he a charlatan?"

"That depends. By charlatan, do you mean someone who pretends to mystical powers he doesn't have? Or one who has no mystical powers, but pretends to?"

"I don't see the distinction, I'm afraid," Annja said.

"Then look again, sweetie. Stern has powers, make no mistake. Just not necessarily the ones he tells his followers he has. He may not even believe he really has any power, in which case he's the most deluded of all. What's most painfully apparent is that he doesn't really know what he's doing."

She ran a hand through her silver-streaked hair, then laughed. "But then, why should he be any different from anybody else, hey? And like all of us, he doesn't let the fact he doesn't know what he's doing slow him down."

Annja chewed her lower lip, trying to not let Tsipporah see the schoolgirlish gesture. She was thinking glumly about how much that aphorism applied to her.

I'm the champion of good, she thought, and I don't really know what that means. Nor what good actually is, for that matter. Am I the schmuck here?

"You seem troubled," Tsipporah said gently.

The words broke the surface tension of Annja's reverie. She realized her own head had drooped toward her chest. She lifted it and looked at Tsipporah. The vague glow of the lamp no doubt softened and flattered the older woman's features, but she looked agelessly beautiful and wise. Like some sort of archetype, Annja thought.

"Well—I don't know if I should talk to you about this," Annja said. "But I need to talk to somebody. And you seem, well, wise."

Tsipporah held up a weary hand, cigarette clipped between two fingers, and drew a zigzag in the air, like Zorro. "I'm just somebody who dragged you in off the street, sweetie. Don't impute more to me than I even pretend to claim for myself." She took a drag. "Bring wisdom into it, how wise are you to trust somebody you met like this? Huh?"

"Humor me, then. You're the closest thing to a sage I've come across in a while." Annja wasn't sure if Roux counted, or to what extent. She wasn't sure how wise it was to trust *him*, for that matter. The more so since he kept hinting she shouldn't, necessarily.

"I wonder if I am worthy. I have shed blood," Annja said.

"In defense of innocence?"

"Yes. And of myself as well."

The older woman laughed. "'If someone comes to kill you, kill him first,' as the great commentator Rashi interprets the Torah. That's the common right of all humans. Do you think you have fewer rights than the meanest goatherd when fighting for good?"

Annja looked at her through wide eyes. "Do you—" There's no tactful way to say this, she realized with a sinking heart "Do you believe in my mission, too?"

"You think I'd be here talking to you if I didn't?" Tsipporah rolled her eyes.

"But I thought—"

I'm not sure what I thought, Annja realized. In spite—or perhaps because—of the ferocious ministrations of the nuns at the orphanage in New Orleans, she did not think of herself as conventionally Christian at all, much less Catholic. To her amazement Roux had assured her, when she'd finally confessed the fact to him, that it didn't matter. She still wasn't sure she believed him....

"You thought Christians had a monopoly on the good, maybe?"

"No—God, no. I mean—that didn't come out right— I mean I'd never..."

Tsipporah reached out and took her hand with one hand and patted it with the other. "Ease up, dearie. I'm only messing with you. Of course you don't. Guess what? Neither do we, chosen people or not.

"Which do you think is more likely? That a given religion is bigger than the Creator, or that the Creator is bigger than any and all religions? Which vessel is the larger, do you reckon, my dear?"

"The Creator, I guess. I don't pretend to know for sure, though."

Tsipporah laughed again. "Right answer, dearie! If you could truly *know* the Creator, you'd *be* the Creator, yes? Who less could understand such a One? Not to mention such a Nothing."

She shook her head. "But enough of my goofy wordplay. We humans cannot really understand the Creator. But it falls to some of us to try, anyway. Some of us call ourselves kabbalists. I don't know which of us has the worse job, my child. Yours is the more athletic, in any event.

"But I do think you're right on track with that concern. You're called on to defend others, as well as yourself, of course. And that's righteous—being given a sword only you can wield is what I'd call pretty clear evidence of some kind of mandate."

Annja felt her eyes widen. "You know?"

Tsipporah patted her cheek. "Of course, dearie. Goes with the territory. And now the word of warning. You need to watch for any tendencies to, ah, freelance."

"Meaning?"

"If you go looking for dragons to slay, it's surprising what'll soon look like a dragon to you. Be always alert to the difference between righteousness and self-righteousness."

Annja smiled a bit tentatively. "I've been told that while saving the world is my job description, I need to prioritize."

"That's true. But it's only part of the truth," Tsipporah stated.

She leaned forward and caught Annja's hands in both of hers. "Listen to me on this. *Hear* me. Demons do their deadliest work through our virtues."

"How do you mean?"

"Even as the strong are more dangerous than the weak," Tsipporah said, "the best are more potentially destructive than the worst. Only those who consider themselves the most selfless are capable of conceiving a notion like cleansing the world by exterminating all the people of a certain race, just to pluck an example out of the air."

"Isn't selfishness wrong?"

"You already know better than that, girl," Tsipporah said, letting go and leaning back. "All things that live are selfish. Anyone who claims otherwise is lying right there—and don't you think it's worse if they don't *know* they're lying? The merely self-interested are far less destructive than the convinced selfless.

"And that's why Mark Peter Stern might be a very dangerous man, my dear. Not because he's a bad man. But because he's so good—and so invincibly *convinced* of it. Such a man is capable of anything. For the good, of course."

Annja felt a sinking sensation in her stomach. "What you're really warning me against," she said quietly, "is myself."

"Both, honey. That said, have faith in yourself." Tsipporah patted her cheek. "You just always have to guard against the temptation to cross the line from defender of the innocent to attacker of the wicked."

Annja sighed. Her burden seemed heavier than the weight of all the masonry above—than the weight of all the noble sanctuary, up there on that mount, that was so drenched in holiness that half the world's people seemed ready to kill each other over it.

"What do I do now?" she asked.

"Sweetie, you know how this mystic-guide shtick works. I can help you find out where you are, and clarify where you've been. I can drop a hint or two about the paths that lie open to you. But you have to choose. Only you."

Annja grimaced. "You can't even give me a *hint?*"

Tsipporah laughed. "I wish I had a mirror! Didn't your parents teach you not to make faces like that?"

"My parents died when I was small," Annja said in a level voice.

"I'm so sorry. I didn't mean—"

"It's okay. Not about my parents, of course. That'll never be okay. I thought I'd get used to it for a long time. But it's never happened. The best I can do is put it away and not think about it.

"But what you said—no harm done, Tsipporah. And as for making faces, the nuns at the orphanage where I was raised used to crack me on the knuckles with a ruler when I made them."

Tsipporah roared with laughter, surprisingly robust, ringing in the womb-like confines of the room. "So naturally you kept doing it! Ladies and gentlemen, we have a winner! Now that I know you, I feel a lot more optimistic about the cause of good than I have in years."

Annja smiled crookedly. "In spite of my problems with authority?"

"Because of them, dearie." She leaned forward across the table, until Annja feared she'd catch her hair on fire from the flickering lamp flame.

"I can tell you this much, the Jar of Solomon must be found. And seen into the proper hands."

Annja laughed. "Gee, thanks. And of course you can't tell me whose hands those are."

Tsipporah sat back. "Of course." She sighed. "Well. Time to be moving along. We each have our destinies." She rose and moved to a wall, made a gesture. Annja heard a slight click.

A light fixture mounted into the ceiling overhead came on. Annja had not noticed it in the gloom.

"A lightbulb?" she said, as scandalized as surprised. She blinked dazzled eyes. "There was an electric light here all along, and I've been sitting squinting in the dark for hours until I'm half blind?" Her voice rose rather higher than she'd intended at the end of the question.

"Of course," Tsipporah said. "This is a modern country, sweetheart. Of course there's electric light."

"Then why?" She could muster no more than a sputter.

Tsipporah laughed. "Because talking about esoteric matters goes much better with that sort of illumination." She gestured toward the oil lamp, whose flame, now guttering low, was scarcely to be seen in the light of what Annja, her eyes somewhat adjusted, realized as a pretty weak bulb. "Don't you have any sense of the mystic?" She shook her head. Her heavy mane swept around her shoulders. "You may be up on the latest fashions, but you need to cultivate a sense of *style*."

"You think I'm fashionable?" Annja asked, perplexed.

"Come on, rouse yourself and give me a hug," the older woman said. "Then I need to lead you out of here."

"Not by the most direct route, I'm guessing."

Tsipporah's smile was radiant. "Of course not! Now you're getting the idea."

11

The night air was cool. It smelled of dust, cooking spices, the inevitable diesel exhaust. Annja realized she had no idea what time it was. The streets of the Old City seemed deserted, or at least the narrow street outside the door Tsipporah held open for her.

"I can't tell you to go safely," the older woman said, "for I know you won't. I could bid you to walk always in the light—but I'm sure you shall. So I'll wish you all the joy it's possible for you to attain."

They embraced, kissing each other on the cheek. Annja wasn't sure whether the warmth she felt toward this woman was more like the feeling for the mother she'd scarcely known or the sister she'd never had. Lack of referents, she guessed.

"One final word about Mark Stern," Tsipporah said. "He's better at stirring up forces than he is at controlling them. And he's got poor judgment in associates."

Annja nodded. "Thank you. I'll keep that in mind. Will I see you again?"

"Unlikely, child." Tsipporah shook her star-blazed mane regretfully. "You will most likely not find this place again, either. You are fated to move through life forming few lasting connections, at least so long as you bear your burden. It is a harsh road for a woman to walk."

She smiled. "But I believe it will have its compensations."

THE OLD CITY SEEMED to have rolled up its sidewalks along with the vendors' rugs. By keeping the well-lit dome of al-Aqsa Mosque atop the Temple Mount at her back Annja knew she was heading west. It was her only reference point in the maze into which Tsipporah had released her.

She had picked her way down no more than three twists of narrow streets and shoulder-width alleys when she heard a growl of angry voices to her right. She moved toward the sound, telling herself she needed to make sure trouble wasn't about to erupt all over her from some unforeseen direction.

She came to a blind alley or small cul-de-sac. She saw six burly men in weathered work clothes with necks as

large as their heads. Three of them held clubs, either ba-
tonlike sticks or metal pipes. Three held big-bladed
weapons, more short swords than knives, at least two
feet long with broad chopping blades. Annja thought of
machetes, although she had no idea if they were that or
some local equivalent. It wasn't exactly an exotic design.

Annja drew in a sharp breath.

They had her pale, black-haired Englishman backed
against the steel-slat shutters covering the front of a
tobacco shop.

"What you want with the jar?" one man said in gut-
tural, heavily accented English. In the gleam of a street-
light the hair cropped close to his head showed hints of
red. He wore some kind of dark band around his throat.
It looked braided. He held one of the broad-bladed
chopping weapons in a ham-sized fist while he prodded
the notch of his captive's collarbone with a sausage-like
finger. "Tell or it will go hard on you."

To Annja, standing unnoticed behind the men, whose
attention was riveted to their prey, it looked as if things
had already gone hard for her unnamed friend. His face,
hanging down toward his open collar, was swollen and
starting to discolor into one giant bruise. One eye was
almost swollen shut; blood from a broken nose made a
dark beard and mustache and had poured down to dye
a messy bib on the front of his shirt.

He looked up. "I told you," he said. His lips were

swollen and split. The words came out half whisper, half mumble. "I'm an archaeological researcher. Such a find would be of inestimable value—"

A beefy fist rammed into his belly from a man standing to the red-haired man's left. The young Englishman doubled over as the air was driven from his body. He gagged, coughed, then tried to straighten.

"He's not saying anything," another man said. "Let's do him. Let the filthy Arabs take the blame. Just another tourist cut up by savages."

"Who cares what he has to say?" said the man who had most recently punched the Englishman. His free hand held a club. "We just need to make sure he can't meddle anymore."

"Hear that, friend?" the red-haired man said, almost avuncular. "You're running out of options pretty quick now. But if you sing me a sweet enough song, who knows? Maybe you will live."

The young Briton tried to stand erect but could only manage a painful half-stoop. "Sorry to disappoint you," he said in a clearer voice. "But I can't carry a tune in a bucket. In good faith, though, I have to warn you—" he turned his head aside and spit blood at the cobblestones "—it's you lot who have the problem now."

And he lifted his head and looked right past them.

His captors stood staring at him a moment, postures redolent of suspicion, leaning forward like hungry dogs.

Apparently none of them wanted to be first to fall for the old "look over there" gag. After a few heartbeats the central man, apparently the leader, slowly turned.

Standing three yards behind him, Annja smiled. His slitted eyes went wide.

She held the sword.

"Throw down your weapons and walk out of here," she told them in a ringing voice. She didn't particularly care if she attracted official attention, at least at this point in the proceedings. Search how they might, the police would never find her in possession of a weapon. Nor would they believe it if they saw it. "I will let you go unharmed."

All six goggled at the cross-hilted steel in her hand. They were having trouble believing, too. But it made an impression; she could see that. They had a sense of history in this part of the world, to understate grandly. The Crusaders' swords with their cruciform hilts were remembered with fear and respect by Muslim and Jew alike.

It had been a reluctant if flash decision to summon the sword before making her presence known. This way there was a chance to avoid bloodshed. These men were serious and their every attitude and action showed they were accustomed to doing violence. Annja knew merely being seen would never make them scuttle away like roaches, as it did many common-thug types. And if an unarmed and obviously American woman challenged them, they'd just laugh.

They did anyway, as she feared they would. "You may believe your actions to be righteous," she told them, words cracking like a whip, "but your actions are evil. Go now and save yourselves a lot of pain."

The Englishman called out something in Hebrew from behind them. The dark-haired man who had earlier gut punched him backhanded him with a casual swipe, not so much as turning his head. The black-furred back of his hand took the young man across the mouth and slammed him back into the shutters with a clanging impact.

"Nice try, girlie," the leader said. "But you have waded in much too deep. Throw that toy down before we take it away and spank you with it, hey?"

With impeccable pack-predator instincts his comrades had begun to move forward slowly. They fanned out so far as the street's width permitted, to take her from the sides. She held her face immobile. She knew there was a reason for the, "charge a gun, run away from a knife" adage.

She was about to teach it to them.

She made herself pull each breath deep down to the center of her body. Adrenaline flowed in her veins like an army of crazed jesters. Part of the mad chorus was due to fear. They were many, strong and seasoned fighters. And part came from anticipation.

"Touch me," she said, "and you will die."

"Listen—" the leader said. The man to his right, the man with the shock of dark hair who had struck the Englishman twice in Annja's sight, suddenly grabbed her right wrist. He pulled hard to yank her into a bear hug.

She didn't move. She had rooted, dropped her weight and sunk into poised relaxation. His slitted eyes went wide.

She turned toward him. The sword flashed. Its blade bit with an ax-on-wood sound.

It flashed between the wrist of the hand that held her and the man's arm, scarcely slowed.

The hand tightened spasmodically on her arm. Without the aid of the muscles of the arm it lacked strength. It was more a nervous jitter.

Blood squirted from between hand and stump. The man screamed as if only realizing a beat late what had befallen him. He staggered back, holding his truncated arm before his eyes, slipping into shock.

Annja sensed a rush of movement from her right. She continued her spin to her left, coming around as the man who had gotten around to her right side rushed in with a wild scream and an overhand cut of his machete. She caught his forearm with her left hand. It was like gripping a telephone pole. Using her hips, driving with her legs, she continued her turn, guiding his downward stroke as she did.

The wide blade of the machete bit with a crunch into the side of the recent amputee's head. His eyes rolled up. He fell like a bag of wet laundry, straight down.

The eyes stood out from the head of the man whose arm Annja had guided to deliver the death blow to his friend. Vomit slopped over his lower lip. Veins stood out on the side of his head in such shocking relief she half expected skyrocketing blood pressure to stroke him dead right there.

She felt no inclination to trust to chance. His gagging turned to a squeal of shock and anguish as she thrust the sword beneath his armpit through his torso.

She put a hiking shoe sole against the man's side and thrust kicked him into a man charging from her left with a raised club. She leaned forward as a machete whistled down past her back. Rising, she turned, holding the sword high. Her opponent's broad blade clacked on the cobbles behind her turning right heel. She slashed down at the wielder.

She felt impact. An instant of resistance.

He dropped to the street bleeding.

A pipe descended from close by. She ducked her head. The club glanced off the back of her skull. She tasted iron on her tongue and her stomach revolted.

But she kept her presence of mind—without which, she knew, she was lost. She cocked her left leg and thrust outward in a side kick, aiming by sheer body sense. Her shoe took a capacious paunch in the middle, sank deep into the flab that cushioned hard muscle. The attacker was driven back against the red-haired leader.

The final man to her left swung his club like a bat at her as she turned to face him. She slipped the home-run cut like a boxer, ducking her body to her right and down. The man used his own momentum to swing the four-foot baton over his head for an ax stroke to her head.

Taking the sword's hilt with both hands, she lunged toward him, slashing across her body. The sword took him under the armpit and opened his chest in a gush of blood. She followed through to clear her blade, then slashed back one-handed to strike the forearms of the pipe wielder she had kicked into his leader. He stared at the bleeding wounds as the club clattered on the cobblestones. He fell to his knees screaming in pain.

"Die, bitch!" The man with the cropped red hair launched a whirlwind attack. He had no more skill than a standard street fighter, whose usual methods were stealth or pack hunting; he hacked at her with his machete as if trying to chop through a log. But he was a strong man, built like a bull, and his own veins were ballooned with the mad adrenaline dump of intolerable fury and fear.

Desperately Annja backpedaled, barely managing to interpose her blade for two glancing impacts that sent sparks dancing in yellow arcs across the narrow street. Had she not used both hands on the hilt he would have beaten down her guard despite her strength.

He cocked his heavy-bladed weapon over his right

shoulder for his own two-handed strike. Screaming, he swung at her face.

A ringing clang sounded with an off-key end. He swung through, then raised his hands to stare in uncomprehending horror at the mirror-bright line where the sword had cut through his machete, a handspan from its hilt.

He raised his face to stare at her with eyes like eggs totally deflated with shock. "What are you?" he asked.

The boiled-egg eyes rolled up to watch the long, straight blade as it descended flat on the top of his head. Then, quite slowly at first, they rolled up and back. His body collapsed at Annja's feet.

Her friend the Englishman was on his knees vomiting. She glanced at the man whose hand she had amputated. He lay with one cheek in the midst of a lake of congealing blood, eyes staring.

She knelt and started to wipe her blade on the back of the unconscious red-haired man. Then she stopped. She'd seen enough forensic-science shows on television to know that her straight two-sided sword would leave a blood smear as distinctive as a fingerprint. One that could not possibly have come from any of the wide single-edged chopping weapons of her assailants.

I wonder if the blood and dirt would even go with the sword to wherever, she thought. Now seems like a pretty poor time to experiment.

The dead man's shirt had come out of his slacks. She used the hem to clean her blade. Then she willed it away.

Suddenly the full impact of what she had just done struck her. She had just spilled human lives into a blood lake on the ancient cobblestones of the Holy City. Her head turned. She had to exert all the will she had not to emulate the man she had rescued. The hot smell of his vomit made it all the harder.

She moved to the Englishman's side. She stepped gingerly, not wanting to slip and do a pratfall in congealing blood. Although it would be appropriate penance, somehow, she felt.

His spasms had blessedly passed. He had settled down so that his buttocks rested on his calves as he stared at the dead men. He looked at Annja with his eyes wide as the puffiness and incipient shiners would allow. Even in the dubious half light of the distant street lamps they were an amazing blue.

"Did you *have* to do that?" he demanded.

"Yes," she said. She knelt beside him. He flinched away from her touch. "Are you all right?" she asked.

"What the bloody hell do you think?" he flared. "Of course I'm not all right. Are you quite mad?"

"Probably." She reached down, grabbed a handful of his shirt and hauled him to his feet.

"Would you please stop doing that?" he demanded. Then he swayed. She kept him upright.

"Don't mean to make a habit of it," she said. "Now, come on. We need to get far away from here—and see if we can clean up a bit before anybody sees us."

12

"Bloody hell," the young man said, slopping coffee over the brim of his mug to stream down the back of his hand and drip between the metal meshwork of the tabletop. "I'm all over nerves, and this whole wretched town has never heard of decaf."

He looked indignantly at her. They had picked sidewalk tables well back from the dubious yellow puddle of light from the street lamp up the block, as well as the more substantial shine from the West Jerusalem coffee shop's front window. After slinking out through the crenellated Jaffa Gate and cleaning themselves in a fountain as best they could, they had by tacit agreement chosen to regroup—and discreetly probe each other's motivations. They looked, Annja thought and hoped, no more damply disheveled than any other pair of tourists who'd spent the day touring in the hot Mediterranean sun. At least in light this uncertain.

"I'm still afraid of trying to get back into my hotel," Annja confessed. "I must look like the last survivor from a slasher film."

Her companion barked a laugh. It had a hard and brittle clang to it, like the gleam in his eyes. "Don't bother yourself. This is Jerusalem, city of conflict holy and otherwise. Hoteliers have a couple millennia experience in seeing their guests straggle back in looking as if the cat dropped them off on the stoop. Besides, should a bellhop or concierge spot you and raise an eyebrow, your American dollar isn't yet so depreciated that throwing twenty of them his or her way won't induce the desired degree of amnesia." He hoisted his mug. "Bribery, the universal language."

"Good point," Annja said.

He looked up at the mug, sighed, lowered it gingerly to the table. "The only reason I'm as calm as I am is that I don't really believe what I saw," he said. "Did you have to kill them?"

"Yes," she said. "They would have killed both of us. Would you rather I'd let them?"

He shook his head. "Perhaps I'm not properly civilized, but I'm not so soft as all that. Before you got there they were talking to each other in Hebrew, and made altogether clear their intention to carve me up like a Christmas goose no matter what I said or did."

He smiled, or made a brave attempt anyway. She gave him full credit.

"They made the standard mistake," he said, "of believing the bloody tourist didn't know the local lingo. Especially one as tricky for a native English-speaker as Hebrew. Still, you didn't kill any of those Russians chasing us all over Amsterdam with guns. Even though they killed that poor shopkeeper."

"But they didn't," Annja said, shaking her head.

He halted with his mug to his mouth. "I beg your pardon?"

"The Russians didn't kill Trees. The antiques shop proprietor. They'd never have come back the way they did if they had."

"I rather thought of them like jackals returning to their spew—if you can forgive the coarseness of the simile." He sipped. "I thought they'd just decided to take us up and see what we knew."

"That much is correct, I'm pretty sure, as subsequent events showed. But while I can't pretend to know much about them, the impression that I get is that the *mafiya* are pretty professional. If they committed a murder they wouldn't risk exposure by traipsing blithely back to the scene of the crime—even if they own an assortment of Amsterdam police officials, as I kind of presume they do. That'd be pushing their luck. Besides, it was pretty apparent they were at least as surprised to see us as we were to see them. And every bit as surprised to find the shopkeeper had been murdered."

He shrugged. "I suppose you're more up on these criminal undertakings than I am."

She sighed inwardly at the dig. He was upset, on edge and mistrustful, despite the polite sheen dictated by his upbringing and some sense of gratitude for her saving of his bacon. She couldn't blame him, not by any stretch. But she couldn't help regretting it.

She was struggling to contain her emotions. Now that the adrenaline in her blood was beginning to break down she felt sandbagged by her own reaction to the violence in the cul-de-sac. She knew her actions had been justified. She did not regret the deaths of the men she had killed. Not as such. But she knew there would be family and friends to mourn them, and did regret the choices they had made that had led them to earn such an end.

She was also feeling, keenly, the truth of Tsipporah's prophesy about her going through life without lasting attachments. Her companion was an intelligent young man, obviously, quick-witted and not without charm, even under reasonably dire circumstances. Manifestly they shared some interests. And yes, he was easy on the eyes.

Even if she didn't know his name.

"I'm Annja Creed, by the way," she told him. Though she had entered Israel using a false identity provided by Roux, she felt she could trust this young man with that truth. It's important to trust your instincts, she told herself.

His chin had sunk to his chest, in reverie or just plain nervous exhaustion. He snapped it up and blinked at her owlishly. "Oh. Forgive me. I've quite forgotten my manners. It's a pleasure to meet you, Ms. Creed. I'm Aidan Pascoe."

"I'm not sure it really is a pleasure for you, under the circumstances," she said, "but points for saying so."

He laughed briefly. Then his brows drew together again and he leaned forward. "Where on earth," he said in conspiratorial tones, "did you get that sword?"

"I beg your pardon?" Annja had expected the question.

"The implement with which you dispatched my tormentors—and to give you your due, no avenging angel could have wielded it with more aplomb."

I suppose I should consider that a high professional compliment, she thought, considering.

"I'm sorry," she said, shaking her head. "I don't know what you're talking about."

His laugh was high-pitched. "Don't be stupid! You chopped those men to chutney. I'm no martial-arts expert, but I know you didn't do it with your bladelike hands. Anyway, I was there, if you'll recall."

"Of course. But you weren't in the best position to

see what really happened, what with blood in your eyes and your head spinning. I picked up a slat of wood to have some sort of weapon when I confronted them— that was what you saw in my hand. Then when they attacked me with those machetes or whatever they were—" she shrugged "I didn't see I had much choice but take one away and defend myself with it."

"But I saw a *sword*," he persisted. "A cross-hilted broadsword. In your hands."

Annja smiled. "I think you said it yourself earlier. In your state I must have appeared like, well, a rescuing angel. Quite a misidentification, but understandable under the circumstances."

He shook his head and muttered under his breath. "Be bloody-minded, then."

Her smile got sweeter. "I just wouldn't want you to have any false notions. Now, why do you happen to be interested in the legendary jar of King Solomon?"

As a flying subject change, it was outstandingly clumsy, she knew. But its very ham-handedness served the purpose of bringing home to Aidan that the subject of the sword was not just closed, but sealed. And anyway, she needed to know.

A tightening of his somewhat full lips told her he saw through the ruse. Also that he had dimples.

"I'm an archaeologist," he said. "I read the subject and biblical antiquities at Oxford. Although the truth is

I've a lifelong fascination, bordering upon obsession, for the fringe areas of archaeology. Indeed, I have actively crusaded to open the minds of my colleagues—albeit, in a cowardly way, making use of the anonymity of the Internet. Or perhaps, *pseudonymity*, should such a word exist."

"You're seeker23!" she exclaimed.

He performed a mock genuflection. "Guilty, *mademoiselle*."

"*Parlez-vous français?*" she asked.

"*Oui,*" he said with a nasal Parisian accent that made it almost *way*. "Bloody badly, as befits an Englishman."

He took a sip of coffee and studied her. "It seems to me I might have seen your name, once or twice."

"Sometimes I ask a question or two. I usually try to stay clear of the flame wars," she said.

"Wise of you." He took another drink, eyeing her with a slight pensive frown.

She leaned her elbows on the metal table, holding her mug in both hands. She had to adjust her weight to keep the off-balance table from tipping. She resisted the urge to improvise a shim; her tendency to want to fix things that were wrong could distract her at key moments.

"Tell me about yourself," she said. Lame! she thought. Growing up in the orphanage and then a career in research hadn't exactly prepared her to make small talk.

"As I said, I've long been fascinated with the way-out and wonderful," Pascoe said. "I've no particular fondness for biblical archaeology, however."

She cocked an eyebrow. "Really?"

He smiled self-deprecatingly, shaking his head. "My father was a solicitor in Weston-super-Mare," he said. "Not a highly remunerative job."

That surprised her. She knew a solicitor was a kind of lawyer.

"I've an uncle, though, who made a few bob in sum through trade." He pronounced the word *trade* with evident contempt. "He's rather a bug on the literal truth of the Bible. The Old Testament in particular—all the Sturm und Drang and bearded prophets and she-bears rending the wicked appeals to him more than parables of a gentle Christ, I'm afraid."

He shrugged. "He should have been a Yank, really."

"We're all fundamentalists, of course," Annja said with no effort to conceal her sarcasm.

"Sorry, sorry. It's not on to let my prejudices show. *Especially* to a woman who has made such a habit of saving my life the last week or so."

"At least this time I wasn't the one who put it in jeopardy."

"Have I not apologized for my intemperate remarks in Holland? Something about being shot at and then dunked in a canal made me, shall we say, a trifle testy? Anyway, my uncle was willing to subsidize not just my advanced education but actual field researches. I see you cocking your brow skeptically at me. I'd be tempted to say it's rather fetching, but I'll refrain for fear of making myself a sexist pig."

She laughed. "Don't hold back for that. I have a pretty high sexual-harassment threshold."

"And some rather brisk penalties for crossing the line, I imagine."

She shrugged. "Accept as a ground rule that compliments are safe. So long as they're tasteful."

"Ah." He touched a fingertip to the side of his nose. "I've wanted to do that since childhood. Well, a nod is as good as a wink to a blind bat, say no more, as Monty Python said. In any event, I note your skepticism, and in fairness to the old gent—yes, and to myself, as well—I have to say that so far he has been quite scrupulous in accepting what I've been able to discover, whether it happens to harmonize with the bees in his bonnet or not."

"Do you get to publish your results?" Annja asked.

"As long as I send regular reports about my progress on areas of his interest, I'm free to pursue such other matters as I desire. Those tend to be more…interesting to the journals."

"I see." She sipped from her mug. The coffee, which she drank with a healthy dollop of milk and artificial sweetener, had gone cold. She didn't really need the concentrated caffeine blast of Middle Eastern coffee at this hour either, but she was coming down from an extreme adrenal high. She'd crash and burn soon enough despite the stimulant. "So your uncle is interested in Solomon's Jar?"

"Not at all. He'd suspect the whole legend of binding demons to build the temple smacked of black magic, actually. The particular bee in his bonnet I'm feeding now concerns demonstrating the factual existence of the Garden of Eden. Bit of a bother, really, since the location most reliably alleged is in Mesopotamia."

"That could prove inconvenient. Does your uncle expect you to do your research in a war zone?" Annja asked.

"I'm not sure the old boy's aware there's a war on," Pascoe said. "Unlike your American fundamentalists, like the ones who back Mark Peter Stern, he doesn't believe that we're living in the end times. Aside from his precious bottom line, he has trouble concentrating on anything later than Malachi 4:6."

"'And he will turn the heart of fathers to their children and the hearts of children to their fathers, lest I come and smite the land with a curse,'" Annja quoted the Old Testament's last verse. "Are you sure he's not into millenarianism?"

"He doesn't foresee the return of Elijah the prophet or the 'coming of the great and dreadful day of the Lord' anytime soon. As a matter of fact I suspect he half believes Christ himself was more than a bit of a dangerous radical."

"What's your interest in the jar, then? Care to dabble in demon binding?" She smiled as she asked, and hoped he couldn't see her eyes clearly in the gloom.

"What? Oh, that's all poppycock, of course. I do believe such a jar exists. I do believe it's been found—as, sadly, one or more far less scrupulous parties likewise appear to believe, as well."

"But you don't think King Solomon used it to bind demons?"

"As much as I believe in the Easter Bunny, Annja dear. Charming name, that—if it's really your name." He didn't wait for her reaction. "I do believe in the historical existence of Solomon, and the empire he built in the biblical story—which is itself controversial in archaeological circles these days, although don't say so aloud where any of the local savants can hear you. As you no doubt recall, since a woman who can quote the final verse of the rather obscure Book of Malachi clearly knows her Old Testament, Solomon was renowned for his wisdom, as well as for his habit of building pagan temples to gratify some of his numberless foreign wives, which quite scandalized the religious establishment, then and since.

"Now, one thing I believe our occult navel gazers and fire leapers get right is that Solomon was a highly regarded sorcerer of his time. Indeed, rather in the manner of the first speaker of the Aztec, I suspect that even though he was not of the priestly caste, he was looked to as a central spiritual leader by the Israelites of his day. Being a magician was part and parcel of being a powerful and popular king. So what could be more natural, especially in some time of unrecorded hardship such as drought or pestilence, than for the nation's chief figure, political and spiritual, to perform a public ritual of binding the evil spirits responsible for the nation's hardships in a vessel, suitably inscribed with their symbols, and then with appropriate ceremony casting it into the Red Sea?"

He sipped his coffee again and grimaced. "Cold as ice. I expect it worked, too, Solomon's public gesture. Kings whose luck runs bad at moments such as that aren't remembered for reigning record amounts of time and dying in bed, are they?"

"I suppose not. But the account you posted online claims the jar was fished out of the Mediterranean by those hapless fishermen—the news services confirmed that the deaths took place, by the way," Annja said.

"Ah, there I think vulgar legend comes to our rescue." He leaned forward and his eyes seemed to shine. "In time, the story arose that King Solomon had employed demons to build his great temple. Although that wasn't really necessary to what came next—treasure hunters, who believed that demons had the power to discover hidden treasure, and either convey it to their human masters or lead their masters to it."

"And so they fished out the jar," Annja said. "And pried it open. And then when, presumably, no treasure was forthcoming—"

"They got browned off and pitched the thing into the nearest body of water! Precisely. How it happened to be the Mediterranean is anybody's guess. But like the water in the watershed, everything that happens in the Mediterranean littoral tends inevitably to roll down to the sea. It's certainly no contradiction to the basic theory."

"I suppose not," Annja said. It's as good a theory as any, she thought. But then, I have some information he doesn't. "But why so much violence now, over a purely ceremonial bauble?"

He shrugged. "There are plenty of gits in the world who believe the fairy story about binding demons. Some of them have fortunes—speaking as the happy, or at least fortunate, beneficiary of one such git, albeit not one who'd give any yarn about Solomon trafficking with devils the time of day. They could easily pursue the jar themselves, or hire minions who may or may not believe any of the rubbish, but are quite willing to take a human life for sixpence. And, of course, such an item would be of inestimable value as an artifact, leaving aside all the mystic gibble-gabble. The world's full of pothunters. By nature they're unscrupulous—why would some of them stop short of murder, if the price were right?"

He leaned back, folded his arms and regarded her with eyes narrowed beneath a furrowed brow. "What about yourself, Ms. Annja Creed? What's *your* interest in Solomon's Jar?"

Her heart sank. She'd cleverly maneuvered him into returning to his early suspicion of her and her motives. Even if it was the last thing she wanted.

"I'm an archaeologist, too," she said, honestly.

"So I gathered." His tone was anything but friendly now.

"Like you, I have an interest in the more esoteric realms of the discipline. The jar would be more than just a part of history…."

She let her words trail away to nothing but the background murmur of traffic. Unlike the Old City, West Jerusalem seemed to thrive after dark, although there was a muted, furtive quality to its nightlife. Great, she thought. Now I sound just like Belloq talking to Indy about the Ark.

Her companion had seen that movie, too, it seemed. Scowling openly now, he tossed off the dregs of his coffee and rose. The rubber feet of his white-enameled metal chair stuttered unpleasantly on the pavement.

"My motive for seeking the jar is clear enough, in any event," Pascoe said. "I intend that it be handed over to the proper authorities. Not be stolen as so many of the world's priceless antiquities have been by immoral, money-grubbing pothunters. Or should I say, hunt-resses?"

He slammed the mug down on the table, making it teeter precariously. Annja winced.

"Good evening to you, Ms. Creed. I hope for both our sakes that our paths never cross again."

13

Returning to her modest West Jerusalem hotel after her less than satisfactory leave-taking from Aidan Pascoe, Annja was cautious.

Though it was late at night, a surprising amount of activity stirred in the Tower Hotel lobby. A party of Japanese tourists was checking in and some Italians were arguing theology among the potted-palm fronds in the seats by the front window. As Pascoe had predicted she aroused no interest walking through. Catching a glimpse of her reflection in a segment of mirrored wall, though, she almost lost a step.

When she drenched herself in the fountain, the blood spattered so liberally across her once-white blouse had run and faded until it looked like nothing more than

pinkish orange swirls or surrealistic flower patterns.
Somehow it struck her now as far more horrific than
obvious bloodstains would have been. Frowning, she
made it to the elevator and then her fourth-floor room
before running to the bathroom and throwing up.

A shower helped her compose herself. Baths and
showers tended to soothe her mind and spirit, as well as
her body. Still, dressed in a fluffy white-and-blue hotel
terrycloth robe with a towel wrapped around her hair,
she found herself too jangled by the day's events to
contemplate sleep.

Needing something to occupy her brain, and fend off
random crying jags, she sat down on the bed and popped
the top on her notebook computer. The hotel offered free
Internet access through its wireless network. In a moment she was looking at page one of over 180,000
Google hits for Mark Peter Stern.

She made an indeterminate noise low in her throat
and set the computer aside. The bedside clock-radio
offered a selection of Moroccan-roll, Israeli hip-hop
and bland Europop, all of which struck her ears as about
equally unlistenable at her current space-time coordi-
nates. Finally she found a classical station. Mozart was
always good. Rearranging the towel around her still wet
hair, she piled up pillows at the head of the bed, picked
up the computer again and lay back for some serious
data mining.

First she scanned news items relating to Stern and his foundation. There were thousands to choose from. She read of his cutting the ribbon to open a literacy center he had endowed in São Paulo, Brazil, with six-foot-tall blond supermodel Eliete von Hauptstark on his arm. She watched in streaming video as he trudged through an earthquake-ravaged zone in Pakistan in his shirtsleeves, even helping rescuers move rubble off a victim trapped beneath a collapsed wall. It didn't seem to be staged.

She saw pictures of him attending some Hollywood film opening, laughing with the likes of Warren Beatty and Jack Nicholson—both of whom, she was quickly able to find, openly expressed scathing opinions of him, his movement and even their celebrity friends who had fallen under his sway.

One common thread became apparent, especially paging through pictures and videos. Mark Peter Stern was seldom seen, or at least photographed, without at least one strikingly beautiful woman in his company. Most of them were famous to one degree or another, from a teenage-sex-bomb A-list actress who claimed he had rescued her from dependency on drugs and alcohol to tae kwon do black belt Hauptstark, the current rave supermodel, whose grandfather, allegedly, was a Nazi war criminal who had fled to Brazil, where he'd lived to a ripe old age. All these women wore around their gorgeous throats the braided green collar that symbolized committed Malkuth adherents.

On the sites that offered actual words concerning Stern, as opposed to strictly images, Annja found glitz, innuendo, vituperation and outright flackery.

He did profess a keen interest in biblical antiquities. Annja knew how to check on that. One thing you learned to do as an archaeology student was track down grant money like a bloodhound. The foundations and expeditions funded either by the Malkuth Foundation or Stern in person proved he backed his words abundantly with cash.

Interesting but inconclusive, she thought.

She saw three possibilities. He sought the jar for reasons she could accept as benign, in which case they might well find themselves allies. Provided, of course, he could convince her that whatever he intended was really likely to work more good than harm. That would take some doing.

Or he might want to use the jar in a way she deemed destructive—whether or not from motives he believed pure. Idealistic motives had led Sir Martin Highsmith to murder, after all, as well as to order her own execution. If, wittingly or not, Stern meant to use the jar to work evil in the world, she would find him a powerful foe. And vice versa.

Finally, he might have no interest in the jar, at which point she would cross him off the list.

Annja hadn't expected the puff pieces or the hit jobs to give her any reliable clues. After surfing various news sites, blogs and variations on the theme "markpeter-sternsucks.com" she took a breath and dived into the official Malkuth Foundation site.

It was professionally done, and unlike a lot of professionally designed sites, actually *well* done. It was not just visually arresting but lucid and easy to navigate, without oversize images, gimmicky hard-to-find menus or eye-itching Flash animations.

As to what it was all about…that she found somewhat less accessible.

She quickly discovered some concise and readable descriptions of the Tree of Life, the arrangement of the ten *sephiroth* and the various pathways between them, a colorful representation of which was the foundation's logo. She glossed over it, as well as a history of both the Jewish and Gentile traditions of the kabbalah. The latter read like respectable popular history, and where it impinged on Annja's expertise, such as discussing the Renaissance-age origins of modern kabbalistic study, she found it to be accurate. But neither a description of the Tree of Life nor the brief story of kabbalism was what she was after.

What she really wanted to know was what the foundation stood for that set it apart from other mystic groups.

She waded through pages of fairly standard common-sense self-improvement advice, most of it unobjectionable and probably even useful, taken in the proper perspective. And the usual peace and love to all human-kind, environmental consciousness, tolerance and the like.

After two hours of diligent reading she had gained nothing but a headache. She didn't have any clearer idea of what the actual core message of Mark Peter Stern and his Malkuth Foundation might be.

Going back to her searches she was certainly able to find plenty who purported to tell her the foundation was a cult, it was sinister, it was evil, it brainwashed its acolytes.

She could find as many sites praising Stern and Mal-kuth to the skies. And all the sites, for and against, sported message boards wherein roared flames of such prodigious heat and volume that she reckoned Dante needed resurrecting from the dead to write up a whole new annex to Hell—a concept he, far more than Scrip-ture, had visualized and inserted into the world's reli-gious imagination.

When she could practically smell the brimstone she sat back and let her eyes go to soft focus. What has been learned, and what revealed? she wondered, remember-ing a catchphrase from an author she had gone to hear read as an undergraduate.

For all his flaws, she seemed to sense in Stern a gen-uine avocation, a sense of true mystic calling. It was hard for her to see at first. He was obviously a showman to a pretty unhealthy degree and, if she were any judge, a charlatan in many ways.

Is it possible, she asked herself, to be both a charlatan and the real thing? A true mystic, a true spiritual leader?

She thought of Roux. He was as fraudulent an old fart as she had ever met. But he was genuine. She had seen and heard and experienced too much to doubt he was what he said he was; if anything, there were depths to him she had yet to so much as glimpse. He *was* at least five hundred years old. He *had* witnessed the burning of St. Joan in person. He was a mystical being by virtue of his longevity; she guessed he had been, and likely still was, a sorcerer of some sort. He was also her mentor, a mighty teacher—if often by way of bad example.

That someone lied, and was caught lying, did not mean they didn't sometimes tell the truth, she reasoned. Even truths that conflicted with all Annja had been taught of science.

She shook her head. This is no time to get sidetracked, she told herself sternly.

None of what she had seen said anything useful about why Stern might want the jar, and whether he would prove foe or friend.

She took a deep breath, sighed it out to the sounds of a Strauss waltz. Well, that clarifies my immediate destiny, she told herself.

She was going to have to go, again, to the source.

Stern was a public figure, easily one of the hundred best-known names and faces in the current world. She reckoned that meant that each and every day a tiny but measurable percentage of all the world's population was vying for his attention.

Annja knew, even had he not been associated with controversial groups such as radical Israeli settler movements and American Christian fundamentalists, he would require layers of intense security. More than physical security, he would also surround himself with phalanxes of specialists to help him run his organization and to keep people out of his well-coiffed hair.

She had to get past all that to see him. She sighed. It would be only slightly more challenging than getting access to the vaults of Fort Knox with a front-end loader and a bunch of empty crates.

She drew in another deep breath and made a disgusted face. "You know perfectly well what you need to do," she said aloud. "You're just in denial."

She sighed again. "And if I want to swim in it, it's just one country over." She began to compose an e-mail.

14

Engine off, the launch coasted into the pier on big folds of green water, their tops trickled with slightly greasy, yellowish foam. Annja took a last slurp at the straw stuck in the chilled orange juice she had been sipping at the dockside café and stood up. She wobbled slightly on her high heels. Whoa, balance, she told herself.

She started walking. It took total concentration to keep her ankles from buckling outward and making her lurch like a sailor in port after six straight weeks in high seas. She couldn't believe models could strut so confidently in such painful footwear.

Gazes followed her from the sidewalk café and among the dockside idlers. She cut a striking figure, she was willing to acknowledge to herself: her considerable height defiantly accentuated by the heels and a light yellow cotton sundress that showed off her legs in the late-morning Mediterranean heat and sunlight.

She had to work the wardrobe angle to appeal to Stern, she reckoned. She had been told often enough by eager men—young and old—that she was attractive. While she never gave her appearance much thought, she was clever enough to know how to use her natural gifts if necessary.

At the moment she felt confident the eyes following her progress toward the pier were admiring. Unless behind them their owners were snickering to themselves at the way she walked in the heels and laying odds on when she'd lose it altogether and pitch into the sea.

The launch was twenty feet long and open. A pilot sat up front with two failed-NFL-linebacker types in dark suits, and a sleek aide. On second thought Annja wondered if they were even failed; maybe they were actual players, Malkuth devotees serving their guru in the off-season. She didn't follow the game so she didn't know. They certainly looked imposing enough.

Attendants at the dock caught a line one linebacker threw and helped draw the craft into a fairly smooth landing against the big orange-and-black rubber bumpers cushioning the concrete pier. They tied it fast and the aide stepped ashore. The bodyguards stood on the boat with their hands folded in front of them. It gave them a ridiculously demure look.

The aide would have been shorter than she was even if it hadn't been for her accursed heels. He was tread-mill slender, his off-white summerweight suit expensively tailored to show his form, a yarmulke not quite hiding a bald spot in his dark hair. He and the football-types all wore the green braided necklaces.

"Ms. Creed?" the aide said, approaching. "I'm Charles Sanders."

She nodded. "I'm Annja," she said. "Pleased to meet you." She extended a hand. He shook it once. To her relief his grip was as firm and dry as it was brief; she feared from the looks of him it'd be damp.

Once again her brilliant disguise was herself. She had spent the morning adding altogether too much to the burden of sorrows of her credit-card balance in a Tel Aviv boutique dressing herself in at least semifashionable mode, when constitutionally and by professional habit she was most at ease dressed in battered khakis and a boonie hat.

Sanders extended a hand to help her into the launch. Liberation be damned, she thought, and she took it and was glad. Spike heels plus rolling boat equaled unsteady Annja. She was not going to risk taking a spill and winding up in the bilge on her backside, with her legs in the air and her pretty skirt up around her waist. That would gratify the grizzled old lechers slurping their lattes at the café entirely too much. She pictured how Roux would react. Concentrate, she reminded herself.

Sanders saw her seated. The bodyguards with the pneumatic necks cast the boat off. The pilot, a wiry little guy with a big nose and white stubble on his cheeks and no cord around his scrawny neck, backed away from the pier, then turned the boat back toward Crete and wound out the engine. The leather seat pressed against Annja's back and away they went.

Charles, as he graciously permitted her to call him, used his cell phone briefly. Then he sat down across from Annja and made small talk. She answered simply, perfectly aware that she was being vetted to make sure she was who, or at least what, she portrayed herself as being before she was admitted to the presence of the great man. Yes, the 3500-year-old Egyptian gate on Jaffa Hill was a wonder; yes, it was exciting working on *Chasing History's Monsters*. No, she had never considered becoming a model….

She looked back. Beyond wake and waterfront the town tumbled almost into the water down the Jaffa Hill headland. She saw a collection of sand-colored buildings of sundry sizes stuffed way too close together. Some of the crowding was deliberate, she was moderately sure, to enhance that old-timey Middle Eastern–village flair for the tourists. Jaffa was far older than Tel

Aviv, of which it was more or less a suburb—although
Tel Aviv had started as a suburb of Jaffa. It was a bit
more organic and relaxed. But what you mostly saw of
it now was not so old. It also struck Annja as more than
a little self-consciously quaint, sort of like Santa Fe. And
as in the New Mexican capital, municipal codes
required buildings to *look* old, even if they went up last
month. They were likely as not to hold an artist's studio,
a Starbuck's with wireless Internet access or a twee
boutique.

She looked forward again. The pilot threaded his
way among a plentiful flock of pleasure craft, mostly
riding to anchor in the easy swell. One of the world's
most ancient seaports, Jaffa hadn't been a serious com-
mercial anchorage for a century or so. Now it was
mostly a tourist trap. A fair number of the tourists
arrived by water, or so it appeared.

Mark Peter Stern's yacht lay out to sea beyond the
common herd of the pleasure craft of the merely rich.
Zohar II surprised Annja somewhat. A ketch with two
masts, white with blue trim, fore-and-aft rigged and
sails furled, showing a superstructure housing bridge
and cabin above deck. At eighty feet over waterline, it
was far from *modest* by any means. But it was nowhere
near the ostentatious showboat Stern's flamboyant public persona had led her to expect.

So far as Annja could see, no supermodels or barely

legal Hollywood actresses lounged topless on deck. That's a relief, she thought.

"IT'S HARD for most Westerners to think of 'nothing' as a positive thing—the ultimate creative force," Mark Peter Stern said, gazing out the porthole of the compartment he used as his office. Outside the sky was an almost painful blue. Cloudless. "Yet it is. From primal nothing, which is really *no-thing,* derives that which is without limits. And from there—light. Limitless light."

He turned. "From there derives our human potential, Ms. Creed. We are sprung from the light, and we know no limits. If only we let ourselves *see.*"

The office, while spacious, was surprisingly spare in furnishings. There was dark-stained oak paneling to sternum height, cream-painted bulkheads above, a large desk with a globe and a computer on it, a rendering of the Tree of Life behind it. Given Stern's notorious love affair with the camera, Annja was surprised to find no photographs at all in evidence.

Sitting on a tubular-steel-and-black-leather chair that was far more comfortable than it looked, Annja let herself smile tentatively. "I'm afraid I don't follow, Dr. Stern."

He laughed, smiled, waved a hand. "Please forgive me. I have a tendency to preach. I have so much to share with a human race that needs the truth so badly." He shook his head. "I'm sure your viewers would prefer to be spared the proselytization. Or your producers at any rate."

Thinking of boy-wonder producer Doug Morrell, who held the world's "my eyes glaze over" land-speed record, she said, "That's for sure."

She tried to remember to keep her knees closed tight. She didn't want any embarrassing moments.

Unlike her famous predecessor she was no virgin. Nor did she think of herself as a prude. But she was using her sexuality as a dodge here, as bait, and it made her feel cheap.

"You're known for your financing of archaeological researches and expeditions," Annja said.

Stern smiled. He was a handsome man who looked much younger than his forty-one years, with open features, green eyes, a shock of straw-colored hair. Indeed in person he seemed more compelling. The camera, no matter how artfully plied, could not capture the full impact of his personality.

He wore a light tan suit, cream shirt, black-and-gold silk tie. All impeccably tailored, of course; renunciation of worldly things wasn't part of his teachings—exactly. As near as Annja could tell from visiting the Malkuth Foundation's Web site, Stern's conception was that materialism was something humans had to get out of their systems before advancing upward along the spiritual path, rather like a childhood sweet tooth or adolescent acne. She wasn't clear, really.

"If you're interested, I'm always open to proposals for new digs," he said.

She smiled back. "Thank you, Doctor."

"Mark."

"Mark. Thank you. But right now I'm most interested in exploring possibilities for doing a show."

"I hope I'm not considered one of history's monsters," he said with an engaging grin. "Other than by some of my detractors, of course."

Annja laughed. She didn't have to force it. He was unquestionably likable. And something more. She remembered that the men who brutalized Aidan Pascoe in that alley wore the same green leather braids around their necks as Stern. Not that she was convinced he was complicit in the attack, but she had to keep perspective.

She was trying to channel Sabine Ehrenfeld, the German-born model who did the Overstock.com commercials. As little as Annja watched television, the model had made an impression. A woman in her forties, Ehrenfeld struck Annja as both beautiful and devastatingly sexy in a sophisticated way, without being flashy or cheap. Annja also admired the woman because she had a pilot's license and had learned how to use a handgun. Obviously, she was not afraid of her own competence.

Annja was well aware of her own sexual nature, despite wondering periodically just how it squared with her destiny as the keeper of Joan's sword. She had grown up with little by way of role models in being sexy. At least in any dignified way; plenty of the girls at the orphanage oozed overt sexuality, precisely to aggravate the nuns. Annja hadn't exactly majored in partying at college. Her studies happily obsessed her. Despite her lifelong affinity for exercise and athleticism she was at core a nerd, and knew it. So she found the most appropriate role model she could and ran with her.

"Were someone to discover an artifact such as King Solomon's fabled jar," she asked, "wouldn't that interest you?"

He raised an eyebrow at her.

"You don't think of King Solomon's Jar as monstrous in any way, surely?"

"No, no. But it is reputed that Solomon bound demons within it. That's the connection for our show. The demon aspect," Annja explained.

He studied her a moment. "If the actual jar was found, I'd be delighted, of course." He smiled warmly. "I'd like nothing better than to see it on display at the Rockefeller or the Israel Museum in Jerusalem."

Annja had the sense he was playing to an unseen audience—out of habit, perhaps, not necessarily bugs.

Although she wouldn't put it past him to videotape his own interviews out of sheer vanity.

"Do you have evidence the jar has been found, Ms. Creed?" Stern asked.

"Nothing more than rumors at this point," she said. "What I wonder, from the standpoint of *Chasing History's Monsters*, is what you as a professed mystic make of the legends of the jar? They say Solomon bound the demons within it after employing them to build his temple in Jerusalem and that the jar was thrown into the Red Sea and later found by parties who released the demons to find treasure for them. What's your take on those?"

He shrugged. "I'm familiar with the legend, of course. Like much of what Christians call the Old Testament, I believe it's an allegory composed by early kabbalists. It represents Solomon's quest for spiritual mastery. It was never intended to be taken literally."

He gave her a rogue's grin. It made him look even more boyish. She felt a stirring inside, and experienced a certain epiphany as to why so many glamorous actresses and supermodels were so attracted to his teachings.

"Trust me, Ms. Creed," he said.

Whatever embers had been smoldering to life damped at once to cold embers. With Tsipporah's warning echoing in her brain, Annja bit her lip for a moment. This isn't going the way I expected at all she thought. She took a deep breath and then the plunge.

"Why was the phone number of your New York central office found on the caller ID list on the telephone of a murdered shopkeeper in Amsterdam, Mr. Stern?"

He stood looking at her in silence for a long moment. She could not truly say that his facade slipped—and regardless of guilt or innocence in this matter, she knew full well he was showing her a facade. Certainly the question, with its implicit accusation, must have been like a bucket of ice water dumped on his head.

I sure feel as if I've dived into ice water, she thought. I think I just led with my chin again. But her intuition had told her to ask the question.

"I had no idea that it had been," he said in a measured voice. "If your information is correct, it's certainly unsettling news. I hope I scarcely need to assure you that my respect for antiquities, not to mention the sorely needed international laws and treaties controlling traffic in them, tends to keep me from pursuing ancient relics in curio shops. Most likely someone in my organization has allowed commendable zeal to get the better of their judgment."

He shook his head. "It can only be coincidence in any event. No one involved with the Malkuth Foundation, with its well-known commitment to peace and justice, could conceivably have been involved in a murder over an alleged artifact."

He checked his Rolex. "If you will forgive me, I have

an important phone call incoming in a few minutes. I must ask you to excuse me. You'll find it pleasant waiting on the afterdeck for the launch to take you back to shore, I trust."

She stood up. "The program—"

"Have your producer call Charles. He'll help set something up. And now, good day to you, Annja Creed."

THE GLEAMING UPPER DECK of the big white boat was deserted when Annja emerged, blinking at more than the dazzling Mediterranean sunlight. Not even a seagull perched on the rail.

She wandered aft from the hatchway. What went wrong? she wondered. I totally struck out. Was it my hair? I know I'm not a raving beauty, but I usually get more response than that. Maybe I was playing out of my league. How could I think I could compete with all those international sex symbols? What was I thinking?

Maybe it had been the blunt query about Trees's death. Not too tactful, she had to admit. Yet even before she asked the question she had sensed the conversation slipping out of control. The bold stroke, to give it a better name than it deserved, had been an all but desperate attempt to get more out of the famed religious figure than the same sort of cotton-candy-and-maple-syrup platitudes he exuded for his celebrity patrons.

She walked toward the stern alongside a boom with

a sail bound to it by nylon cords. What had her totally flustered was that everything had started so well. She had expected to have to spend days if not weeks trying to contrive a meeting with Stern. Instead she'd succeeded before she'd even properly tried.

Then she'd done a face plant into a brick wall. If that wasn't mixing metaphors. She had never gotten quite clear on that concept.

Before she could fully comprehend what had happened a hand seized her hair from behind and snapped her head around.

15

Annja gasped from surprise. The stinging at the back of her scalp brought unwelcome tears to the corners of her eyes. The morning sun shone on the white deck and housing like liquid incandescence, beating furnace heat against her cheeks.

Her jaw dropped. Through the dazzle she stared into a pair of angry green eyes glaring at her from a perfect face. Glaring *down* at her.

To her utter amazement she recognized the face. It belonged to up-and-coming Brazilian supermodel Eliete von Hauptstark. Her name was pronounced "Ellie-etchy," as Annja had discovered during her research about Mark Peter Stern. She was six feet tall with skin and hair like different shades of honey.

Under normal circumstances Annja would have known no more about those details than she did about the workings of a printed-circuit fabrication plant. But she'd seen much of Hauptstark online recently, as the latest addition to Stern's celebrity retinue.

Hauptstark's arm lay across Annja's shoulder. A strong hand was still wrapped in Annja's hair at the back of her head. The Brazilian woman wore a white man's shirt open over a red bikini top, pale turquoise Capri pants and white deck shoes. She looked angry.

"I beg your pardon," Annja said as politely as she could. "Please let me go. I was leaving anyway—this isn't necessary."

The supermodel let go with her right hand. Her left struck in a jab. Annja blinked furiously at the tears that sprang up in her eyes as her head snapped back. It hurt, especially since her nose had scarcely healed from her South American escapade.

She stepped back. She felt more astonishment than anger or even outrage. "What on earth do you think you're doing?" she asked.

The taller woman spun and fired a back kick into her midsection. Annja flew backward. She landed on her hip, then shoulders and slid across the smooth white deck. She stopped against something solid but slightly yielding.

Thoughts jostled for preeminence in her mind. *Why is she attacking me? What the hell does she think she's* doing? She got her bearings and realized she had struck a truncated cone of wrist-thick nylon rope with a grapnel-style anchor with a nasty-looking blade sticking out stacked on top of it.

Annja kicked off her shoes. Shaking her head free of the whirl of confusion, she jumped to her feet, willing her mind to clear. She drew in a deep breath to calm and center herself.

The other woman was advancing on her. Her face had now twisted with rage. Yet her eyes looked strangely blank.

"What exactly do you think you're doing?" Annja said in Portuguese, grateful for her knowledge of many languages.

If the supermodel felt surprise at being addressed in Portuguese, she showed no sign. She showed no sign of comprehension at all. Or even of being aware that Annja had spoken. She only came on, not fast, but implacably.

Annja waited with legs slightly flexed. She realized she had slid all the way to the edge of the yacht's deck. Her head was full of the smell of paint, of sun-heated synthetic and steel, even the soap with which her dark blond nemesis had bathed recently, and the slight sweat of exertion she had worked up.

She remembered that Eliete von Hauptstark was a third-degree black belt in tae kwon do. Annja herself had studied martial arts and she knew full well that formal martial arts had little to do with real fighting, but if advanced practitioners had real-world fighting experience, they could be extraordinarily formidable foes.

When she was less than ten feet away from Annja, Hauptstark did a sort of stutter step, skipping forward to launch a front kick to Annja's sternum with a force that might have shoved the front of her rib cage right through her heart.

Annja met it with a left forearm held out at a forty-five-degree angle. It was a simple technique, powered by a turn of the hips. Had she tried to block the kick directly, her forearm would have been broken. But the beauty of the counter, along with simplicity, was that it simply added a side vector and guided the fearsome thrust past her. *A force of four ounces deflects a thousand pounds*, Annja recalled learning.

Annja felt her opponent overbalance. Using the same hip twist that powered the deflection, she drove a Phoenix-eye fist, first knuckle extended, in under the supermodel's short ribs on the left-hand side.

The tall blonde exhaled violently. It didn't slow her down, although it did take the force out of the follow-through blow, another spinning back kick, this time off the foot that had delivered the deflected front kick. The second wouldn't have landed true because she hadn't knocked Annja back with the first kick, and her opponent had closed instead. The combination attack was aborted. Hauptstark had to bend her knee to land the strike at all. She could do no more than push Annja in the small of her back with the rope sole of her deck shoe.

But it was a powerful push. Annja went flying past her in a graceless windmill of arms and legs. She felt like the coltish adolescent she had once been—not all that long ago—running out of control down a steep slope.

She regained control of her hurtling body when she accidentally ran into the side of the cabin. It knocked the breath from her. She turned, fearing a rib had cracked, as her first labored inhalation felt like a nail being driven into her side.

The taller woman was all over her like a tigress. A high kick flashing for Annja's face was a feint for a flurry of punches and elbow-strikes. Had Annja reacted by trying to block this time, instead of simply leaning her upper body back and to the side, slipping the first feigned attack like a boxer, at least one sledgehammer impact would have landed and quite possibly incapacitated her.

She stayed close to her opponent to keep her enemy's blows from having pace to gain momentum, using her forearms against the insides of the model's forearms to foul the jackhammer blows. At the same time she attempted to land short, hooking, hip-turning strikes of her own. She was still deficient in jabs, and would have to spend more time training with a Western-style boxer to master them.

If she survived.

The exchange was delivered in silence except for little cries as Hauptstark explosively expelled her breath by clenching the astonishingly well-defined muscles of her stomach at each strike. Annja slipped aside from a vicious cross and the supermodel's right fist blasted through the planking of the cabin's outer bulkhead like a harpoon. The woman seemed impervious to pain.

The hole's jagged jaws momentarily seized the supermodel's forearm like a bear trap. Annja used the opening to slam a brutal palm-heel uppercut up under Hauptstark's somewhat broad chin. The blow made her teeth clack together and lifted her slightly into the air.

Eyes literally reddened with rage, Eliete von Hauptstark uttered the first actual vocalization Annja had heard from her since the unexplained attack had begun. A furious roar, rising to a predator's unbridled scream, it was so piercing that something inside of Annja quailed. As the voice soared in pitch through better than two octaves, the Brazilian ripped her arm loose by yanking it out roundhouse, ripping a yard-long gash in the wood.

Annja gaped, stunned by violence of the move. Blood flew in scarlet strings from great furrows clawed by wood splinters in the tan satin skin of Hauptstark's forearm. An eight-inch sliver penetrated the arm like a spear. Ignoring what must have been blinding pain, Hauptstark continued the motion that had ripped her arm free into an ox-mouth blow, delivered with the back of her right wrist. It was another one of those showy traditional martial-arts moves, superpowerful but way too unwieldy to use in a real fight.

Except it came at an already off-guard opponent at bullet speed. Annja barely got both forearms up in time to save her jaw from being shattered, and likely her neck from being snapped like kindling.

The impact stunned her arms. It knocked her bodily through the air again, toward the stern. She bounced off the starboard quarter rail in lieu of tumbling over into the sea and landed in a heap on her side on the deck.

She looked up. Her opponent moved toward her with fierce deliberation. Her face, once inhumanly beautiful, was now merely inhuman, her exotic features a demon mask.

Annja leaped to her feet. Her body felt like one big bruise. She'd had enough. She concentrated her will.

SINCE SHE HAD BEEN made aware of her connection to Joan of Arc's sword, Annja had spent many odd moments trying to puzzle out under what circumstances it might rightfully be employed. Roux had so far proved of little help. His relationship to the cause of good was as puzzling as everything else about him. He tended to blend ruthlessness with an eye for the main chance that she guessed was all his own. His advice ran along the lines of quoting the words Abbot Arnaud-Amaury uttered during the Albigensian Crusade: "Slay them all! God will know his own." Or, as Roux gleefully translated it into more modern terms, "Kill 'em all and let God sort 'em out."

Killing women, children, noncombatants, the odd household pet or anything else that happened to wander into the circle of her swinging blade had little appeal to Annja's modern sensibilities. She did wonder if Roux's bloody-mindedness—which she knew from voracious childhood reading was actually British slang for extreme willfulness, nothing to do with bloodshed per se, but still doubly appropriate applied to her ancient mentor—was in part a harsh if veiled reminder that as a force for good she had to make her own moral choices and live with the consequences. Just like everyone who *didn't* have a magic sword.

She had vowed to summon the sword only in defense of herself or innocents—and only in extremis.

Eliete von Hauptstark plainly meant to kill her. It seemed likely she could, that she was about to, unless Annja did something radical.

The time had come.

ANNJA COMPOSED herself. She gave her head a slight shake. The sword gleamed in her hands.

Surprised, Hauptstark checked and recoiled slightly.

"Stay back," Annja said. "This has gone far enough. If you attack me again, I will kill you to defend myself. If you turn and walk away, we can forget this ever ha—"

With a hawk scream of fury Hauptstark launched herself.

The bull rush caught Annja unprepared. Before her reflexes could respond, Hauptstark had planted a powerful shoulder in her midriff and wrapped arms like iron bands around her upper thighs.

The air exploded out of Annja's lungs. She felt herself lifted off the deck. Then she was falling backward, seemingly in slow motion.

She collapsed herself, slightly rounding her back in hopes of taking the fall across her shoulders and not on the back of her skull.

Annja hit the deck with considerable force. Her teeth crashed together with a squeal. Had she not had the presence of mind to tuck her tongue well back against the roof of her mouth she would have bitten it in two. Her right elbow came down hard on the deck. The nerve center was struck. The arm went limp.

As she watched, the sword somersaulted out of her nerveless hand.

16

For an instant terror seized Annja. This isn't supposed to happen! she thought desperately. I've failed!

A sense of betrayal flooded her like fire. No one is supposed to be able to take it from me!

The sword had vanished.

With a flash of near manic relief Annja realized her sword had gone back to the pocket universe where it customarily awaited her summons. Then momentum slammed the back of her skull against the deck. Purple-and-scarlet lightning shot through her brain. A black fog swirled behind her eyes.

She snapped back to herself at once.

A concussion might yet be on the agenda, even a potentially lethal subdural hematoma, but she was able to focus enough to perceive that Eliete von Hauptstark sat straddling her hips, hands on her shoulders, pinning her to the deck.

The animal fury that had propelled the supermodel seemed to have subsided into systematically murderous intent. She cocked a fist.

Annja jerked her head to the right. She felt a wind of passage, then heard a terrifying crunch and felt a sting at the back of her scalp as some of her hair was driven through the deck along with Hauptstark's fist.

The power she had packed into the blow—and possibly the surprise that she had missed—made the tall woman loosen her grip on Annja's right arm. Annja moved quickly. She twisted free and drove a punch against the side of the Brazilian's jaw. Pinned as she was, she could get none of her body mass behind it; it was a pure arm punch.

Annja had very strong arms. But the model's head merely jerked to the side. Her expression didn't change as she ripped her hand free of the deck in a shower of dust and splinters.

With a convulsion of back and belly muscles Annja lifted her upper body off the deck, trying to writhe free. With her hips immobilized she had little force. Hauptstark slammed her head down into Annja's. It struck too high; they clashed forehead to forehead, instead of Annja's nose being smashed. More sparks shot through Annja's brain.

The Brazilian supermodel shook her shaggy blond mane. Annja got her feet planted and thrust upward with all the strength in her legs.

Hauptstark folded herself against Annja, wrapping her arms around her neck and shoulders. Annja heard the bestial panting behind her head, felt the woman's breath on her neck. It was like the wind from a blast furnace, hot and damp.

Momentarily freed, Annja's arms flailed. Her right hand encountered something of smooth texture but rumpled feel. She realized it was the anchor rope.

Her left arm struck her foe's forearm. She felt blood, sticky on the model's skin. Her fingers brushed sharp hardness. It was the wood splinter that had been driven through Hauptstark's forearm when she punched through the cabin wall.

Annja grabbed it and twisted as hard as she could.

Hauptstark threw back her head and howled in agony.

With the force of desperation Annja heaved her shoulders off the deck. Her right hand scrabbled like a terrified animal at the coiled rope. As the supermodel raised her free hand to chamber a hammer-fist blow that would smash Annja's skull a strand of rope came loose in Annja's hand. She hauled on it for all she was worth.

She didn't know exactly what the anchor lying atop the rope coil was for. Despite having been raised within spitting distance of Lake Pontchartrain, in a town that spent a certain amount of time underwater even before Katrina brought much of the Gulf of Mexico to town for a protracted visit, Annja knew almost nothing about boats. The anchor seemed too light to make a vessel this size stay put. She figured other anchors must have been deployed.

It was still a good-sized hunk of iron. It felt as if it must have weighed eighty pounds. Under most circumstances Annja knew she would have strained to lift it one-handed.

But these weren't most circumstances. The rope snapped taut as she yanked. The anchor flew through the air, the point of its wedge blade descending like a pickax between Eliete von Hauptstark's shoulder blades.

Annja was already moving. Her right hand whipped a coil of the rope, still rippling the air, around her opponent's neck. The weight of the anchor had pushed back Hauptstark's center of mass. With a heave of the muscles of her lower back and abdomen that sent pain shooting through her belly, Annja thrust her pelvis into the air.

The supermodel was thrown bodily off her. Bleeding and weakened, Hauptstark was momentarily stunned.

Annja jackknifed. She came forward onto her own feet facing her foe. With a scream of pent-up frustration and rage of her own she skipped forward and fired a side-thrust kick into the front of Hauptstark's pelvis with all her strength.

The supermodel was long and lean, but no one could

have accused her of being gaunt. Annja knew the woman was incredibly strong and still very dangerous. She also knew something more than simple jealousy was fueling her killer rage.

A voice deep inside her head was telling her what had driven the insane, and insanely powerful, attack. But she wasn't ready to listen to the voice. For all the miracles she had witnessed—had taken part in, had performed herself—there were some vestiges of her rational world-view she wasn't willing to surrender just yet.

And there were some things she didn't want to believe.

Annja turned to lean on the rail and look off across the water while she recovered her breath. She knew she had to take some decisive actions immediately. But her mind and spirit had taken as brutal a battering as her body.

The water was a lovely deep blue between the sailing vessel and the shore, with its buildings marching up Jaffa Hill. Gulls and terns wheeled and called out to each other overhead. Below them, a variety of water-craft, mostly smallish vessels, rocked gently at anchor or swooped to the impetus of sails or small engines. She gave herself over to a deliberately thought-free contemplation of the postcard prettiness of the scene.

Then, before Hauptstark could attack again, Annja climbed over the rail and jumped into the sea. She swam as hard as her tired muscles would allow. Her instincts told her to get as far from Mark Peter Stern as possible.

A sudden flash caught the corner of her eye. She turned her head to see a puff like a cotton ball, pure white, roll away from one of those pretty little water-craft, perhaps a quarter mile away across the crowded water. In the midst of it blazed a spark like a miniature blue sun. It moved. It seemed to be circling slightly, and drew behind it a corkscrew trail.

Annja dived deep.

17

Above her head a yellow glow spread like a blanket. It had a benign, almost comforting appearance.

Annja wasn't fooled by that for a nanosecond. Apparently Stern's yacht had an engine with fairly substantial fuel tanks. They had just exploded. If Annja surfaced through that deceptively gentle glow she knew she'd functionally be necklaced like a South African informer.

Having some warning about what was about to happen, she'd drawn a good deep breath. She set out swimming underwater with strong strokes of arms and legs. She may not have grown up with boats, but she'd swum like an otter since she was four years old.

She swam until the yellow glow from the surface

lay well behind her. Then, lungs burning, she swam some more.

When she could no longer stand the pain, she surfaced. Behind her the *Zohar II* wallowed in the soft swell with its deck just above water. Everything from there up was a great compound billow of yellow fire, with dense, greasy black smoke roiling out of the midst of it and fouling up the sky.

She let out the deep breath she'd gasped down without volition and shook water from her nose and eyes. "Wow," she said.

For some reason the only thing she could think about for a moment was that her spike heels were still aboard the blazing yacht. "Good riddance," she said aloud.

She looked around. She was all alone in the water. If any survivors had leaped from the boat they were bobbing around on the far side of it. She turned to look toward shore. It lay perhaps half a mile off. A somewhat tedious swim, but well within her capabilities.

She heard the whine of an outboard motor. She immediately thought someone had seen her bail and had come out to finish the job. Her head and shoulders rose from the sea as she sucked down a deep breath, increasing her buoyancy, ready to dive fast and deep. She reckoned her best and probably only shot was to remain submerged until her persecutors decided she must've drowned....

"Wait! Don't be a bloody fool!" a voice called over the snarl of the approaching boat. It was a familiar voice, with a distinct educated-middle-class English accent.

She looked around. A small white powerboat slid toward her, riding a rolling crest. The driver was waving vigorously to her from behind the wheel.

"Aidan? What on earth are you doing out here?"

The engine's sound diminished as the boat approached broadside to her and stopped just a few feet away. She bobbed in the surge that rolled from it.

"I believe you Yanks have some less polite terms for it," the young man called, half standing to lean over and extend a hand to her, "but I'd call it a rescue."

He helped haul her aboard. She lay dripping puddles into what she thought might be called the scuppers. Or was it a bilge?

"The shoe is on the other foot," he said. "Or some such rubbish."

"That's fair," she said.

Annja's dress was plastered to her body revealing more skin than she would have liked. Pascoe chivalrously looked away as she tried to wrestle it back into place. He revved the engine and turned the boat around, heading into the crowd of watercraft clustered closer to shore.

"Where are we going?" she asked, sitting on the seat behind Pascoe.

"Somewhere fast," he said, "in the faint hope that we can lose ourselves. In a pinch—if the authorities nip us, say—I can claim with perfect honesty to be taking a survivor of the explosion to shore for emergency medical examination."

As he spoke she heard the warbling of electronic sirens from shore.

"You don't really need medical attention, do you?" he asked, looking concerned.

"No," she said. "You're not worried about the authorities?"

"Not half so much as I am about the lot that did in Stern and his floating pleasure palace."

Luxurious as its appointments had been, the *Zohar II* struck Annja as having been on the small side to be a "palace" of any stripe. She didn't say so. Now that survival did not require immediate action and reaction, she felt mostly stunned.

"Good point. What are you doing here, anyway?" she asked, realizing her rescuer could hardly have been nearby in any kind of coincidence.

"Keeping an eye on our friend Mark Peter Stern," Pascoe said, with a nod of his head to a big camera case that lay by Annja's feet. It sat half open, a camera with a long lens visible inside.

"Subtle," she said, watching a white-and-yellow helicopter with a shrouded tail rotor that had begun to prowl toward the blazing wreck from the shore. Her interest was abstract. Weariness descended on her like lead fog.

"But not too easy to pick up among all the other boats around unless someone was keeping a lookout specifically for such surveillance—which in Stern's case would mostly consist of paparazzi. Nobody noticed the crew on another boat setting up to fire that antitank missile, for instance."

Annja sat dripping and stared at nothing in particular. She felt numb. She knew that she needed desperately to sort out any number of things that had just happened. But somehow she couldn't muster the urgency.

Something, though, pierced her lassitude. She raised her head and looked in the direction of the smoking wreck. Other boats had begun to swarm around it in vain hopes of rescuing somebody.

"Right now! Turn hard!" she shouted.

Without hesitation Pascoe cranked the wheel hard right. A line of water spouts six feet high marched across their curving wake. Bullets would have raked the boat stem to stern had he turned a half second later.

"Bloody hell!" he shouted as the whine of the helicopter's engines and rotor chop became audible above the roar of the boat's motor. "What is it now?"

"Somebody in that helicopter flying toward the wreck is shooting at us," she called, looking back at the chopper. It hovered broadside to them now, a sleek Aerospatiale Dolphin SA-366, not twenty yards up. A man was visible in the open doorway, aiming what looked like an AK at them. "Swerve," she shouted another order.

Pascoe obligingly cranked the wheel left. Again bullets ripped the water where they would have been but for the rapid course change.

"Sod this for a game of soldiers," Pascoe shouted, barely audible above the roar of their motor. Annja didn't have the slightest notion what it meant. Their latest turn aimed them toward a variety of anchored boats. Pascoe rolled the throttle full out to put theirs among them.

"Will you check my eyes?" Annja asked suddenly.

"What? What?"

Boats flashed by to either side, rocking gently in the powerboat's wake. "My eyes. I'm afraid I've got a concussion."

"You may just be mad. They're shooting at us, woman!"

Pascoe glanced back. The chopper was approaching them slowly from behind. The gunner in the doorway seemed reluctant to fire with all the other vessels so close, just as the Briton had hoped.

Annja stood behind him, bracing herself with one hand holding the back of the seat. She flexed her legs as Pascoe turned the wheel over hard again, this time to port. They passed between a schooner-rigged catamaran and a big white power cruiser. A topless woman who had been sunbathing on the cruiser's afterdeck rose up and shook her fist after the boat whose wake had carelessly drenched her.

"Please," Annja said. "I need to know."

Pascoe's handsome face scowled ferociously. He looked intently into Annja's eyes. "Both pupils the same size. Now will you let me drive?"

"Sorry," she said. "It was important. Break left!"

Pascoe had turned them back into open water. The helicopter now prowled alongside them to their port side. The gunner raised his rifle.

The powerboat veered hard as Pascoe complied. For a moment Annja feared he turned too tightly, that inertia would have its way and break them over the berm of swell that had built up along the hull outside the turn. She feared they'd be scattered across the waves like rag dolls. If that happened they'd either be killed outright, or too hurt to do anything when the helicopter dived in close and the gunman pumped bullets into their floating bodies....

But Pascoe kept the boat on her keel. Annja was impressed at his skill. The boat passed beneath the helicopter, which turned on its axis to pursue.

"Head us straight out to sea," Annja suggested.

"What? Maybe you took too hard a crack on the head after all. That chopper's faster than we are!" Pascoe said.

But the cobwebs had cleared from Annja's brain.

Perhaps it was a brand-new adrenaline dump on top of the old one. She felt much better, almost exhilarated.

"I've got it," she said.

The helicopter had spun round. A line of bullet holes appeared in the prow of the powerboat. Pascoe turned the small craft back to starboard and lit out for open water.

Annja heard the gunner's bellow of rage even above all the rotor chop and surf hiss and engine noise. Pascoe had the throttle wide open. The small boat banged across the tops of the waves, each impact like a sledgehammer to the bare soles of Annja's feet.

Suppressing a thrill of alarm that the small craft might break apart from the violence of its own passage, she crouched down in the stern. The helicopter was overtaking them rapidly. Its pilot, she guessed, was as sick of his quarry's disobliging antics as his gunner. If they did what she anticipated, the chopper would zip past them and then flare into hover mode broadside to them, so that whether they broke left, right or came straight on, they couldn't escape getting hosed down by copper-jacketed bullets.

As the Dolphin closed in, nose down to drive with its main rotor's maximum thrust, Annja stood abruptly. In her hand she held a loop of a nylon rope that lay coiled in the stern. Dangling from the end was another grapnel-style anchor. It was a much more modest anchor than the one she'd struggled with on Stern's yacht.

Well, anchors have been lucky for me today, she thought, and cast.

In a long underarm lob the anchor rose toward the oncoming rotor disk. The pilot apparently saw something flash toward his face and responded by reflex. The helicopter banked hard left. The man in the door, seemingly oblivious to anything wrong, raised his rifle to his shoulder. The chopper was close enough that Annja could see him grin beneath his dark aviator glasses.

The anchor passed between rotor blades. The trailing blade caught the rope high up near the hub.

Instantly Annja heard a change in the rotor sound. The rotor, rather than severing the tough synthetic rope, wrapped it tightly around the shaft. The anchor, brought up short, bounced upward again. This time it struck a blade.

The thin composite sandwich sheared with a crack and a screech. The face staring at Annja over the Kalashnikov's sights went pale as the helicopter rolled rapidly counterclockwise around its long axis. The pale yellow flames that leaped from the muzzle brake when the gunner's finger tightened on the trigger stabbed impotently into the sky.

The Dolphin rolled onto its back and pancaked onto the Mediterranean. Annja heard a loud crack as its backbone broke. As it began to settle in the water a yellow glow of flame began to shine from within the cockpit.

The speedboat fell away to one side, engine idling. "Bloody hell," Aidan Pascoe said. "That's impossible."

"Just dumb luck," Annja said. He stared at her, blue eyes wild.

She grabbed him by arm and shoulder and pushed him back into the driver's seat. "Drive," she said. "Or do you want to try explaining this to the Israeli port police?"

The engine snarled back to full throttle. Annja rocked back as the little craft took off across the blue-green water.

18

"Either Israeli search and rescue has some pretty harsh ideas about how to go about their business," Annja called out from the bathroom, "or we've got a new player in the game."

She dashed cold water from the tap on her face. She wanted a shower. Her dress felt like papier-mâché molded to her body, and her skin itched from dried salts and less desirable substances from the Jaffa anchorage. But there were some things to be cleared up first.

"I don't know." Aidan Pascoe sat in a chair in a corner facing the twin beds. With the curtains drawn and the light off a twilight gloom pervaded the modest hotel room. Only a buttery glow at top and bottom of the reinforced drapes showed that the sun was setting over Tel

Aviv. "But I'd guess we've just had another run-in with our friends the Russian *mafiya*. It's about the right approach for brutal completists, mopping up after the way they did with the helicopter."

"You're probably right." Annja said.

The television was on with the sound muted. For about the tenth time since they'd turned it on, it showed a past-prime pop diva in London, peroxide curls awry, mascara tear-smeared, sobbing about the loss of her adored spiritual leader Mark Peter Stern as her Pakistani soccer-player husband hovered in the background looking vaguely scandalized by the proceedings.

"What does the news say?" Annja asked.

"Still blaming terrorists, of course," Pascoe replied. The screen now showed burly yarmulke-clad settlers rioting at the Temple Mount. "If it was the Russians, I suspect that terrorists will remain the official explanation, and the story won't have many legs."

"Why do you say that?"

"The *mafiya* has its influence, after all. There's been never a peep in the international media about that slight unpleasantness we were embroiled in over in Amsterdam, has there? 'Terrorism' is a useful catchword, always available to swallow inconvenient loose ends," he said.

He took a sip of the whiskey he'd bought in the hotel lobby and shook his head. "Bah. Vile stuff. Not as bad as their gin, but there you have it."

Annja splashed more tepid water on her face. It made her feel a little better. It cut the salt sting if nothing else. It didn't improve what she saw in the slightly cloudy glass, however.

"Could it have been?" she asked.

"What?"

"Terrorists?"

"Not a chance. Who'd rent a helicopter like that to a Palestinian? An expensive bit of work, that Dolphin. And also if one was positively frantic to get put under a microscope by the Israeli security service, that would be just the ticket, wouldn't it?"

"You're right." Her arms braced on the sink, Annja drew a deep sigh and considered her reflection in the mirror. She sported two black eyes and looked like a raccoon. Her cheeks were puffy and her upper lip split. Her nose had, amazingly, not been broken again.

"It's all right," Pascoe called out. "You look beautiful. Relax."

She laughed ruefully. "I look as if I just had a not very promising debut in the middleweight division."

"You should see the other guy." Pascoe joked.

She shuddered and turned away from the mirror. "Please don't say that."

"Ah. Sorry. Just trying to sound like a Yank. I wasn't thinking. Forgive me, please."

Smoothing back her hair, which felt as if it were

pulling at her scalp with a thousand little hands as all the salt dried in it, she came into the main room. "It's all right," she said. "I can't hide from things I do. That way lies madness—of one kind or another."

He tipped his head and looked at her like a curious bird in the gloom. She sat on the edge of a bed.

"What was that thing that blew up Stern's yacht?" she asked. "Some kind of rocket?"

"Antitank missile. Almost certainly laser guided. It was much too big for a free-flight rocket such as an Armbrust or a Milán. And a wire-guidance system won't work over open water. Shorts out, you see."

He set his drink on the little round table by his armchair and leaned forward, knitting his hands together. For the first time she noticed they were large hands, substantial hands. They looked strong. They looked out of place with the rest of his pink-cheeked, almost juvenile appearance, although she of all people knew a working archaeologist wasn't going to have the fine, soft hands she'd somehow expected to find on the ends of the pretty young man's arms.

She put her arms straight back to either side and leaned back on them. She raised an eyebrow at him. "How come you know so much about it?"

"I was with a Javelin antitank team in Northern Ireland for a year," he said, "Royal Fusiliers. Bloody foolishness, really, since the Provos never managed to come up with any tanks."

"Was it dangerous?"

"Not for us. It was after the Provos started negotiating with Downing Street. There were a lot of nasty incidents that never made it to the telly, but they were directed almost exclusively against rival drug dealers. Lucky for me I mustered out before First Battalion got stuck into that mess over in Iraq."

"Why were you keeping watch on Stern?"

"Same reason you are," he said. "We're all looking for Solomon's Jar, aren't we?"

"What put you onto Stern in the first place?"

"You didn't think you were the only one to know about that last-call recall trick, surely? Although to be wholly candid, I merely read the telephone number over your shoulder."

She laughed. "I didn't really think about it until now. I guess I should've connected it all once I learned you were seeker23."

"You took your own sweet time coming to the Holy Land," he told her. "Did you try the Malkuth offices in New York?"

"The White Tree Lodge, in Kent," she said. "You saw the card, too, I'm sure."

"Yes. How'd that turn out?"

She felt her expression harden without intention. How much dare I tell him? she wondered.

She kept it terse. She admitted having been forced to kill to escape a death sentence in the churchyard behind Ravenwood Manor. She did skip past exactly *how* she'd fought her way free of her would-be executioners.

He leaned toward her, blue eyes intent. "We need to talk," he said.

She smiled faintly and pushed back a stray lock of hair that was tickling her forehead. She was very aware of her own stale smell of dried seawater, sweat and petroleum fractions. "I thought we were talking," she said.

He picked up his glass, looked into it. An inch of brown liquid stood at the base of a small pile of slumping ice cubes. He took the glass in both hands and, leaning forward, swirled it between his legs, elbows on thighs. The ice made tinkling music in the glass.

"Who are you?" he asked.

"I'm an archaeologist. Although I believe you once characterized me as a pothunter." She couldn't help the last coming out with some asperity; it was the ultimate insult one archaeologist could pay another.

"I think that whatever my suspicions were, they've moved well past that, Annja my dear," Aidan Pascoe said. She found she didn't mind him calling her that, even though he said it with an edge of sarcasm. "What I meant to ask was rather more along the lines of, are you human?"

She laughed. "Do you expect me to turn into some kind of reptilian alien before your eyes?"

"I'm not sure what to expect. I'd have said rubbish to all that about aliens passing as humans when I woke up this morning. That was before I saw what appears to be a very attractive and intelligent but otherwise altogether unremarkable young woman bring down an SA-366 helicopter by chucking an anchor at it."

"I told you, that was just a lucky—"

He showed her a forestalling palm. "Please. I suspect we need to trust each other. To start, I'd like to be able to trust you not to insult my intelligence. Too much has gone on, from your astonishing presence of mind, not to mention competence, during our escape in Amsterdam, to that distinctively European cross-hilted broadsword you made such short work of those bully-boys with in the Old City, which mysteriously appeared and just as mysteriously vanished. What are you, Annja?"

She sighed. "I'm afraid if I tell you the truth, you'll *really* believe I'm insulting your intelligence."

"Try me," he said.

"What would you guess, if you had to?"

"I don't believe in superheros. Although you'd look smashing in a cape and tights. Or tights, anyway. Then again, I no longer pretend to know. I accused you of being some kind of CIA agent or special-operations type, back in that canal in Amsterdam, but that doesn't answer it, either. There's not a training course in the world that could teach you to make a cast like that with the anchor. Much less summon a sword out of thin bloody air. I was never the sort to swot for the SAS. But even I know that much," he said. "So suppose you tell me, Ms. Creed."

"I'm on a mission from God."

He blinked. "You and the Blues Brothers?"

She shrugged helplessly. "Believe it or not, that's the least…silly…way I can think to put it. I'm not even formally religious. I was raised in a Catholic orphanage, mostly, but like a lot of kids who went through parochial school growing up, that tended to make me more defiant and antireligious than anything. Or at least mistrustful of organized religion."

"Very well. Go on."

She explained how she had found the medallion in the cave in France, how she had, without conscious intent, much less knowing how, spontaneously restored the broken blade with her touch. She mentioned Roux and what he had told her about her legacy as successor to Joan of Arc. She didn't see any good reason to mention Garin Braden. She wasn't sure she believed the story any more than she'd expect Pascoe would. She shrugged and looked at him.

"Good Lord!" Pascoe exclaimed when she'd finished. "You make it sound as if I've been serially rescued by Buffy the Vampire Slayer!"

"Well—not really. There hasn't been any unbroken succession of champions or anything. After they lost Joan, it basically took half a millennium for conditions to be right to appoint a new champion of good. Or anoint. Whatever."

It was not, of course, either the whole truth or nothing but the truth. But Annja felt guilty telling him even this much. He certainly didn't have a proverbial need to know more details—or even more correct ones. As it was she'd told him this edited version of the truth because she could only see worse problems arising from trying to stonewall him. He was keen and analytical enough to arrive at the truth on his own—and imaginative enough to concoct potentially disruptive theories if he missed the mark.

"That's the most preposterous thing I've ever heard," he said finally. "Then again, nothing less preposterous would begin to account for what I've experienced in your company."

He rubbed his forehead. She sat in silence in the gloom and gave him time to think. It was hard. She liked him. She felt a need to be understood by him. Yet she didn't dare give him more details than she had already. And though she didn't think of herself as particularly adroit at relations with living people, she realized at some level the best thing she could do was bite down and hold her peace, whatever it cost, and let him sort out what he'd choose to believe.

He raised his head. His eye met hers. They were large and luminous in the dim. After a moment he smiled.

"Let's get cleaned up and go for dinner," he said. "Adventuring is hungry work, I find."

"How DOES a self-professed agnostic get selected to be the champion of good?" Pascoe asked after they returned to the room. Once more he sat on the chair while she lay on one of the beds, propped on pillows. She'd had a tougher day than he had. They had turned on the lights by the beds. It still wasn't very bright. That seemed to suit both of them.

Dinner had passed in uncontroversial conversation. That had been by tacit agreement. Once Pascoe accepted the situation he was in, he either had a proper sense of discretion or was taking boyish delight in playing secret agent. Or, she reckoned, both.

"You aren't the first one to ask that question," she told him. "You're not the first to get an entirely unsatisfactory answer to it, either."

He looked at her a moment, then laughed. "Do you believe in Him now?"

"Well, I sort of have to. I guess. Although the impression I'm getting is that our religions don't necessarily get all the details exactly right, let's say."

"What would your illustrious predecessor say if she heard you talking like that? The angels talked to her on a regular basis, didn't they?"

"I think she may have been delusional," Annja said. "Roux never really contradicted me when I suggested that to him. Although I did feel bad about it after the fact because Joan's such a painful subject for him."

"So no angelic voices for you, eh?"

She shrugged. "If angels did try to talk to Joan, they might have had their work cut out getting a word in edgewise, if you catch my meaning. That may have been what led to her downfall—trouble sorting out the signal from the background noise and all. May the spirit of my revered predecessor forgive my saying so.

"You know, all of this isn't any easier for me to digest than it must be for you," she said.

"I suppose not," Pascoe said thoughtfully.

"In any event, no angels have spoken to me so far that I know of."

"What happens if they start?"

She smiled almost shyly. "Cross that bridge when I come to it?"

He laughed. He had a good laugh. Solid, louder and fuller than she'd expect to come out of his somewhat slight frame.

"What about you?" she asked.

He blinked. "Me? No, no angels have spoken to me, either. Not that it's ever occurred to me to listen," he said.

"No. I mean, what drives you? You seem just as determined as I am to find the jar. You'd have to be, to keep at it after all that's happened to you so far."

"Well, I do seem to have acquired my very own guardian angel, have I not?" He smiled. "Still, I'd like to think I'd have persevered in spite of what's happened had you never intervened. Provided I *survived*, of course, which I'm realistic enough to know is far from a given."

He sat back with his chin sunk to his chest a moment, contemplating. "I could give you a load of rubbish about desire to keep a priceless artifact out of the hands of unscrupulous men but I'll spare you reciting the whole laundry list. I'm sure we both know it by heart by now."

"If we even know all the players in the game," she said.

"Lovely thought, that. It's true enough, of course. Like any responsible archaeologist I detest pothunters."

For a moment he fell quiet. Annja had closed her eyes, resting them, but she could feel his scrutiny like the glow from a heat lamp on her cheek. He still doesn't altogether trust me, she thought. Well, who could blame him?

"But I have to admit, thoroughgoing rationalist and modernist that I am, I've always harbored a hope, deep down inside, that things like the jar are *real*," he said quietly.

"I think most of us feel that way—if we're honest

with ourselves," Annja said, opening her eyes. "Not many of us are brave enough to say so."

"You think? You might be right, judging from the postings on alt.archaeo.esoterica. Then again I'm sure archaeologists aren't any more prone to self-honesty than all the rest of the ruck. I frankly doubt I'd believe a word of your story if I hadn't repeatedly seen you do things which defy what I once considered rational explanation. But if I'm forced to swallow one impossibility, to say nothing of an entire set of them, others become more palatable, somehow," Pascoe said.

"All my life I've wanted to make a difference, Annja. I've always been appalled by how much ugliness I've seen in the world, how much evil. War, starvation, neglect. It's naive, I suppose, but I've never been able to see people suffering without wanting to help them."

"You're kind," she said.

He leaned forward. "Think what it would be like if the jar is *real*, Annja. That kind of power. What couldn't we do to make the world a better place?" His cheeks were flushed. His eyes glowed like beacons.

"With demons, Aidan?"

He laughed. "It sounds improbable, I know. But Solomon was a great man, a wise man. A good man, even if a lot of his contemporaries thought the worst of him for building pagan temples for his favorite wives. He didn't use the power for evil. Perhaps he even built the temple in Jerusalem using the demons, and that's a righteous thing, to be sure. It must be possible to subordinate the demons to one's will for good, as well as for wicked purposes."

Annja thought back to what Tsipporah had told her. She hadn't shared anything about the mysterious American-born kabbalist sage with Pascoe. But from the information she had provided, Annja suspected he was correct.

She felt a certain disquiet.

You're just tired, she told herself. Being silly. He's an innocent.

Pascoe had relaxed for a moment. Then his intensity returned. "What do *you* intend to do with the jar if you get your hands on it?" he asked, eyes narrowed.

She drew in a deep breath and let it out slowly. "I don't know yet."

19

"Ah." The man's teeth were brown and crooked surrounded by his short, grizzled beard. "You must mean Mad Spyros."

The quayside watering hole was not one of your quaint tourist tavernas. Nor did the clientele consist of tourists, glossy and well-scrubbed. Womb dark after the brilliant Ionian Sea sunshine outside, the tavern smelled of the same things its patrons did: fish, varnish, sweat and brutally harsh tobacco. It was a mixture nearly as potent as tear gas. Annja found it hard to keep smiling and not blink incessantly at the stinging in her eyes.

Pascoe gave her a look. His blue eyes were clear. I'm surprised they're not bloodshot, she thought.

"Spyros?" she said tentatively. "Could that be your cousin, Aidan?"

He shrugged. "Well, he's a bit on the distant side. And I've never actually met him in person, you know."

"It is short for Spyridon," their informant said helpfully. He was a short, thick man with bright black eyes shining from red cheeks, and a cloth cap mashed down on graying curls.

Annja and Pascoe had spent a sweaty, footsore day tramping the dives along the waterfront in Corfu, where the hills crowded with whitewashed buildings tumbled down almost into Mandouki Harbor. They had climbed up the Kanoni road past the archaeological museum and the old fort on its island across a causeway, along the esplanade and around the tip of the peninsula to Arseniou, then along the north shore past the container-ship fleet landing of the old port, past the late-sixteenth-century Venetian new fort toward the new fleet landing and the Hippodrome. They were posing as a pair of tourists on a genealogical vacation, tracking down a missing relative of Aidan's. Despite the fairness of his skin, his curly black hair made it plausible he had Levantine ancestry.

To Annja's eyes he looked rather Byronic, in his white shirt with open collar and sleeves rolled up and his faded blue jeans. She knew George Gordon, the sixth Baron Byron, had come to the nearby Ionian island of Cephalonia to fight in the Greek war of independence against the Ottoman Turks. Indeed to Annja's eye her companion bore a slight resemblance to the infamous poet.

The man who had mentioned Mad Spyros spoke in Greek to his companions. They were a tough-looking lot, professional fishermen like the object of Annja and Aidan's search. They all laughed and nodded. Most of them were short, some wiry, some wide. One tall man with a touch of bronze to his beard loomed over Annja and rumbled something in a voice like thunder. He finished his speaking with the word "Nomiki," suggesting to Annja that was their informant's name.

"Surely it must be, as my friend Petros says," Nomiki said, jutting a thumb back over his shoulder at the big man.

"There's an appropriate name," Annja heard Aidan mutter beneath his breath. She agreed. She knew very little Greek, but she knew *petros* meant "rock."

"Spyros is our friend. But, poor man, he has taken to the drinking, to seeing bad things everywhere. He is, what you say, paranoid," Nomiki said.

He looked expectant, with his head cocked to one side. His eyes glittered like obsidian beads.

"Uh, yes," Annja said. "I think that is the word you're looking for."

"So my cousin's name is Spyridon," Pascoe said. "I don't know if I'd say he's paranoid. After all, something did kill his shipmates." The men made the sign of the cross, in the Orthodox manner that looked backward to Annja, accustomed as she was to the Catholic version.

IT WAS MURDER that had brought them to Corfu. The island was a riot of hills, intensely green with olive trees, shaped like a horse's haunch and snuggled up next to the Greek mainland in the Ionian Sea at the mouth of the Adriatic, altogether too close for comfort to the coast of turbulent Albania. Rumor had connected the discovery of King Solomon's Jar to the mysterious, violent deaths of six local fishermen reported on the wire services worldwide.

Annja and Aidan had started out that day asking about the killings. They first posed as crime tourists, what some pundits were calling the new ecotourists, people with a morbid fascination with forensic pathology from watching too many television shows.

It was not an occupation that had ever appealed to Annja. While her own profession brought her into frequent contact with human remains, like most archaeologists and physical anthropologists, she had a marked distaste for dealing with specimens that were fresh.

Not unexpectedly, the locals they questioned at first had regarded them with fascination mixed with loathing. Annja suspected that only Aidan's liberality in buying drinks for the house wherever they went—with handfuls of cash to prevent leaving plastic tracks—kept them from having to fight their way free of some places.

But gossip is a powerful force in human affairs, as Annja had discovered as a child. They soon started hearing a persistent rumor that the six crewmen who had been murdered on the boat were not the same six who had been aboard when the ancient jar was found. One member of the original crew had somehow survived.

The pair switched their focus to trying to find that lone survivor. To cover the fact they didn't know his name, Aidan claimed to be an Englishmen of Greek extraction who had heard rumors from an estranged branch of his family that a distant cousin had been involved in the horrible business of the fishing-boat murders. He told their listeners since he and his female friend had already planned a Greek holiday, he agreed to his aging mother's request to check in on Corfu and see if they could track the poor man down and bring him comfort from his displaced family in the British Isles. It was thin at best, but as far as Annja could see, it was their only option.

"WHERE MIGHT WE FIND poor cousin Spyros, then?" Pascoe asked.

Nomiki cocked his head to one side. A calculating look came into his eyes. Aidan reached for his wallet. Not quite sure why, Annja stopped him with a touch on his arm.

The Greek man spoke again to his friends. His manner was earnest. The ensuing conversation was low and intense. Annja had the impression of general disagreement, of men not accustomed to muting their emotions trying, for reasons unknown to her, to keep the argument from rising to the boisterous levels it ordinarily might. As they argued Aidan stood by smiling vaguely and humming to himself, as if oblivious to the passions being kept simmering below the surface.

Finally Nomiki turned back to the pair. "The boat was the *Athanasia*." He and his companions crossed themselves again. "It is to be found on a beach a few kilometers south of town. There you may find poor Spyros, as well. He cannot leave it behind, it seems."

Pascoe's smile widened. "Splendid! Thank you so much." Now he did dig in his pocket. "Allow me to buy a round of drinks for the house."

Nomiki leaped back as if afraid the mad young Englishman was going for a gun. "No, no!' he exclaimed, holding up callused hands with fingers twisted from being broken repeatedly hauling in water-heavy and stiffened nets.

Then he smiled. It was forced, ghastly. "It is not necessary. We do this as a favor to kinfolk of our friend Spyridon."

He spoke quickly to the others. They all seemed to draw back, then nod and smile fixedly.

Pascoe shrugged. "Well, thank you all, and good day."

He waited a moment, then turned and walked out. Annja stayed close to him. She felt a tingling sensation at the nape of her neck.

Out on the street an old man in a dark wool suit tee-tered past them on a bicycle. Away to the north bruise-dark storm clouds gathered above Albania. The sky was clear and achingly bright blue above them, the water a deep green inshore and a royal blue so intense it seemed almost self-luminous farther out.

"Odd," Pascoe muttered.

"What?" Annja asked.

"I've never known working men in a pub to turn down free drinks," he said.

"Maybe they felt it would be bad luck, for some reason. They were obviously still feeling the effects of the murders." Annja said.

"I can understand why." He shrugged. "Ah, well. Let's rent a car and nip down to this beach to find the boat. I don't fancy poking around a scene like that in the dark."

Annja laughed. "What? You're not superstitious, are you?"

Aidan laughed louder. He thrust his elbow out from his side.

After a moment Annja threaded her arm through his. Side by side they began the lengthy hike back to the car-rental office.

THE HILLS OF CORFU WERE a deep and beautiful green. That was the good part. Looked at more closely a note of monotony came to the fore. Most of the island's copious verdure, wild as well as cultivated, consisted of olive trees. They were the island's main, close to only crop. Export of olives to the mainland and fishing were key sources of income for the islanders, although both came well behind tourism.

Now the green, made into different hues and values by the island's vigorous relief, had begun to take on a dark uniformity as the sun declined toward the rugged mountains inland.

Gravel turned and shingle crunched beneath their feet as they made their way down the beach. At its southern extremity a boat lay beached on the shingle, heeled over onto its port side. Its bottom and screws had rusted red.

"*Athanasia,*" Aidan said, looking at the characters painted on the stern. "That's the boat we're looking for."

"You know Greek?" Annja asked, a trifle suspicious, and ready to be more than a trifle put out if for some reason he had withheld knowledge and allowed them to struggle through the whole day trying subtly to interrogate people who spoke dribs and wisps of English if any at all.

But he only laughed. "The dire consequences of a classical education," he said. "I speak a few words and understand next to nothing of the spoken tongue. But

I read it fair enough. Well enough to transliterate, surely."

He walked up to the boat and rapped on the hull. It did not ring so much but echo hollowly. "Besides, this is a big craft. Maybe thirty feet long. A substantial investment, especially on a poor island such as this one. Do you see any holes in her hull? I don't. So there must be some serious reason she's moldering here on the beach with nobody trying to take her to sea."

"I guess you're right," she said. "She's a lot bigger than I thought she'd be."

"She's not even being used to dry nets," Pascoe said. Several other craft, obviously also fishing boats, bobbed at anchor not far out from the little beach. Wet nets had been spread out over upturned dinghies and stretched out on the shingle and held down with large rocks. "People are afraid of her," he stated.

Annja glanced toward the sun, which hung low and swollen above the steep green hills. "I guess we'd better take a look aboard while there's still some light," she said.

Throughout the day they had not yet found it necessary to refer to the jar itself. This was good, Annja thought. Whoever or whatever had killed those men might still be in the area, or have spies on the ground. The guilty party or parties might or might not be fooled by touristy preoccupation with the macabre, or goofy genealogical enthusiasms. But the killer's putatively pointed ears would definitely prick up if somebody turned up asking about the priceless, supernaturally powerful relic the hapless crew had pulled from the sea in its nets. Provided, of course, the murders had actually been connected to Solomon's Jar, and not some semi-random element. Such as drug smuggling gone bad, as follow-up articles said the Greek police surmised. That was the catchall of bad, lazy, or simply stymied police investigations, Annja knew full well.

Scrambling over the port rail was easy. Climbing up-hill into the wheelhouse was something of a challenge, although nothing daunting to a pair as fit as Annja and her companion. Pulling herself through the open hatch-way, though, she came up short.

The stench struck her like an invisible barrier.

"Ghastly," Aidan muttered. "I didn't imagine it would smell this foul after so much time."

"Neither did I," Annja said. Her cheek rode up in response to the stink, squinting her amber-green eyes. "The humid climate must keep the smell active. I guess that's why we're archaeologists instead of med-ical examiners."

"We're wimps," Aidan said, holding on to a stanchion right behind her. "I can live with that."

By force of will she thrust herself into the reeking dimness. Flies swarmed up to meet her. Their bodies fuzzed the air like a living haze. The sunset light shone almost directly through the cracked front port, yet it made little impression on the gloom within.

She could still see enough. More than enough.

The first impression, which did not particularly surprise her, was that someone had tossed buckets of dark paint liberally around the compartment. Copious buckets. Her stomach began a slow roll.

You've seen blood splatter like this before, she reminded herself sternly. You've even caused it. So you'd better learn to face up to the consequences of your actions, no matter how righteous.

Lest they become too easy. The voices of Roux and Tsipporah sounded in her head.

Beneath the irregular coating of dried blood the compartment was a shambles. Chair seats and backs had been ripped in parallel slashes and bled yellowed stuffing. An obvious radar screen and other navigation instruments were smashed. The chart table lay broken against the bulkhead below. Charts and logs had been torn to pieces and strewed around. The papers had mildewed and crumpled in the humidity, and some had begun to melt into the varnished wood and painted metal of the deck and bulkheads.

The sound of the flies was like an idling engine's growl.

"My God," Aidan said, coming in behind her. "A charnel house."

"Literally," Annja whispered.

He gestured around at the shambles. "Did vandals do some of this?"

"I doubt it." She pointed to a volume lying open against the juncture of deck and bulkhead. A ragged streak of blood crossed it at a violent angle. "At least some of the destruction probably happened before the murders. Or during. Anyway, as you just pointed out, nobody's tried to reclaim this vessel, despite the fact it's still probably worth the life's savings of an entire fishing crew. Who'd dare to vandalize it?"

"Not I," Pascoe said.

Her foot began to slip on the canted deck. She reached out reflexively and grabbed the back of the pilot's chair, which was fixed on a pedestal.

She felt a shock as her skin contacted the slashed leather. It was as if she had completed an electric circuit, though not unpleasant. Inside herself she seemed to perceive a hint of golden glow.

She felt a chill as if the sun had gone out instead of set. She shuddered.

"Annja!" Pascoe exclaimed, exquisitely sensitive. She felt the reassurance of his hand on her shoulder. The strength of his grip surprised her. "Are you all right?"

She shook her head as if shedding water. "Yes," in a shaky voice.

"What is it?"

"It was here."

"The jar?"

She nodded.

"That's what made you shudder like that? You looked as if you'd seen a ghost."

"Not seen, Aidan. The jar was here. I'm sure of it. But it's long gone."

He nodded. "We reckoned that."

"It's not the only thing. There was something here. Something I've sensed before. At Ravenwood Manor and the Wailing Wall. And, oh, on Mark Stern's yacht, when Eliete von Hauptstark attacked me. I just realized what it is."

"And that is…?"

"Evil." The word had force precisely because she said it quietly, with utter lack of inflection.

Pascoe looked around quickly. "Is it still here?" She could see from his frown that his trained skepticism was warring with his emotions. And losing.

"No. All I'm feeling are the traces it left behind."

"Months ago? It must have been a pretty potent evil."

Wordlessly she waved her hand around the blood-splashed cabin.

"Right," Aidan said. "Forgive my being a git."

Pupils dilated more than the gloom justified, Pascoe's eyes scanned the interior, even the overhead, which was likewise liberally streaked with blood spray. "Do we need to search any further into the bloody boat?" His tone said that he fairly urgently didn't want to.

"No point," she said. "We're not crime scene investigators, thank goodness. We know what we came to learn."

Before she finished the last word he had slipped backward out the hatch. She joined him before saying, with a shaky smile, "I'm just as glad as you are."

He stood with his feet at the joining of deck and gunwale, head down with chin on clavicle and moving side to side like a bull's, drawing deep, quavering gasps of air in through his open mouth. She recognized the signs of a desperate fight against nausea.

The wind was blessedly coming in from the sea. The warm, humid air felt almost air-conditioned on Annja's face, which she realized was streaming sweat in a way the day's exertion in the sun had not been able to achieve. The moist sea breeze smelled sweet, like life itself.

Aidan clambered over the rail and jumped down to the sand. Then he reached up a hand to help Annja. She hid a smile at that. Some women she knew might have angrily spurned the gesture as chauvinistic—and it was certainly unnecessary, given that she was as strong or stronger than he was. It struck her as archaic, gallant and altogether sweet. Just the sort of thing, she thought, a well-bred and very handsome young British archaeologist ought to do. She took his hand and jumped lightly down beside him.

He withdrew it as if it were hot. "Sorry," he said, eyes down. "I think I've just been a right Charlie again."

"Not at all," she said. "I thought it was sweet."

"What now?" he asked awkwardly.

She looked to the west. The sun was almost out of sight, just a blazing white arc backlighting a rounded peak. Around them she felt the velvet mauve darkness, the cooling of the heavy air.

"Better see if we can find our friend Spyridon before he drinks himself to sleep," she said.

He touched her arm, lightly and deliberately. "Don't move," he said softly. "We may have a spot of bother."

She turned to look at him. Light and movement drew her focus beyond him, north up the beach, to where an irregular line of torches slowly approached.

They were borne by half a dozen or more shabbily dressed men. They held knives and makeshift clubs in their other hands.

20

"They've surrounded us," Aidan said through clenched teeth.

She turned to look south. A similar group approached from down the beach. Their dark, bearded faces were grim in the wavering orange light of their driftwood torches.

"Nice traditional touch, that. Torches," Pascoe said. "Pity it's not an agrarian enough setting for them to have pitchforks. Still one supposes it's the thought that counts."

Annja felt a stab of admiration for his insouciance. She felt little herself.

She recognized the approaching men weren't carrying torches to act out a classic monster-movie scene. Rather, it was because of the traditional role of fire in cleansing evil.

"If we've trespassed, we apologize," she called out to the nearer group, the one coming from the south. "We mean no harm."

Her eyes darted—her head unmoving so as not to reveal her desperation. The beach was isolated. A small scatter of shacks lay several hundred yards up the beach to the north. To the south a jutting headland walled it off. A few more little warped-plank buildings leaned in various directions across the road, a hundred yards or so inland. Help was far distant—if anyone in the vicinity would care to help them against their own neighbors.

Pebbles crunched ominously beneath boots. The torch flames were gaudy in the heavy twilight.

"You've done enough harm," called a voice. To Annja's shock it was familiar. The voice of Nomiki had coarsened to a raven's croak. "You devils killed our friends, our kin. Now the time has come for you to pay."

With a scream of jet engines, an airplane lifted off from Corfu International Airport just across the narrow mouth of the inlet. It sounded to Annja like a lost soul fleeing.

Someone cried out hoarsely. With a rush the fishermen were on them. Any doubts Annja entertained as to their seriousness were dispelled in a blink when one man took a horizontal swipe at her face with a torch. Its head blazed a meteor orange trail as she ducked back. A piece of her hair passed through the flame and she smelled the stench of it burning.

She moved quickly, tweaking the torch from its wielder's grasp and throwing it end over end to fall with a hiss and a fizz into the foam of a retreating wave. It was a small gesture, and only momentarily satisfying as more angry men crowded around.

She punched the man who had swung the torch in the face. He sat down hard with a crackle of shingle and an aggrieved outcry. "Stay behind me," she called to Pascoe without looking back.

If the fishermen felt any Old World compunctions about attacking a woman they took care not to let them show. Annja pirouetted around a clumsy knife slash, smelling a waft of alcohol breath that accounted for much of the clumsiness. She dropped its originator sprawling and gasping with an elbow at the back of the neck. Somehow she sensed it as a club swung for the back of her head. She bent forward sharply at the waist. The club swished behind her skull. She mule-kicked straight back, caught an ample abdomen with hard muscle beneath and elicited a whoosh of forced-out air as its owner was launched back several feet.

Another man rushed her, bellowing, club raised to crush her skull. She turned and charged past him, catching him with a forearm high on his chest that dumped him hard on his back and left him stunned and breathless. She stiff-armed a second attacker.

Annja moved through the crowd of attackers in a

controlled frenzy, allowing her training and reflexes free rein. Rather than block, she dodged, ducked and weaved. In preference to kicking and punching she grabbed and swung or simply pushed. She kept moving through her assailants, directing blows away from her, thrusting men into one another. Then she heard Aidan shouting angrily to the men to keep their hands off of him and she turned to glance back.

The move undid her. Strong arms thrust beneath her armpits from behind. Huge hands clasped the nape of her neck. She was lifted kicking off the ground, knowing the bronze-bearded giant, Petros, had caught her.

A man closed with her from the front, empty handed. She raised her knees and kicked him hard in the gut with both feet. He flew back, out of her sight beyond the ring of torches that had walled her in with barracuda suddenness. She became aware of various smells. Indifferently washed bodies, wool steeped in sweat, grease, sea salt and fish scales, garlic, decaying teeth, and resinous Greek wine and Albanian beer that smelled like formaldehyde, all mingled to cause a bit of sting for the eyes. She also sensed an edge of fear.

Then Nomiki himself was before her, bandy-legged and mysterious as Pan in the shifting of dark and torchlight. A snarl of hatred bared his brown and jumbled teeth. A blade protruded from his hand, with torchlight sluicing along it like the premonition of blood.

Annja kicked the knife from his hand.

Nomiki fell back with a curse as she kicked him in the face. But then her leg was seized, followed by the other, and more men piled on than she could kick away with all her strength.

She realized she had made a potentially fatal mistake. She'd been holding back when her opponents were not.

Petros's monster hands thrust her head forward, intending to snap her neck. Her neck muscles strained, popped, seemed to groan aloud as she fought his strength. She would not give in. She couldn't win, but that meant nothing to her resolve....

A voice cried, "Stop!"

It called out in English. It was a male voice, high-pitched, harsh with an accent and something more. As it penetrated Annja's fog, in which she had been aware of almost no sound since the fight began, it must have penetrated the consciousnesses of the mob swarming over her. The men actually did stop and paused in their sinister intent.

A man hobbled forward, using a broken oar as a sort of crutch. The men at the back of the mob surrounding her fell back with torches in hand like an inadvertent honor guard, producing an illuminated aisle for his approach.

Nomiki stood before Annja rubbing his jaw. He spit what looked suspiciously like a fragment of brown tooth onto the slate shingle at his feet. "Spyros?" he croaked.

At first glimpse Annja had thought the newcomer was an ancient, so hitched and painful were his movements. Now she realized the hair surrounding his head like a clumped and matted halo was dark. His naturally lean features were drawn further by pain as though stretched on a frame. His dark eyes were pits of sorrow, black in the torchlight.

Someone barked at him in Greek. He replied in a low voice, more dead than deliberately soft, it seemed to Annja.

"But Spyros," Nomiki said with a touch of whine in his voice. "They killed your mates."

"No," the lame young man answered in English. "They did not. Now go."

Petros protested. The young man's face twisted as if he had been struck. "Enough killing! Enough pain. Spare my soul more burden! Go!"

He cried out again in Greek, his tone desperate, yet angry rather than pleading. Annja felt the self-righteous energy of the mob drain away. Where they had been a pack of raging predators half a minute before, now they were just normal men, rapidly feeling themselves overtaken by shame. Like a clot of muck being washed from a deck with a hose, the erstwhile lynch mob began to come apart, and then flowed away down the beach in separating streams, as if the men were too ashamed even for one another's continued company.

Aidan knelt on the shingle by the *Athanasia*'s red

hull, fists down like a sprinter's on the line, breathing heavily through his mouth. Annja knelt beside him. "You're hurt," she said.

"You oughta see the other guy," he joked through split and puffed lips. "Actually, the other guys look splendid, if you leave aside the effects of hard living and doubtful hygiene. I never laid a finger on them. Not for want of trying, though."

Despite her protests he started to rise. When his determination became obvious she helped him stand and let him lean half surreptitiously against her. His body was warm, flushed perhaps by effort and fear, against hers.

Aside from bruised cheeks and puffy eyes he didn't seem badly hurt. Apparently all that had struck him had been fists, not wood or steel. Not that fists alone couldn't do severe damage.

"You're Spyridon, then?" Aidan said to the young man who stood before them, leaning on his crutch and panting from the effects of his own passionate outburst.

"I am."

The young Englishman forced himself by visibly painful degrees to stand fully upright. Not for the first time, Annja was surprised by his toughness. He looked so boyish and—tender, perhaps, not soft exactly, she thought. But he had steel in his spine.

"We owe you our thanks," Pascoe said.

"Thank you," Annja added.

But the wild-haired head shook decisively. "You owe me nothing," Spyros said. "I do it for me. I am doomed. I hope to not be damned."

He turned and stumped off. Bats swooped overhead, taking flittering tiny insects as they followed him up the darkened beach. A gibbous moon was rising across the waves. Pollution haze or something else stained it red around the rim, like dilute blood.

They followed. "How did you know we weren't who your friends thought we were?" Pascoe called after him.

"You tourist couple, very nice," he said over his shoulder. "Who killed my crewmates—not nice."

"Might be some holes to that logic," Annja said to Aidan, quietly.

He shrugged. "Roll with it, I say."

Spyros led them to a rough shelter at the south end of the beach, masked from view by some large rocks covered in brushy arbutus and fragrant bay. Knocked together out of planks and tarpaper, it was little more than a lean-to. He lowered himself painfully to the ground, set aside his broken oar, gestured for them to sit. Annja and Aidan looked at each other, then perched side by side on a chunk of driftwood perhaps eight feet long that seemed to serve as a sort of boundary for the young man's living space.

Rummaging around in litter piled beside the shelter Spyros made a little stack of newspaper and dry twigs, broke some small bits of driftwood onto it and lit a fire from a plastic lighter. By its uneasy orange light he dug in a mound of reeking cloth Annja realized must be his bed. He came up with a bottle, upended it. She smelled the turpentine-like scent of cheap ouzo as it ran down both sides of his narrow stubbled chin.

In the firelight she studied him as he drank. He had a triangular head and hunted-fox eyes. He was wiry to the point of emaciation. His eyes were sunken deep in pits of blackness.

At last he lowered the bottle and wiped his mouth with the back of his hand. "What you want with Spyros?" he asked. He sounded sad. An undercurrent in his voice, the way he held himself, ever poised as if for flight, the way the firelight flickered from eyeballs turning restlessly this way and that spoke eloquently of a fear that nagged with ceaseless rodent teeth.

"You were part of a crew that dredged an ancient jar from the sea," Aidan said without preamble. "Is that correct?"

Spyros nodded. He looked even less happy. "King Solomon's Jar," he said.

"Why do you say that?" Annja asked.

"When it came up in our nets it look like nothing but big lump. Like lava, but green, you know? But Ioannis, my brother-in-law's cousin, he scrape some corrosion away with his knife. Beneath was yellow metal. Brass."

Next to her Annja felt Aidan shudder at such desecration of an ancient artifact. She felt some of the same thing. She couldn't muster quite the same outrage. For some reason she found herself seeing different points of view with a lot more clarity and empathy these days.

Isn't that kind of an occupational impediment for a champion of good? she wondered. It would make sense for her to start to see everything in black and white.

But that would be too easy, she thought.

"Once he clean up some, in the brass we saw drawings." Spyros said. "Engraved, very fine, but we could just see them. Almost like letters, but not like any letters I see. Not even Chinese. Not Egyptian hieroglyphs." He shook his head.

"Then Georgios, our captain, he get very excited. He had seen writing like that in some book he read once. He said it was used to write the name of spirits. He said it meant we had found jar of King Solomon himself, that he used to put spirits in.

"We laughed at him, even if he was captain. He reads too much! But he was so serious. He got angry that we laughed, so angry he threaten to heave Ioannis over the rail into the sea. Vasilios, he was our mechanic, he thought he knew too much because he lived for a time in America. He said if there were ever spirits in the jar, they were not there now, for there was no stopper. Georgios, he say that not matter. He knows someone pay much for the jar!"

For a moment the young man sat cross-legged staring into the fire. "I grew up with Vasilios," he said. "He was a year older than me, bigger. He stayed bigger when we grew. He used to catch me, rub mud in my hair, laugh and laugh. But it was just fun. He was my friend."

He looked up. "So we sailed to Haifa. A Jew met us in a launch, an Israeli. Doctor from Ministry of Antiquities. Ehud Dror his name. He was man who studies old things, a scientist, you know—what is word—?"

"An archaeologist," Pascoe said in a tight voice.

Spyros nodded. "That's right. Archaeologist. From the government. Georgios does business with him before. Sometimes we bring other things up in our nets, you know? Old things. And he paid us well, just like the captain say. American dollars."

He took another pull from his bottle. For a moment he sat staring into the small pale flames of his fire.

"Then a month ago," he said, "a lifeboat broke loose in a bad sea. It broke my ankle. I was in hospital. I have to use this—" he held up the sawed-off oar "—because the crutch the health service gave me keeps folding up. But at least they did not give me saltwater injection and call it antibiotic."

He drew a deep breath, as if nerving himself to go on. "My nephew Akakios took my place. It was his first voyage—he was sixteen. He could not believe his luck."

Emotion choked him. He tipped his head and drank

again. As he lowered the bottle, Annja saw firelight glisten in a tear track down his cheek.

"It happened just offshore," he said, "when *Athanasia* returned with the catch that evening and dropped anchor. It killed them all. Akakios, Ioannis, Vasilios, Pavlos, Stamatios, Georgios the captain. It took them all."

"It?" Aidan asked gently.

Spyros wept openly now. He shook his head as he spoke—as if denying himself hope, not denying the tragedy that had haunted his every waking thought, his every dream, since it happened. That was something he had no power to deny.

"A devil," he sobbed. "A devil killed them."

Glancing aside, Annja saw Aidan's face working in an effort to restrain his skepticism from emitting a sarcastic blurt. "Surely it was a man. Or men," he said.

"A man who did such a thing," Spyros said, "must be a devil. Or have a devil in him."

A driftwood chunk shifted, fell into the fire. Yellow sparks flew up. Aidan jumped, then cursed under his breath.

Annja leaned forward. "Why do you blame yourself, Spyridon?"

Disconsolately he shook his shaggy head. "I should have been there to meet my fate with them. Instead my nephew died in my place. And I must live knowing that

I have cheated death—cheated the devil. And death and the devil, they always collect their due."

They sat a moment in silence. The night had settled in around them. Tree frogs trilled softly. The stars shone overhead.

"I have one question, Spyridon," Pascoe said. "How did word of your discovery get out? This Dr. Dror certainly made no official announcement."

"Oh, no. It was my nephew. Akakios used the Internet. He wrote about it there after some of the other crew bragged to him. I think his friends online thought he make it all up."

"But somebody took him seriously," Annja said.

Miserably, Spyridon nodded. "May the saints forgive me," he whispered brokenly. "I never believe in them. Saints. But they are all I have now."

"But what happened wasn't your fault," Annja said.

"We were cursed," the young man said almost matter-of-factly. "It was a holy artifact, but not meant to be…troubled. We did wrong to bring it up. And I did wrong by escaping punishment." His voice sounded hollow.

"And soon the devil who took my friends will find me!" He upended his bottle and emptied it with a gurgle. Then he threw it into the night. It smashed on the shingle.

Annja rose and moved toward him. He stared up at her with empty eyes. She took his hands.

"Spyros, listen to me. You can't hide from evil in a bottle. You know that, don't you?"

He looked away. "Man cannot hide from devil at all."

"But the evil has passed you by! Don't do the devil's work for him by drinking yourself to death," she said.

He looked up at her. She took his face in both hands. "Don't you see? You were spared for some purpose. You're alive. *Stay* alive. Find your purpose. Follow it. Shame the devil and honor your friends and relatives."

Sincere as she was, her words sounded lame in her own ears. Yet a strange thing happened. She felt a sense of strength, as if a golden radiance shone within her. She felt a tingling, then, in her palms, a sense of flow as from her to him.

He stared at her a moment longer. He sighed, and she had to steel herself not to grimace at the rush of breath redolent of stale wine and long uncleaned teeth. At last he began to weep, great heaving sobs. She hunkered down beside him and put her arm around his shoulder, feeling awkward.

Aidan sat across the fire from them, gazing at her, blue eyes thoughtful. She mentally dared him to say something flippant, modern, cynical and biting. But he didn't. He only watched.

At length Spyros cried himself out. Annja held him a few minutes longer as he relaxed against her. Eventually he began to snore.

She eased him down beside the fire and pulled a blanket over him. The night was still warm but she had no idea whether it would stay that way. Better a filthy blanket—the same one he used every night, anyway, it seemed—than to let him get cold. She stood and kicked the small fire apart and smothered the embers as best she could with brittle plates of shingle and some dirt she was able to scrape from beneath it. Aidan came to help. She brushed back a stray lock of hair and smiled at him.

Then they stood away from the gently snoring Spyros. "You think he'll be okay out here?" she asked.

"He's done well enough so far," Aidan said. "And anyway, would *you* want to try something with him, after what happened to us earlier? I don't doubt someone's been watching the whole time."

"Oh."

He looked up at the stars. "Do you really think it'll work?"

"What?"

"What you said to him. *Did* to him. There was something that passed between you. I felt it, but I don't know what it was. Do you think it'll help him, then?"

"I have no idea," she said. In thoughtful silence they walked back toward their rented car.

21

"Do you know," Aidan said as rain pattered down on the broad-brimmed hats he and Annja wore, "there are some most splendid Neanderthal sites in the region of Mount Carmel?"

Haifa was a somewhat gray industrial city in north Israel, tucked between the mass of Mount Carmel and busy Haifa Bay. An overcast sky occasionally spitting rain onto steaming streets may have unfairly emphasized the grayness. If the city lacked the melodrama of Jerusalem and the self-conscious quaintness of Jaffa, it felt less sterile than Tel Aviv. And it also lacked something of the tension you felt in the air like an unseasonable chill in Tel Aviv or Jerusalem, despite the city's proximity to Lebanon and the Golan Heights. Its residents, Jewish, Arab and foreign, seemed to have their minds mainly on business.

Although she knew the Old Testament used the fifteen-hundred-foot Mount Carmel as something of a standard of beauty, Annja found its gray limestone palisades a bit on the forbidding side. The green terraces of the Baha'i World Center overlooking the town were nice, though.

It was late in the morning. Wearing their usual inconspicuous garb, Aidan a blue chambray shirt and jeans, Annja a light tan cotton blouse with black-and-white streaks like Japanese brushstrokes and khaki cargo pants, they walked a little-trafficked street on the northern side of the industrial and waterfront district known as the lower city. The buildings were mostly one-story offices and shops. Though they had the low, boxy profile and dust-colored stucco of the basic adobe structures you saw at these latitudes around the world, they looked like modern cinder-block construction, with edges too raw and angles too sharp for mud brick.

"It's a little hard to believe," she said to him. "It's just, on the whole, we could be on the outskirts of Phoenix right now, if it weren't for the humidity. And come to think of it, Phoenix is pretty humid, thanks to irrigation and all those swimming pools."

"I'll take your word for it." He had a Borsalino hat or a good imitation on to protect against the weather, the brim low over his blue eyes—a pricey-looking hat, and if real, possibly one of the few affectations she'd been able to discern. His eyes lacked something of their customary glitter today, she'd noticed. He had been subdued since the campfire conference with Spyridon on Corfu.

He stopped and nodded his head. "I think we're here."

A discreet bronze plaque beside a door read Israel Antiquities Authority in English and Hebrew with a logo that looked like a stylized menorah. Annja looked over the building, which appeared no different from the others on the block, and frowned.

"I thought with all their terrorism troubles, Israeli public buildings would be well fortified," she said.

"Undoubtedly the high muckety-mucks don't think the place is worth defending," Aidan said. "You know how governments feel—archaeologists are expendable." He was making no effort to hide his bitterness.

Annja laughed because she was pleased to see him get a bit of his sparkle back. Actually, if she understood correctly, Pascoe was wrong. Israel was obsessed with archaeology. From the earliest days of its existence as a modern state some of its most prominent political and even military figures had displayed fanatic interest in antiquity, at levels ranging from impassioned amateurs to world-renowned archaeologists.

She knew Israel was also a heavily socialist country that loved its bureaucracy. And it had revered sites galore. You couldn't sink a spade in the soil without disturbing ground walked on by some notable personage from the Mideast's long and somewhat depressing history. As a consequence of all these things, a *lot* of Israel Antiquities Authority buildings dotted the landscape. But she supposed it may not have been especially useful or even affordable to defend them all like Cheyenne Mountain.

"Shall we?" Aidan asked.

They pushed in through the white-painted door. Inside it was cool and fluorescent bright. The dark-wood-and-metal desk in the reception area was unoccupied. It sported a computer, a phone and a half-full mug of coffee, showing a cartoon boy and girl leaning against each other with moonily romantic expressions. Hebrew characters were indecipherable above their heads. The air was tart with an astringent smell of dust and cleaning chemicals.

"Ah," said Aidan, sniffing. "Smells like they do archaeology here."

"Strange there's nobody here," Annja said. A door opened into a brightly lit hall behind the unoccupied desk.

"But that means there's no one to tell us not to go on back," Aidan said with a twinkle. "Easier to get forgiveness than permission, as you Yanks say."

They took off their damp hats and placed them on the desk. She walked past him through the door. The hallway beyond consisted of half walls, with glass from waist height to ceiling on either side. To the right was an office with a bookcase on the far wall stocked with books with thick, age-cracked and darkened spines.

In the larger room to the left a long table had a chunk of sandstone lying on it. An obviously ancient human rib cage and what appeared to be a curved reddish surface, apparently part of an earthenware pot or vase, had been painstaking half-liberated from a slab of sandstone. Tools—magnifying glass, steel pick like a dentist's, a cordless Makita drill with a cotton disk buffer mounted in the chuck—lay next to the slab.

Gradually Annja was becoming aware of a strange, cloying odor underlying the dust and disinfectant. At the same time she realized the tip of her left walking shoe seemed to be sticking to the floor. She looked down.

A face looked up at her from a pool of blood spilling through the doorway.

Aidan came into the anteroom door behind her and saw what she saw.

It was a head of almost stupefying normality—if you left aside the expression. And the fact it was by itself—there was that, of course. It was the head of an elderly woman, with waved gray-white hair surrounding a plumpish face, the cheeks rouged, the lips painted.

The eyes were wide in horror. The tongue, bluish, protruding from a lipstick-smeared hole of a mouth.

The skin was sallow from the loss of the blood that had drained from the head to the vinyl floor.

With the pallid jowls sagging into the wide pool of blood—shockingly red with bluish undertints in the uneasy light of the overheads—it was impossible to tell how the head had been removed from the body. *Violently* seemed a good guess.

For a moment Annja's vision—her whole existence, really—was tightly focused onto the severed head of what she presumed had been a receptionist or secretary. Drawing in a deep breath through her mouth, to avoid smelling more than necessary, she widened her vision field enough to take in the fact that visible not far beyond the head, a pair of thick, dough-pale legs protruded into view on the floor between worktable and half-window front wall. They ended in sagging wool socks and stodgy black shoes. Toes down. Annja swallowed hard at the realization that the body, presuming it belonged to the head, was pointing *away* from the door. Whatever had removed the head had carried it a short distance before depositing it near the door.

She felt a chill.

Suddenly, from the corridor's far end came a wild cry of panic. Annja focused her will. The sword came into her hand as a man burst through the door at the end of the hall, emerging from a darkness that suggested a poorly illuminated stairway. The man was tall and gaunt, with gray hair streaming in a wild nimbus to either side of a dome of olive skull. He wore a lab coat over a shirt and tie. The tie was askew. The lab coat was spattered in red.

He skidded as he broke from the doorway. He saw Annja and Aidan and called out to them in Hebrew, half-slumped against the wall as if trying to catch his breath. His eyes, already standing out of his head in terror, seemed to focus. For a moment Annja saw an expression of something like hope flicker across his face.

A growl from the stairway washed it away. He bolted toward them, arms and legs flying in a transport of panic.

A black shape shot from the doorway behind him, already waist high when it came into view, and rising. Light seemed to be sucked into it. It struck him on the left shoulder and slammed him back into the wall, pressing the side of his face into the glass. He screamed shrilly as he was dragged down to the floor.

It was a dog, huge, 120 pounds at least. Against its matte-black hide its eyes were visibly outlined in red, rolling in its big broad head. Its teeth were brilliant white.

Blood fountained around its muzzle, driven under high pressure from a severed carotid artery. The man's outcries abruptly ceased.

The dog let its prey fall to lie twitching on the speckled gray-white tiles. It raised its burning eyes to Annja. They almost seemed to widen when they saw the sword. Then they narrowed with a hatred so intelligent, so human seeming, that it struck Annja like a blow. The dog growled again.

To the depths of her being she was stricken with the most total horror she had ever known. Fear clamped like asthma on her windpipe and threatened to let go the set screws of her knees, drop her choking and weeping and crippled to the floor. She had never imagined such fear.

"Annja," Aidan said from behind her.

She made herself step forward and to her right to put herself in the middle of the corridor, squarely between the hellish creature with the gore-dripping muzzle and Aidan. "Stay back," she said without turning her head.

It seemed for a moment that she saw ghost shapes, shimmers in air above the dog's shoulders. Like a pair of shadowy wings. She did not dare even blink, but shook her head violently. The shadows vanished.

The dog darted forward. Its claws clacked on the vinyl flooring. Its snarling rose in a crescendo as it galloped toward Annja with tremendous speed, looking huge. Its upper lip was pulled back from its teeth, white swimming in red.

It was as terrifying a sight as anything Annja had seen in her life. Yet the blinding-fast attack released her from the fear that threatened to disable her. She steeled herself to face it. I've got to trust the sword, she thought. And myself, she thought.

Halfway down the hall and still a dozen feet away, the beast sprang for her. She met it with a diagonal step forward to her right and a two-handed cut that began behind her right shoulder.

She feared to strike the thing head-on. That huge sloped skull would shed a blow that didn't hit squarely, even from a preternaturally sharp blade.

Fanged jaws flew at her face, spread wide. Her stroke took the creature at the juncture of left shoulder and trunk-thick neck, angling inward toward the center of its chest.

The jaws clashed futilely beside her left ear.

Blood spurted over Annja's face. It seemed unnaturally hot. Her gut revolted. She had bared her teeth as she cut. Blood had sprayed into her mouth.

But she followed through, turning her hips, driving from her powerful legs.

She felt the sword spring free. She saw the beast strike the floor with a sodden thump.

Annja kept herself from going over backward but had to drop to a knee to do so. She held the sword raised before her.

The animal lay thrashing on the floor, one lung a deflated ruin, the other pumping its final breaths. Its other organs spilled out on the floor. Impossibly it lifted its head from the floor to stare at her. Its teeth chattered horribly in its blood-slavering jaws.

For an instant Annja had the horrific sense it was

trying to *speak* to her. Then the light went out from its eyes and the head fell to the floor with a thump, the tongue lolling motionless over the teeth of the lower jaw.

She felt as if a hideous presence had vanished—and an enormous weight had lifted from her soul.

"My God," Aidan said quietly.

Slowly Annja rose. She felt the blood drying on her face, getting tacky, starting to itch. The front of her blouse and pants were sodden; she could feel the dampness against her breasts and belly and the fronts of her thighs. She became aware of a salty taste in her mouth and spit violently. It took an effort of will not to vomit.

"You killed a dog," Aidan said accusingly.

"Yes," she said. She felt a stab of remorse for the animal. "It killed that man," she said, sounding more defensive than she intended.

He shook his head. "Isn't that a bit thick?" he asked. "It was just a dog."

She drew a deep breath. He's shaken, she realized. And no surprise. It's made him irrational.

Sword in hand, she moved cautiously into the lab to the left. It was a bloody shambles. She avoided looking at the dead woman. There wasn't anything to do for her. And whatever had killed her had made a ragged job of decapitating her.

The lab was splashed liberally with blood. More surprising, notebooks had been torn and a stool and a chrome-and-leather chair had been slashed open so that stuffing swelled from them like puffy white excrescences. This scene is starting to look familiar, she thought.

Aidan stood in the hall staring in through the window at her. She backed out, moved quickly to the door across the way. "Keep an eye on that door," she suggested, nodding as she passed to the end of the hallway. "We don't know what else might come through it."

Aidan's normally pink complexion had gone ashen and green around the edges. He was breathing rapidly through his mouth. "And take deep breaths," she added. "Into the abdomen."

The office on the far side looked curiously untouched. She backed out of there and went to kneel gingerly by the side of the man who lay slumped against the corridor wall. Still keeping the sword in her right hand, she went quickly through his pockets, feeling more than a bit like a ghoul.

"It's Dror," she said, holding up a wallet unfolded to show a credit card in a plastic carrier with the archaeologist's name embossed on it.

"Hmm," Aidan grunted. His eyes weren't quite tracking. Even after all he'd been through in the past week, what he had witnessed since entering the corridor had shaken him like a fist wrapped around his spine.

He shook his head. "I'm sorry," he said, stepping

around the body of the huge black dog. "I'm having trouble with the dog. I can't help it; it just seems harsh to treat an animal so, no matter what it's done. It's just a poor animal. It has no moral judgment. It can't be blamed, after all."

"You don't know the half of it," she told him, rubbing the wallet clean of fingerprints with her shirttail, or so she hoped, and slipping it back into the dead man's pocket. She straightened. "Doesn't this strike you as somehow familiar?"

He gaped at her.

"The scene on the bridge of that fishing boat in Corfu," she said. "The blood splashes. The ripping up of the furniture and the logbooks, apparently out of sheer fury." She nodded her head at the window opening onto the long lab chamber. "Same thing happened here. Not to mention two brutal murders. At least."

"You think that dog killed the crew of the *Athanasia*?" Pascoe's voice curled and cut like a whip of sarcasm. "And then what? It swam across the Mediterranean to assassinate Dror?"

"No. Not *this* dog," Annja said.

"So you suspect an outbreak of some kind of madness—mutated avian flu perhaps—that's making domestic animals run amok and rip up people and commit random acts of vandalism?"

She took a deep breath. "I agreed with you that the

dog wasn't to blame," she said. "That's because the dog isn't responsible."

"But you just said—"

"But the same guiding agency did. The same entity. Do you get what I'm driving at, Aidan?"

He glared at her for a moment as if suspecting she was making fun of him. His nostrils were flared.

Then he shook himself, so violently she feared for a moment he was having a seizure. He sighed gustily. "You're speaking of demonic possession."

"I'm afraid so."

He shook his head. "It's hard to assimilate something like that."

"Yes," she agreed, "it is. Let's look around. We came here to learn some things. We need to get out of here before the authorities arrive, unless you feel like discussing demonic possession with the cops."

"Right," he said. "And perhaps we'd best discover if there are any more demonic dogs about."

"Good point," Annja said.

The room next to the office was a little storeroom filled with boxes of specimens and overstuffed filing cabinets. A door stood ajar, letting in a slice of sunlight shining down through a break in the heavy overcast. A quick glance showed it opened onto a narrow alley.

Annja caught Aidan's eye with a meaningful look. It

explained how the dog had gotten inside. Or at least, it offered one explanation.

It took all her will and physical courage for Annja to grip the sword in both hands and go down the stairs through the door at hallway's end. The mere physical danger scared her, certainly. But she had faced greater danger—although the horrible savagery of the dog's attack had shaken her as few assaults from humans had. But she felt a creeping conviction that they faced a menace that was more than physical. The dread that had almost overwhelmed her when she faced the animal down clung to her like wisps of fog.

Above all she feared what she might find at the bottom of the stairs.

Her fears were realized.

The stairs turned once. The walls were cool stone and smelled of it; a relief after the abattoir upstairs. "Obviously the modern building's been built on a preexisting site," she murmured. She wasn't vastly concerned about making noise. If anything awaited them downstairs, it—or they—already knew they were coming.

"Looks nineteenth century, to hazard a guess," Pascoe said, reaching out to brush the stone with his fingertips. Though he spoke quietly, as she had, his voice was steadier, more controlled than before. In a small way she was tempted to smile. Thinking professionally was an excellent way to break the spasm of shock and horror.

But the respite was brief. The stairs emptied into a small chamber with metal shelves to either side bowing beneath the weight of the customary dusty artifacts, some wrapped in plastic, some exposed. The floor was concrete, laid when the upper structure was built, Annja guessed.

An arm lay in the middle of it. It looked male, to judge by the dark, hairy hand jutting from the blue sleeve. A heavy gold band, probably a wedding ring, encircled one finger. The other end of the sleeve was soaked in purplish blood. A raw bit of bone jutted out, yellow in the single electric bulb hanging from the ceiling.

A similar light illuminated a scene of fresh horror through the doorway. Beyond lay a storeroom with crates and boxes, many of which had been shattered or ripped open. Amid artifacts, many of shiny yellow metal, sundry body parts were strewed. By the usual mathematics—chiefly that she quickly saw two heads— she guessed at a pair of victims, including the original owner of the arm in the outer room.

"Nothing down here," Annja said. "Nothing alive." She willed the sword away.

"God," Aidan said in a choked voice. He held a handkerchief to his mouth, either in an attempt to prevent himself from vomiting or to ward off the stench in the damp basement. "Such rage."

Annja was aware of conflicting sensations, again

reminiscent of what she had felt on the *Athanasia,* both a sense of intense evil and of power.

"The jar was here," she said. "I can feel it. But it's not here now. Perhaps the creature expected to find it, and was enraged by its disappointment."

"The jar itself may not be here," Aidan said, voice muffled by the handkerchief, "but there are certainly jars here. In plenty."

Preoccupied initially with assessing the casualties, Annja realized with a shock he was right. The yellow metal objects lying on the floor among the human wreckage were jars of bright brass. She knelt and picked one up that lay well away from one of the several broad pools of blood. It had the shape of a globe with a narrow funnel thrust into it from above, with two surprisingly delicate handles curving down away from the top, ending in upward-curled knobs.

"It's the same as the one I found on Sir Martin High-smith's mantel in Kent," she said, holding it out toward Aidan. "Down to the characters engraved on it."

He slipped past her. Either he had reasserted his self-control or simply gone numb; he moved in a brisk, businesslike fashion. "They're all identical," he said.

He hunkered by a wooden crate whose lid had been pushed in. Inside stood a dozen of the jars, encased in bubble wrap. "And look at this," he said. "A shipping manifest."

22

It was raining heavily when they emerged from the front door. But the street wasn't deserted, as a quick check had indicated. As Annja and Aidan ran out, hoping anyone who saw them would believe they were sprinting from doorway to doorway in the downpour, a tall, slim figure stepped out of an alleyway and approached them. The woman was holding an umbrella above a head of long, dark hair with a white streak above the brow.

"Tsipporah?" Annja asked as she and Aidan skidded to a halt.

The older woman smiled. "You were expecting maybe Madonna?"

"Well—not a whole lot less than you," Annja said. "Didn't you tell me I wouldn't see you again?"

"Change of plans. Aren't you going to introduce me to your handsome young man?" she asked.

"Do you have someplace else we could go," Annja said, "out of the rain and out of sight? Like, right now?"

"Of course. Follow me."

She turned and walked at a businesslike pace down the street away from the Israel Antiquities Authority office. Annja and Aidan followed, crowding under her umbrella. In Annja's case, anyway, it was as much because to do otherwise would look suspicious, She was numb and pretty oblivious to getting wet. The young Englishman looked confused and more than a little suspicious, but said nothing.

At the end of the block Annja turned and looked back. Through the blinds on the front window of the building they had just left she saw a blue flash. Then with an almost dainty tinkling of glass the window blew out ahead of a billow of yellow flame.

Tsipporah stopped and turned back. "Natural-gas explosion," she said. "Accidents happen. Or do they?"

Annja looked at Aidan, then at the older woman. "No accident," she said, "as if you didn't know. They had a gas feed for Bunsen burners. It got left open. And somebody left a cigarette burning in an ashtray in the basement."

Fire was billowing upward out the front window, and smoke streamed away from the flat roof. Tsipporah nodded. "I like your style, girl."

"So Dr. Dror was involved with importing and selling fake jars of Solomon," Tsipporah said, sitting back from the card table set in the repair bay of a small garage off Chaim Weizmann Street, east of the now-destroyed antiquities authority office toward Kishon Harbor. The family that owned the garage, Tsipporah assured Annja and Aidan, was on holiday in Jaffa for a few days; no one would disturb them here.

Why exactly Tsipporah had picked the place, or how she had gained access to it—or even known about it—Annja had no clue. For that matter she didn't feel up to hazarding a guess as to why they weren't holding their discussion in the garage's business office. The fact it was small and cluttered and almost every horizontal surface was stacked with papers, work orders, receipts and God knew what else may have had something to do with it. In their brief association Annja had figured out that Tsipporah did things according to her own agenda. She probably had good reasons for them. But she was unlikely to explain. So they sat in the murky gray light filtering out of the rainy sky through windows grimy and fly specked, sipping cheap Negev wine from colorful plastic picnic cups.

"As you're probably aware, various members of the antiquities authority were implicated a couple of years ago in fabricating the fake ossuary alleged to belong to Jesus's brother, James," Aidan said.

"I had heard about that, yes," Tsipporah said with a faintly ironic smile.

"It would appear Dror and his confederates turned the scheme on its head. Or perhaps inverted it, would be more accurate. Coming into possession of the genuine artifact, they contrived to produce replicas of it to sell to avid collectors, New Age aficionados and religious zealots around the world."

Annja shifted on her folding chair, not entirely comfortable in her new lightweight cotton dress, white with little floral prints on it, which she was quite convinced was either transparent in certain light or would become so if she ventured into the rain in it. After stashing her and Aidan in the garage, which smelled inexplicably of boiled cabbage as strongly as automotive grease, Tsipporah had nipped off to find replacements for Annja's shirt and slacks, which were pretty liberally spattered with blood. She had come back in a matter of minutes with the dress, presumably from a local market.

"Why not sell the real thing?" Tsipporah asked, leaning back at ease with her hair spilling in great waves down her shoulders.

Aidan shrugged. "Perhaps a lingering respect for the genuinely unparalleled value of the artifact to archaeology. Maybe after cashing in as much as possible from selling the fakes, Dror intended to see the genuine article discreetly into the possession of the antiquities authority." He shrugged. "Or perhaps I'm giving the good doctor the benefit of too much doubt, and he just realized he could make more money selling fake jars a hundred times than the real one once."

"Why wouldn't he try to make use of its power himself?" Annja wondered.

"Probably he didn't believe in its power. He could have authenticated it readily enough through metallurgy and electron spin resonance dating. But if he had believed, he probably wouldn't have bothered with the counterfeiting, since if I recall correctly legend holds that the reason the jar was dug up in the first place, and the famous seal removed, was to use the demons to find hidden treasure."

"You're a most knowledgeable young man," Tsipporah said with a smile.

Annja stifled a surge of irritation that the smile was returned. It may have been that she kept seeing the older woman in softening light, but she looked more than handsome to Annja. And Aidan seemed more appreciative than she liked. She chided herself for being ridiculous.

"It didn't do him much good in the end, though," Annja said.

"It most certainly did not," Tsipporah said. "It seems he encountered one of the Goetic demons. Marchosias. He's big and bad—one of the worst. But you stood up to him and won. Not everybody could do that. You've justified your role as champion, Annja Creed."

"Thanks. But it wasn't much of a fight. Not really. He—the dog he was possessing—just jumped straight at me. And I—" She shrugged. She was a little uncomfortable repeating the details, for fear of setting off the animal-loving side of Aidan again. "I would've expected him to be a cagier opponent, I guess."

"Don't underestimate either the demon or yourself. Note I don't say his name. I won't again, and I suggest you don't. They can hear their names from a long way off. What you did was confront him and stand. That's what makes you special. Pure moral and spiritual courage.

"I'd say he knew the form he was occupying stood no real chance against you, armed as you were with the sword. So he decided on an all-or-nothing assault that might get lucky—or might intimidate you into not resisting. It's not as if he had anything to lose at that point."

"Nothing to lose?" Aidan burst out. "Annja killed him."

"She killed his host, you mean," Tsipporah said. "Do you think you could hurt a demon, or even cause him serious discomfort, when he's in another's body? If he appeared in his own form as a winged wolf, the sword might do him harm—I can't say, and I'm really unwilling to speculate. It may have caused him physical pain. But only momentarily."

"And the dog?" Annja asked feeling terrible.

"There was no dog. Except the meat shell. It wasn't possessed, girl. What you encountered was a rare phenomenon the *Catholic Encyclopedia* calls demonic *obsession*. It means the original occupant's mind, will and soul have been flat-out evicted. The demon isn't sharing the space, the way it does in possession. You're dead and gone. It's easier with an animal, obviously," Tsipporah explained.

Annja shuddered. She felt a stab of pity for the poor dog, and wondered if it might linger as a ghost, after being turned out of its own body by the demon. But she felt a strange, rather silly sense of relief that she hadn't really been the one to kill the poor thing.

"Do you think someone summoned him and sent him to visit those people?" she asked. Despite sharing Aidan's distaste for artifact forgers, she didn't share his tacit but unmistakable feeling that Dror, at least, had got what was coming to him. Not for the first time she noted that her companion, while a sweet enough young man, and definitely an innocent at heart, still possessed a not altogether attractive self-righteous streak.

"More than likely," Tsipporah said. "It wouldn't be too characteristic for a demon to act so directly on his own. But don't forget the demons have their own stake in this. I can't help wondering if the extreme violence you saw might indicate the demons' own mounting frustration at not being able to find the jar themselves."

"But the demons are supposed to be good at finding treasure," Aidan said. "Why can't they find the jar the same way?"

"The jar has ways of avoiding discovery through magical means. The demons are flying as blind as the rest of us in this." Tsipporah turned her intense dark gaze full on Annja. "You seemed to react pretty strongly to something I said, there."

"Can they do that to anyone?" Annja felt tremendous fear once again.

"Can they tempt you? That's up to you," Tsipporah said.

Annja felt her heart pounding. "But I thought—" Her voice dwindled into futile nothingness.

"You thought you'd be immune?" Laughing softly, Tsipporah patted her cheek. "You're a sweet child. But occasionally, not so bright. You have to choose between right and wrong. Every minute of every day. Just like the rest of us. Only, now, even more so. You think maybe it should be easier on you than on the average shlemiel?"

Annja could find nothing to say.

Tsipporah studied Annja a moment. "Interesting. You may have attracted some unfortunate attention, young lady.

"But believe it or not," Tsipporah said, "the reason I broke my earlier resolve and looked you up again, Annja, had nothing to do with our friends from the jar. Or only peripherally. I have some information about the human players that might prove useful to you."

"Tell me," Annja said.

"First, Sir Martin Highsmith and his White Tree Lodge. He and his little chums desire the power of the jar to remake the planet. They wish to overturn the modern world and restore all to a state of nature."

"He did seem pretty nostalgic for the Paleolithic when I spoke to him," Annja said.

"If not the Pleistocene, before there were any nasty people running around bothering the animals. Since their little plans envision overthrowing the whole order of the world, undoing all of civilization and technology and reducing the Earth's population to a few thousand happy hunter-gatherers, it's safe to assume they won't hesitate to kill anyone who gets in their way. But I guess you've had a bit of firsthand experience of that, haven't you?"

Annja nodded.

"Now, Mark Peter also wants the power to do good for everybody, whether they like it or not."

"Mark Peter?" Annja said. "You mean Stern?"

"He's dead," Aidan said. "I don't know if you follow the news, but someone blew up his yacht off Jaffa with an antitank guided missile. About two minutes after our dear Annja leaped over the rail into the sea."

"What interesting lives you young people lead these days. I do occasionally see a television news broadcast, when I can't help it. I've even been known to go on-line a time or two. As it happens I'm aware of all the things you said. And one thing more. Stern wasn't on the yacht when the *mafiya* blew it up," Tsipporah said.

Annja frowned. "But I had just finished talking to him."

"Really? Just that instant? You walked up on deck and, wham?"

"Well—not exactly." She described her encounter with Eliete von Hauptstark.

"So you might have been a bit distracted for a minute or two. Long enough for Mark Peter to grab a mask and some tanks and roll over the seaward rail, where his Russian minders wouldn't spot him. A resourceful boy, is Mark Peter. Gotta give him that. A certified scuba diver, too."

"But why would he do that?" Annja asked, shocked by the turn of events.

"Maybe because somebody tipped him off," Tsipporah said.

Aidan exhaled loudly. "I thought nobody turned on the Russian *mafiya*," he said.

"Somebody turns on everybody," Tsipporah said. "The *mafiya* have some people in it who are terrifyingly smart and some who are terrifyingly brutal, and sometimes they're the same. They have a total lack of scruples and a healthy respect for the power of terror. All true. But it *isn't* true nobody ever turns on them. That's just propaganda they spread, with plenty of help from various police agencies. The same way the Western defense establishment used to go along with the Soviet army's policy of vastly exaggerating its capabilities and combat worth. It's budget-positive behavior."

"Still, why would anyone risk crossing people like that for the sake of a man like Stern?" Aidan asked.

Tsipporah shrugged. "Why would anyone help the Russians against him, for that matter? You think the *mafiya* ran that hit on Stern's yacht without some sort of cooperation inside the Israeli government? Maybe it was just corruption, maybe it was a disagreement, let's say, with some of Stern's aims and methods—such as the covert way he's been arming radical settler groups to fight the central government. Maybe it was both. Now, I don't know, but I suspect the likeliest answer to how Stern knew to go over the side in advance of that missile was that somebody in government got wind of the plan, didn't like it and tipped him off. Maybe it was even one of his followers. Somebody outside the *mafiya* would, I grant you, have a lot less trepidation about putting a spike in their wheel than an insider."

She shrugged. "We'll never know, likely. Does it matter that much? Stern escaped, he's still in the game as much as before—and now, being officially dead and all, he's got a lot more scope for action, which would be good to keep in mind. Are the ins and outs that important?"

"Not really," Annja admitted.

Aidan was looking at the older woman with his head

tipped to the side and a hard little smile. "If your mystic arts tell you all this," he said, "why don't they show you where Solomon's Jar is?"

Tsipporah laughed. "How do you know they don't, and I'm not telling you? Seriously, I can't trace the jar. It has ways of disguising itself, you might say, from spiritual detection. But the information I'm giving you now isn't quite so esoteric in origin."

"Ha! I knew it!" Aidan leaned forward. "You're intelligence. Or counterintelligence. Mossad or Shin Bet."

Tsipporah laughed again. "Whoa! Slow down, cowboy. You're riding that there horse too far, too fast. Let's just say I have my sources in this plane—and if they're a bit on the occult side, using the actual meaning of the word, well, a girl's entitled to her secrets, isn't she?"

"But you do know for a fact that Stern is still alive?" Annja asked.

"Oh, yes. And not too happy about the loss of his yacht and crew—and his Brazilian supermodel. But he probably writes them all off as sacrifices necessary for spiritual progress—his own. And the good of humanity, of course.

"He's drawn Israeli fanatics, especially among the settlers resisting evacuation of the occupied territories, to help him with promises of magically rebuilding the temple and creating a globe-spanning Israeli empire. He's also got well-heeled, rapture-happy U.S. fundamentalists bankrolling him big time with promises of kicking off Armageddon, also by restoring the temple."

Tsipporah lit a cigarette. "But he has no intention of doing so. What he wants is for the demons to make him king of the world. For the children, of course."

"Did he really do that?" Annja asked.

"Who, sweetie? You got me a bit confused."

"I'm sorry. I wasn't very clear. King Solomon. Did he really use the demons to build the temple in one night?"

For a moment Tsipporah looked at her through a cloud of smoke. "No," she said. "Not literally. The temple yarn is just a metaphor. As we've seen, the demons have a hard time acting directly in our world. Shaping and hoisting blocks of stone is a little hands-on for their capabilities."

"What about our Russian friends?" Aidan asked. "What's their interest in the jar? Or have they strayed so far from dialectic materialism that they're believing in evil spirits now, too?"

"You'd be surprised just what most Russians—including some very highly placed ones—did believe during the Soviet years. But as it happens their interests in the jar are impeccably materialistic enough to satisfy the most doctrinaire Marxist. Money. They've accepted a commission from an oligarch who's a rich and powerful collector. He's a total atheist. He basically wants to put it in his personal museum and leave it there under massive guard, so he and only he can look at it when he wants to. World without end, amen."

Aidan tossed back the last of his drink. "How selfish!" he exclaimed in disgust.

Tsipporah gave him a thoughtful look. "You might consider opening your mind to the possibility selfishness isn't quite as bad as it's cracked up to be."

"Nonsense! With all due respect. It's the root of all evil," Aidan stated.

Tsipporah chuckled. "Ah, the young. Moral certainty comes so easily to you."

23

It was twilight when the big Boeing wound down toward Rio de Janeiro. The city looked like a big bowl of crunchy gray urbanization poured in among a plethora of sharp hills, with green in myriad rich shades busting out through the cracks and gaps.

"It's not all favelas and Carnaval," Annja told her companion as they both leaned forward to peer out the window. "But both are important in their own way."

She laughed. "How sententious is that? Listen to me. I've never even been to the place. I just read the news on-line a lot."

"We're still going to be bloody tourists," Aidan muttered. She noticed his knuckles gleaming blue-white on the back of the hand that gripped the armrest. He was a nervous flier. She had to suppress a giggle. It seemed incongruous given how calmly he had faced terrible danger and soul-wrenching horror. As usual, it seemed to be the smaller things he had trouble coping with in equanimity.

"Hardly that," she said. "Too bad, too. Although I understand Rio's like Mexico City—too big and crowded, not really representative of the country as a whole. Although it's not as big as São Paulo. Or as polluted." She shrugged. "Still, it's a city named after an imaginary river—January River, in fact. That's got to stand for something."

Having allowed Annja to take the window seat, either gallantly or because he was afraid of flying, Aidan sat in the center seat of the row. The third party was a plump, benign-looking German woman who spent the whole tedious trip across the Atlantic bobbing her gray head in response to whatever was being piped through the iPod earbuds she wore.

Annja noticed Aidan craning his head to follow the flight attendant, a willowy young woman with ebony skin, gleaming white smile and brilliant green eyes who had just spoken briefly to their seatmate in what sounded to Annja like flawless German. At the moment she was speaking very good French to a portly gentleman in a rumpled blue suit in the central seat section of the wide-body aircraft. She had several times during the flight spoken in effortless, lightly accented English to Annja and Aidan.

"She's certainly an eyeful," Annja said with more irritation than she intended.

Aidan turned his eyes forward with a shrug. "I don't mean to be impolite. But ye gods! I'm a heterosexual male, after all."

Annja nodded with what she hoped was understanding.

"Anyway, I admit I'm still trying to assimilate a Brazilian woman named Gretchen. What's up with all these German Brazilian women?" he asked.

Annja was wondering what was up not just with German Brazilians, but with women who were taller than she was. Even without the heels the attendant must have stood six feet, like the late Eliete von Hauptstark.

"Santa Catarina," she said. "A state south down the coast a ways, next door to Paraguay. It's full of Germans and Italians."

"Good Lord. Was it settled entirely by Axis fugitives fleeing World War II?" Pascoe asked.

She shrugged. "Not all of them. There are other groups, too, like the descendants of Confederate soldiers who came here after the American Civil War. I understand they enjoy reenacting antebellum Southern life."

Aidan frowned. "What in hell's that?" he asked, leaning forward and pointing out the window. "And I mean that a lot more literally than I might have a fortnight ago."

As the airplane banked toward Galeão-Antonio Carlos Jobim International Airport on Governador Island, the brown haze overlying the city and the hills beyond was underlit by an evil orange color. Scores of individual lights glowed red like gaping wounds bleeding fire.

"Usinas," Annja said. "Metal foundries. They use a lot of open-furnace and crucible techniques down here that are outmoded in most Western countries, if not outlawed." At Aidan's surprised glance she smiled. "I cheated and checked on-line from the hotel in Milano. They do look like vents from hell, don't they?"

Her expression sobered. "Appropriately enough," she said, "they're our destination."

"IT'S A LITTLE BIT like a sauna, isn't it?" Annja said as they walked back from dinner at a restaurant near their hotel. Around them it was very dark. Lights shone brightly all around them and well up the hills of the affluent São Conrado neighborhood, near the southern shore peninsula that jutted into the Atlantic. It had all the subtle restraint of a black velvet painting. Around them music blared from a hundred places, nightclubs, restaurants, even the balconies of exclusive apartment complexes. A thousand beats were vying with each other and the noise of the traffic surging past. While she could make out plenty of Brazilian traditional and popular tunes, Annja was somewhat disappointed that thumping rock and hip hop seemed to be winning the volume battle.

"Too right," Aidan said. "Even after the Mediterranean the heat and humidity is a bit stunning."

"Well, it is the tropics."

"I'd think you'd be used to it, though. I thought you'd spent time down here before getting involved in all this jar madness," he said.

"That was in the high Amazon basin," she said. "Pretty much the foothills of the Andes. Higher, dryer. Cooler."

They came to a stretch of relative darkness, though the street itself was still broad, well lit and traveled. Inland a series of hills rose, their sides encrusted with lights. "Pretty," Aidan murmured.

"By night," Annja said. "That's Roçinha. The largest slum in Latin America. They call them favelas here. That term's politically incorrect now, supposedly, but as far as I can tell it's what everybody actually says."

Aidan shook his head. "I should have known," he said. "Rio's slums are legendary. Do you think we're safe? All the guidebooks are filled with masterful understatements about the risks of being out on the streets. Especially at night."

Annja grinned at him. "Do you really think we have anything to worry about?"

He sucked in his lips. "Well…they might have guns."

She continued to look at him.

"I guess you'd be a bad choice for victimization, even at that."

She laughed.

"I keep forgetting you have all these abilities. You're harmless enough looking. For a strikingly beautiful young woman, that is."

"Flatterer," Annja said smiling.

He shook his head briskly. "Not so. I don't flatter."

"I'm not beautiful. I'm too tall, gangly. Plain," Annja said.

He laughed so loudly a couple of men walking by turned to stare at them. "Nonsense," he said.

"No. really. Don't make fun of me," Annja said seriously.

He looked at her with his head tipped to the side and one eyebrow raised. His eyes were so pale they seemed to glow in the shine of stars and streetlights. "Quite without vanity, are you?"

"About my looks. I guess."

"Then why do you keep fishing for compliments?" And he whooped with laughter again.

"You bastard." Annja laughed as she said it.

Ahead their hotel, the InterContinental Rio, rose

from the parking lot and huge swimming pools the way Sugarloaf Mountain did from the sea off nearby Urca. All lit up by floodlights it looked to Annja like a heavily striated cut face of sandstone or limestone, one of those with the history of aeons laid out for anyone with the requisite geological knowledge to read.

She said so.

"You're such a romantic," Aidan said. "Of course, I was thinking much the same thing."

"Let's face it," Annja said. "We're archaeology dorks."

Laughing, they ran to the light blaze of the great covered entrance.

WITH GREAT RELIEF Annja sat on the foot of her bed to take off her shoes. Their room was spacious, clean and much like any fine hotel room anywhere. Not that Annja had spent much time in hotel rooms as nice as this one. She had been actively uncomfortable with the notion of staying in a five-star establishment. Also it was in the Zona Sul, the South Zone, on the other end of town from their objective of the next morning, as well as from the international airport where they'd landed and from which they'd depart.

If they survived the trip.

But Aidan had insisted. After what they'd been through, including the series of adequate but shabby rooms in Mediterranean motels and down-at-heels *pen-*

siones they'd shared the past few nights since he fished her out of the water off Jaffa, he said they deserved a luxury break. Besides, he paid.

He stood in his sock feet, gazing out the floor-to-ceiling window at Pepino Beach. Despite their elevation on the ninth floor there wasn't much to see beyond the bright lights of the parking lot except the tiny lights of some vessels well out on the water.

"You can go out on the balcony," Annja said.

"If I open the door it will be like being hit in the face with a wet woolen blanket," he said. "I think I'll avail myself of the wonders of modern air conditioning a while longer."

He turned and dropped into a recliner chair with a sigh. Annja lay back on the bed with her own feet, now bare, resting on the carpet. She rolled her eyes to look at him. With only the lamp between the beds lit it wasn't too bright in the room. Despite that she thought he looked troubled, in his posture if not expression.

"Something's bothering you," she said.

He shook his head. "No, no."

They had stopped off in the bar downstairs to sample the national drink, *caipirinha,* made with sugarcane liquor, called *cachaça*, mixed with lemon and ice. Unlike many of their colleagues, neither was much of a drinker. Annja felt more than a little elevated.

"Not a bit of it," Aidan said somewhat grandly.

Rather than keep her from feeling anxious about her companion's mood, her slight buzz seemed to sharpen her anxiety. She wondered at the phenomenon without knowing what to do about it.

"Come on," she said. "Please don't fence me out."

"For some reason I've been thinking about those Greek fishermen who braced us on the beach in Corfu," he said.

"What about them?"

"You didn't kill them?"

She frowned. "Would you prefer I had?"

"No. I was wondering, why not? You killed some of those men attacking me in Jerusalem."

She sat up. "They attacked me, too, if you'll recall."

"Sure. But so did the Greeks. What makes the difference, who lives, who dies?"

He frowned. "It couldn't have made any difference that those men in Jerusalem were Jewish…could it?"

Annja stood up quickly. "You can't seriously believe that about me. And don't you think charges of anti-Semitism are being tossed about just a bit too freely these days? That kind of thing is unworthy of you."

She loomed over him. She was seriously angry.

He held up defensive hands. "Sorry. Sorry, love. I don't know what made me say that. But it's a question that's…been bothering me. That's all. Some men die, some live, and you have the power to make that decision."

Annja turned away. His use of the word *love* had

struck her like the jab of a baton in the belly. She knew it was casual, an English turn of phrase. No doubt it signified little more than he was slightly inebriated, enough to have disregarded the political correctness of using a word that might be deemed sexist. But still—

Nothing gets a girl worked up like reminding her how isolated she really is, she thought. She remembered Tsipporah's prediction or prophecy on taking leave of her in Jerusalem. The fact that the wise woman's other prognostication, that their paths would never cross again, hadn't panned out was small consolation right now.

Aidan was standing behind her. "Look, I know you do the best you can," he told her. "I can't really judge you, because I've no way of sharing your burden. And you saved my life twice, if memory serves. I'm a bloody ingrate and a twice-bloody fool. Please, just forget I spoke."

"No," she said. "It's true. Not that it made any difference to me that those men in Jerusalem were Jewish, if they even were—I have no way of knowing that. Not really. But what is true is that I used the sword without much hesitation and I couldn't make myself use it on those men on the beach. I *couldn't* have summoned the sword. My will was…clouded. I didn't feel in the right."

She felt him standing behind her. His breath stirred the hair at the back of her neck, where she'd tied it up to keep cooler in the muggy heat.

"I understand. I think I do. It was the intent," he said.

She shook her head. "Their intent was to kill us, those fishermen. I mean, I thought that their motives were purer—they were doing it to avenge their dead friends, and also to protect their living one. But what if the men who attacked you in the Old City thought they were doing the right thing, too? They must have, after all."

"Isn't that the burden you have to bear?" he said softly. "Trying as best you can, with imperfect knowledge and poor old human fallibility, to judge what's good and what isn't? We all have to make those decisions, I suppose. But with you there tend to be harsher consequences."

She raised her head and looked out into darkness. "You don't think I'm delusional? Some kind of psychopath, a serial killer who imagines she has a mission to cleanse the world of evil?"

"The sword is a pretty convincing delusion, Annja. And I haven't seen you execute anybody in cold blood, only defend yourself—and me. I don't pretend to understand all the moral ramifications of this mission of yours. Which I guess, now that I step back, makes me understand the pressure you're under even more."

She shook her head. "I wish *I* understood better. Sometimes I don't think I'm suited to this new life. It just sounds impossibly grandiose even to say. I don't know if anybody's up to a role like that. How can I possibly live up to it?"

Her eyes stung, filled with warm tears. Self-pity? a merciless voice reproached her in her head. Too much alcohol?

She felt his hand on her shoulder, firm, gentle. "Perhaps that's why you were chosen," he said softly. "Because you have the strength and integrity to ask questions."

She turned. Her breath seemed to catch in her chest. His eyes were fixed on hers. They seemed to glow.

She grabbed him by the head, almost roughly. She pressed her mouth to his. A frozen moment, in which her mind wheeled with fear and embarrassment. I've pushed it too far. I'll scare him off—

Then his hand was behind her neck. A quick, smooth gesture and he had plucked the long pin she used to tie up her hair. It fell in a cascade to her shoulders. Their tongues twined, their faces pressed together so hard her lips were numbed by unaccustomed pressure.

In a sudden adolescent frenzy their hands were in motion, undressing themselves, undressing each other.

By the time they had finished gracelessly hopping free of their undergarments and landed on the bed together, naked, they both were laughing.

24

"Admiral Cochrane's Forge," Annja said.

Peering through lush green underbrush, Aidan said, "The place itself is a great deal less prepossessing than the name, I have to say." He muttered a curse and swatted some kind of big green fly that had lit on his bare forearm to sink a probe.

They had parked their rented Toyota on the side of a track off the main road, crossing their fingers it wouldn't got bogged down on uncertain ground. Then they had hiked a quarter mile or so through the woods to reach the outskirts of the foundry.

Though she was in superb shape, and used to hiking cross-country, the humid heat and swarming bugs had Annja wondering if they were being paranoid in their approach. The forge, after all, had a marked blacktop road leading, they now saw, to a lot graded out of the surrounding forest. But even though the occasional dark look and scowl from her companion told her his thoughts ran down the same track she was just as glad they had taken a roundabout route. After what they'd experienced the past week or so, *too* paranoid might just prove barely paranoid enough.

The smelter was a sprawling rectangular building and seemed to be mostly metal post and rusty sheet metal in construction. Even in the bright daylight the fiery glare was visibly spilling out the front. They could feel heat on their faces a hundred yards off.

"Charming place to work," Aidan said.

"I'm sure their safety standards are as up-to-date as their equipment, too," Annja said. "Still, I guess the heat is easier to endure than starvation—even if you throw in the risk from the occasional splash of molten metal."

A few cars stood parked by the building's rust-streaked flank, several foreign sedans and a battered white Range Rover. They probably belonged to the technical staff and foremen. Annja guessed the workers probably walked.

"I don't see any sign of trouble," Aidan said. "Maybe we did hike all this way for nothing." He took off his bush hat and wiped sweat from his face with a handkerchief. He wore a light blue cotton short-sleeved shirt, now with big half moons of sweat beneath the arms, and his customary blue jeans.

Annja wore a cheap panama hat and her usual field garb of white man's shirt and khaki cargo pants. She had the sleeves rolled down for the same reason she avoided shorts in the heat—to discourage the plentiful and insolent Brazilian insect life.

"I wonder what it's like in the bloody Amazon, with all these bloody bugs they have down here," Aidan said, slapping his bare arm again. It left a smear of red against his pale skin.

"Worse in the Lower Amazon, I imagine. The Upper Amazon where I've been was not quite so bad. Close call, though," Annja said.

She studied him. She wasn't sure how she felt about the previous night. At breakfast, in one of the hotel's restaurants Aidan had been his usual self, not so much bubbling over with humor as voluble about his interests and passions with a dry backing of humor. She thought there had been an extra flush to his normally pink cheeks, but perhaps she'd imagined that. She felt as if her cheeks were a bit rosier, though. She had, however, studiously avoided letting herself think about what had happened between them. Or what it might portend.

"What do you think?" he asked. One thing you could say for him was that he seemed to have little trouble deferring to a woman in a potentially dangerous situation.

She smiled. "I say we go. Race you?"

He touched two fingers to her arm. "Won't it be less obtrusive if we just walk?"

She looked at him a moment. Then she nodded. "Good point." And that's what I get for getting cocky about my action-babe pose.

They strolled out of the brush as casually as if they came this way every day about this time. Some royal-blue-and-orange birds flew up, squalling indignantly. Annja and Aidan walked at a matter-of-fact pace toward the structure, feeling the heat on their faces grow with every step.

"Think they have surveillance cameras?" he asked.

"The place looks as if they're in there listening to an old radio with vacuum tubes," she said. "But we can't take anything for granted. Not with surveillance equipment so cheap these days. Still, does it really make a difference?"

"I suppose not."

They approached the open front of the building. From inside came a roar of noise. Ignoring a door covered in flaking green paint, they walked to the big opening. Annja leaned forward and peered around the wall.

Furnace heat and the stench of hot metal hit her in the face. Even after the heat of the tropical sunlight it was almost staggering.

"Inferno," Aidan whispered by her shoulder. He sounded truly horror-struck.

Through eyes watering from heat and the chemical smell she got an impression of a vast dark face shot through the glow of fires. Great tangled machines loomed and catwalks strung back and forth like a steel spiderweb above. Vast black cauldrons emerged from an enormous yellow furnace mouth, drooling liquid metal; streams of living flame like lava fell into molds, sparks showering and skittering on the floor as they reddened, faded, winked out. A continuous roar of noise sounded, the whoosh of gas jets, the rush of molten metal being poured, hissing and sizzling, and ruling all the ceaseless bellow of the flame.

Black men, bare to the waist, moved through the hellish tumult with almost desperate purpose, carrying long poles with hooks, and outsized tongs. Wiry torsos ran with sweat. The glare reflected and skittered over their safety helmets. The display might have stirred a favorable response inside Annja, who liked looking at well-muscled scantily-clad men as much as the next woman. Instead she found it somewhat frightening and sad.

"How can anybody work in that?" Aidan asked.

"Necessity." Annja said. "I guess if archaeology teaches us anything, it's just how much humans can learn to tolerate if they have to."

"Poor bastards," Aidan said.

"Amen. Let's get in there," Annja replied.

The brightness of the furnace seemed to make the

shadows darker, defeating the lights hanging from the ceiling high overhead. There were ample hiding places, even had anyone been looking around. But no one was.

They moved toward the back, keeping close to the left wall. Exhausted crucibles, suspended from a track overhead, were conveyed out another wide opening of the far wall into daylight. Before them an enclosed space intruded onto the main floor, its lone story far below the cavernous ceiling. It appeared to contain an office with windows in its flank showing desks and computer monitors with men in shirtsleeves sitting at them. It struck Annja as being way too close for either comfort or safety to where the fuming cauldrons tipped their cargo into the waiting molds. Seven or eight yards beyond the far side of the structure yawned the mouth of the furnace itself.

Annja stopped, heart in throat.

She ducked behind some kind of great rounded gray-painted metal casing. Aidan duckwalked up next to her. "What is it?" He had to put his mouth to her ear and still practically shout to make himself heard over the tumult.

She pointed. A dozen or more men in dark suits stood confronting office workers in shirtsleeves in front of the office area. All of them wore large silver medallions on chains around their necks. One man wore a suit all of white and cream rather than dark fabric. He loomed above the others and appeared thin as a flagpole.

"It's Highsmith," she said.

"My God," Aidan said. "Those men have guns."

It was true. Sir Martin's followers, at least a dozen in view, held a variety of firearms, some handguns, some long arms—machine pistols, shotguns, assault rifles. Looking around, Annja saw more armed men moving around the work floor. The foundry workers themselves paid scant attention to them. They were probably not unaccustomed to seeing heavily armed men. Houses of the wealthy and even exclusive apartment complexes routinely sported guards carrying submachine guns in Brazil. Or maybe in comparison to the tons of two-thousand-degree liquid metal swaying over their heads and pouring out in great glaring streams like lava, the firearms just didn't seem dangerous.

"What now?" Aidan asked.

"We get in closer."

His expression told her what he thought of *that* idea. With a flip of his hand he gave her a mock-courtly "you first" gesture.

The White Tree Lodge members seemed preoccupied with keeping an eye on the foundry employees. They weren't looking around to spot people sneaking through the heavy metal machinery on the floor.

Annja and Aidan got within thirty feet of the two groups in front of the door to the office. A burly young Englishman was shouting at a short, dark man with bulging eyes, hair like Brillo pads flanking a sweat-shiny spire of skull, and his tie askew.

"*Não, não,*" the Brazilian was saying. Annja guessed he was the foundry manager. "I do not know what the foreign gentlemen are talking about—"

"Dennis," Sir Martin said. Though he did not seem to raise his voice the name rang clearly audible above all the volcanic noise.

Without warning a short cultist with a shock of unruly dark hair shot the tall and gawky young Brazilian to the manager's left through the knee. The young man fell down howling and thrashing and clutching his leg.

Blood sprayed the immaculate ivory shins of Sir Martin's trousers. The knobbed face showed no reaction. A slight young cultist quickly knelt before his master and began dabbing at the blood spatter with a handkerchief. It only had the effect of broadening the droplets into dark smears.

Aidan tensed as if to lunge. Annja put a restraining hand on his arm.

"We can't just watch," he hissed.

"What do you suggest we do? They've got us out-manned and outgunned."

Aidan frowned furiously at her. "You've got that magical sword!"

"I can't knock bullets out of the air," she said. She looked around nervously. Though it seemed unlikely anybody could have heard their soft-voiced but intense conversation the odds against them were too high for her to take anything for granted.

"But surely you don't mean to do *nothing?*" Pascoe said.

"We'll do something," she said, wanting to keep things as simple as possible. "But we need to wait for an opportunity."

"But we can't just stand by—"

Annja grabbed him by the arm and put her finger to his lips. His eyes widened in outrage.

"Wait," she said. "The equation just changed."

She tipped her head toward the large front door. After a scowling moment his eyes followed her lead.

More men were striding in out of the brightness of the morning. They were thick-necked men, white, obviously foreigners, though their garb was mostly rough. Their posture suggested arrogance.

They too openly carried guns. Green braided leather thongs circled their thick necks.

Among them walked Mark Peter Stern in a tropical-weight tan suit, a yarmulke on his gleaming gold hair.

25

A White Tree cultist who had worked his way toward the large opening shouted and raised a handgun. One of Stern's followers fired a burst from his hip with an Uzi. The Englishman spun and fell, his weapon unfired.

Annja crouched lower, drawing Aidan down with her. She expected an instant eruption of answering gunfire. Instead the White Tree cultists seemed thunderstruck by the arrival of their rivals and the sudden death of one of their comrades.

"Sir Martin," Stern called out as he strode past Annja and Aidan's hiding place with his burly henchmen spreading out to either side of him. "What a pleasure to find you here. I wish I could say it's unexpected."

Highsmith stared at him with his dramatic white eyebrows flared in fury. "What are you doing here, you mountebank?"

"You mean your divinations didn't tell you that? Any more than it warned you to expect my visitation? Gee, it's too bad. Obviously you're too inept to possess an artifact of the power and majesty of King Solomon's Jar. Jumping naked over fires and hugging trees is more your speed, eh, wot." The last appeared to be a cartoon-ish attempt at parodying an English accent, and Stern had said it with a nasty sneer on his face.

"How typically American," Highsmith said. "Your feeble attempts at humor are of a kind with your so-called mystic teachings—base humbuggery fit to pull the wool over the eyes of self-besotted simpletons."

"Are they going to try to talk each other to death?" Aidan demanded. The color had dropped from his face at the murder of his countryman. His cheeks were re-gaining their usual hue, and his insouciance seemed to be springing back.

Annja was relieved. "I'm afraid not," she said. "I don't know if that's good or bad."

"I see your point. I deplore bloodshed. But it couldn't happen to a nicer—"

She gripped his arm and put a finger to her lips. She had begun to sense a change in the atmosphere—over the hot-metal stink and booming noise of the foundry.

Another crucible came to a stop and poured its contents in an arc of liquid fire into a mold, where it ran in rivulets into the depressions awaiting it. Now looking somewhat nervously at the invaders, with sparks cascading unnoticed around them and dancing by their feet, the workmen plied the flow with their long tools, seemingly more to make sure it behaved as expected than because they needed actively to push the process along.

By reflex Stern and his men glanced toward the fire fountain. "Take them!" Highsmith shouted.

The White Tree cultists opened fire. Two of Stern's men fell. Another backed away, firing an Uzi machine pistol from the hip. He screamed as bullets hit him but kept firing until he tripped backward over the edge of the molds and fell into the stream of molten metal cascading from the crucible. His scream rose in a crescendo, impossibly shrill. Steam gouted from his body as his flesh became fluid and sluiced from his bones. His body, half-skeletonized, sprawled across the glowing molds.

Annja ducked as random bullets cracked overhead and whined in ricochets off the machinery around them. She wished she had ducked when the shooting first began, and not seen what she had just seen. Aidan hunkered beside her, looking sick.

"What now?" he mouthed over the crackle of gunfire and shouts and screams.

"We can't just hide," she shouted back to him. "They'll find us if we do."

He nodded, swallowing spasmodically as if trying to control his emotions. Her stomach was churning. She turned away. She knew she could not afford to be incapacitated by a fit of nausea, however briefly.

Without any dignified course coming to mind, Annja crawled on all fours toward the office where it protruded onto the shop floor. Coming within ten feet of it, with what she thought might be a lathe shielding her from the interior of the building where most of the action was, and a big red toolbox on wheels between her and the office, she cautiously reared up and peered over.

Throughout the smelter, men fought furiously. Some fired at each other from behind cover. No one was having much success. Much of the equipment and even general clutter inside the vast building was steel or iron, massive enough to stop bullets. Other men whaled at each other with wrenches, metal rods, bits of scrap as far as Annja could tell. Some simply pummeled each other, wrestled, shrieked, gouged eyes and tore at throats with their teeth.

"My God," Aidan gasped from her side. "I've never seen anything like this."

They both ducked as a burst of gunfire raked across the top of the lathe table, bullets howling like lost souls as they tumbled to rip irregular holes in the thin sheet-metal wall above their heads.

"The rage and passion—they're increasing it, trying

to use it to manipulate them. But at the same time all that emotion is working on them, too. They're getting themselves into a frenzy, losing control," Annja said.

A figure loomed up at the other end of the lathe. It was one of Stern's men in a torn tan shirt with epaulettes. His forehead had been cut open, turning his face to a mask of blood, making the green-dyed braid around his neck a brown-and-purplish mess. He aimed an Uzi at them, pulled the trigger.

Nothing happened. He had fired his magazine dry. Screaming with frustration, he raised the Uzi above his head as if to smash them with it. His eyes rolled in pits of blood.

From his crouch Aidan lashed out with his boot and caught the man squarely in the groin. The kick lifted the soles of the Malkuth devotee's heavy work shoes an inch off the greasy concrete floor.

Annja's close-combat instructors had warned her the famous crotch-kick did not always work. Whether he was too adrenalized for the neural overload associated with a blow to the testicles to have much effect, or just wasn't susceptible, the kick did no more than stagger the man. He came on again growling incoherently.

"Bloody stay *down*, will you?" Aidan said. He jumped up and smashed an overhand right into the man's face. Annja heard the buckling crunch as the cartilage in the man's nose broke. He went over backward with blood pulsing from his nostrils, slammed the back of his head hard on the pavement and lay moaning and moving feebly.

"Good shot," Annja said. Aidan waved his hand in the air, grimacing. "You didn't break it?" she asked.

He flexed his fingers. "No. No thanks to myself. Stupid bloody stunt to pull."

"It worked," Annja pointed out.

A violent heave of shadow caught Annja's eye in the gloom. Another figure appeared twenty feet behind them, back toward the entrance. It leveled a long-barreled weapon at them. Annja threw her arms around Aidan and half vaulted, half rolled with him over the top of the lathe. A shotgun boomed, yellow muzzle-flare blooming. Lead pellets skittered across the floor and against the lathe's metal pedestal where the two had crouched an eyeblink before.

Annja landed hard and Aidan's weight came down on top of her and squashed the breath from her body.

By force of will alone she sucked air back into her lungs with a great convulsive inhalation. She shoved Aidan aside, rolled to her feet, gathered herself and sprang.

She heard the shotgun slide being racked as she jumped over some kind of waist-high mechanism covered in black plastic and curling duct tape. She steeled herself to receive the next charge of shot at contact range. Instead she cleared the plastic-wrapped machine unopposed and the sole of her boot caught the gunman in the chest in a flying kick. He windmilled backward, the shotgun flying from his hand.

Annja did a graceless three-point landing. Pain shot from her knee where it struck the concrete floor. The impact was so savage that white lightning seemed to thread through her brain. Across the main floor someone shouted and opened up on her with an automatic weapon of some sort. To her intense relief her knee did not lock or give way when she came up on hands and feet and scrambled like a four-legged spider back to cover.

Aidan awaited her, crouched down in a narrow aisle, hair and eyes wild. With a white-knuckled hand he brandished a crescent wrench he'd found somewhere. Unfortunately the tool was no more than ten inches long and did not make a threatening weapon.

"Listen," she told him, breathing hard and massaging her right knee, which throbbed. "You just stay here until everybody's distracted. Then try to find the jar."

"What are you going to do?" Pascoe asked.

"Something showy and stupid enough to make sure everybody's looking at me," she said.

"Wait—"

She didn't. She couldn't. Bent low she scrambled several feet deeper into the foundry, back toward the office, and peered over a steel table with a shelf beneath it piled thick with rusty junk.

The fight raged unabated. She guessed both the White Tree and the Malkuth contingents had called in reinforcements. At least eight bodies were lying in her field of vision, on the floor, draped over equipment, sprawled at the base of a metal stair up to the catwalk. Meanwhile pairs and groups still shot and screamed and fought. She wasn't even sure they were paying attention to whether the person they raged and raved and struggled to destroy was on their own side or not.

Men brandishing firearms had made little impression on the foundry workers. Men *firing* firearms made quite the impression indeed. Wisely the wiry-muscled men in the hard hats had vanished. The white-collar types had retreated within the office and locked the door, leaving two of their number lying unmoving outside. One was the skinny youngster who had been shot in the knee. He had apparently bled out or been finished off somehow. Possibly he'd just stopped a stray round; it was clearly not his day, Annja thought.

Wreathed in pink ghostly flames a new crucible swung out of the furnace, white-hot metal slopping over the sides. It was an alarming sight. It would have dumped its load across the already filled mold pallet, which had not been removed out the side door along the steel track laid into the concrete floor when the last crucible had emptied itself into it. But instead of flooding the shop floor with liquid metal the vessel stopped to swing perilously midway between furnace and mold. Someone out of Annja's sight must have thrown a cutoff switch.

A man, one of Highsmith's devotees by his clothing, which looked as if it had been expensively tailored before it had been torn and yanked every which way, began hacking at the office door with a fire ax. It was a bizarre gesture. To either side the walls were mostly window and many of them had been shot out. He could have simply scrambled through with little effort. Evidently the violent frenzy had so gripped him he never even considered the possibility.

Is he possessed? Annja wondered. Maybe he's done it all himself, indulging himself in an ecstasy of pure destruction. It came to her to wonder, with a shock, whether the demons everyone spoke of were actual entities, possessed of any separate existence of their own, or were merely projections of human anger and fear and hatred.

Something possessed that poor dog in Haifa, she thought. But couldn't it have been worked into a frenzy by human rage and cruelty?

She shook herself. There was no time for metaphysical speculation—especially since the office door gave way after no more than three good whacks. The White Tree cultist charged inside, making for half a dozen office workers cowering from him. His ax was raised and an expression of mad joy twisted what otherwise might have been a handsome young face.

Annja raced forward. She jumped, easily clearing the office structure's low side wall, ducking her head so as to fit through the vacant window. Her boots skidded with a crunch on the broken glass littering the floor. She had to flex her legs deeply to keep from falling over in it.

The crazed man swung the ax at her. She jumped aside. The axhead rang on concrete, throwing up chips. With wild speed he raised it again and chopped at her.

She ducked. The axe struck a heavy wooden table littered with drawings by the wall. The blade bit deep. It stuck.

Annja shifted her balance, intending to disarm the man and then put him down, maybe dislocate his shoulder and take him out of the fight—or the fight out of him, in any case. But with mad strength he yanked the ax free in a shower of splinters, throwing it up and back over his head with such violence he almost overbalanced.

It was too much. Annja concentrated. The sword was in her hand. The man screamed and started to swing at her.

Blood gouted from his chest as she slashed horizontally through his torso, right below where his nipples must have been. He went to his knees. Blood welled up and slopped over his chin as it sprayed out to the sides from the wound. The ax fell from his hands with a clatter. His eyes rolled up and he fell forward at her feet.

From the corner of her eye she saw someone point a weapon at her. She ducked as a shot crashed. Where the bullet went she didn't know.

"Keep low," she said in Portuguese to the terrified office workers, who stared at her as if she were covered with green scales. She saw there were doors at the back of the office, apparently leading outside. "Get out of the building if you can. Lock yourselves in someplace out of sight if you can't."

It was the woman who warned her. She hadn't noticed before that there was a slender middle-aged woman in the group huddled in the office. She looked past Annja and her dark eyes went wide.

Annja spun toward the door and uncoiled from the floor like a striking rattlesnake, thrusting the sword in a long lunge.

26

The sword's tip caught a man wearing a Malkuth necklace in the center of his broad chest.

He lowered the Jericho 941 Baby Eagle handgun he had been pointing at her as if his arm was suddenly too tired to support its two-plus pounds. For a moment Annja stood face-to-face with him. He looked no older than thirty. His eyes were blue and wide. They seemed to stare through Annja without seeing her. His mouth opened but only blood came out.

His legs sagged. His jaw worked. Annja pushed him out into the cacophony of the smelter.

His body jerked as a bullet struck it. The man winced and his eyes rolled up in his head. She pushed him farther away. With the last capability of his own legs he staggered back three steps. From all around the foundry's cavernous interior the firefly lights of muzzle-flashes winked as at least twenty firearms opened up on him. The hammering noise of gunshots was like the devil's own forge, echoing within the metal walls.

As the already dying man performed his jerking dance of death Annja willed the sword back to the otherwhere. Taking a step out from the doorway, she jumped up. With hands reversed she caught the edge of the office space's low roof and pulled herself up.

The shooting suddenly stopped. As Annja had hoped, many of the gunmen had exhausted their magazines and needed to reload. She hoped to make use of the lull in the gunfight.

"Listen to me," she shouted in English. "You've got to stop this! Can't you see you're being used?"

"My, my," called an American-accented voice. Mark Peter Stern stepped into view from a side niche near the open maw of the furnace. It must have been wiltingly hot but he looked fresh, and his tropical-weight suit didn't seem to have lost a bit from the sharpness of its creases. "You're a woman of unusual talents for a TV archaeologist," he said.

"I'm a *real* archaeologist," Annja declared with a defiant toss of her head.

"You are the inconvenient young woman who came to my manor in the guise of a researcher," a voice boomed from up high. Annja raised her head. Up on the catwalk Sir Martin Highsmith stood, his own shades-of-white suit gleaming as if spotlit in the glare of the halted crucible, whose contents had only cooled to yellow from near white. Its sides glowed red. "Enlighten us, then. Used by whom?"

"Demons," she said.

The devotees of the warring sects had given off their wrestling and sniping to stare at her openmouthed. Her heart was pounding. She could see a good thirty of them still standing.

Stern laughed. "That's a good one. Demons." His followers looked at each other, then voiced an uncertain laugh of their own.

"Don't be ridiculous," Stern called out.

"You think when you get the jar you'll control them," she called. She fought to keep desperation out of her voice. She was losing them, she knew. I hope this is providing enough of a diversion for Aidan, she thought. "But you're already in mortal peril of your souls."

"Foolish young woman!" Highsmith declared in tones that rang like a great bronze bell. "Do you really think we have no means of protecting ourselves?"

She looked up at him. For a moment he seemed surrounded by a nimbus of blackness.

Suddenly she understood what was happening.

Stern and Highsmith were willing participants in creating the frenzy. Their followers truly believed they were following a righteous path. And in the quest for power everyone had been possessed by evil.

Up on the catwalk, surrounded by heat shimmer and flitting darkness, Sir Martin Highsmith began to laugh. It was a deep, rich, melodious laugh.

Mark Peter Stern joined in. His laugh was harsh and rang throughout the metal sepulcher, clearly audible above the still hungry roaring of the furnace.

One by one the men of the rival sects joined in.

Maybe I should consider switching to a career in stand-up comedy, Annja thought.

"Listen to me, please," she cried, shouting to make herself heard above the foundry sounds and the roar of laughter, now showing clear manic overtones. "We can work together. We can work things out like reasonable people."

Sir Martin's laugh cut off as if he'd been chopped across the throat. Instantly his face was suffused with blood. "You're just like all of us," he screamed, spittle flying from his mouth. "You just want the jar for yourself. Kill the meddling bitch!" he screamed.

Annja launched herself up and out as guns spoke. A great iron hook hung from the metal ceiling girders by a chain, ten feet from the lip of the office roof and about three feet above Annja's head. She grabbed the hook and swung on it.

A half-dozen rival cultists stood clumped together by the foot of the stairway up to the catwalk along the far wall. They had been brutalizing one another with fists and makeshift clubs when Annja put in her appearance. They seemed to have all been able to put their hands on firearms, though. Their aim was thrown off by Annja's unexpected—and unexpectedly swift—movement. In fact when she let go the hook and came swooping down on them they were all too startled to track and shoot at her.

It was the very response she'd been hoping for.

She came down with both feet in the well-padded midsection of a blue-collar Malkuth hardman. The man staggered and sat down hard. Suitably braked, Annja landed with both feet on the concrete in the midst of the five still standing. She had hopes of preventing more bloodshed. She strongly suspected that the high-frequency emotion of combat and the actual spilling of life force were both feeding the demons in everyone.

Taking full advantage of her skill and speed, Annja targeted two of the goons, plucking a handgun and a shotgun from surprise-slack hands before their owners could react. She pitched the weapons out into daylight through the opening yawning nearby. She kicked a second pistol from the grasp of a pasty-faced White Tree member who was pointing it at her sideways, American gangsta style. Then she spun and grabbed the flash suppressor of an FN-FAL 7.62 mm military rifle, twitched the long weapon out of its owner's hands and hit him in the jaw with it. He went down moaning and clutching his face.

That left two with guns in their hands. One man wearing a silver medallion fired a handgun. The noise and recoil so startled him that he immediately punched off a second shot on the light trigger, unintentionally to judge by the astonished look on his face. Both shots missed Annja, but one of the fat bullets hit a fellow Lodge member, one of the first pair Annja had disarmed on landing. He dropped to his knees and toppled on his face. His comrade dropped the big handgun as if it had turned red-hot.

The stout Malkuth follower Annja had used to cushion her landing had gotten his feet under him. As he raised his pistol, still hunched over and clutching his gut with his other hand, Annja did a sideways stutter-step toward him and side kicked him in the groin once more. This time she put a hip thrust into it and sent him flying right out into the sunlight.

With a wild scream a White Tree devotee cut loose from the hip with a 9 mm Franchi machine pistol, sweeping it left to right. A Malkuth enforcer and one of the gunner's lodge mates spun down in a welter of blood. Annja turned and sprinted toward the front entrance with bullets letting in daylight in a sort of irregular sine wave behind her. She dived behind a large machine and heard bullets ring off its far side like trip-hammer blows.

Baying like a pack of hounds, zealots of both stripes converged on her. She lay on her stomach trying to listen for footsteps. With all the noise and the echoing properties of the vast enclosed space, it wasn't easy to sort them out.

She saw a pair of oxblood shoes on the floor on the other side of a wheeled device that might have been a generator or portable power supply by her head. She prepared herself.

The White Tree fanatic spun around holding a beefy SPAS riot shotgun. Annja rolled hard, flung out a leg, caught him right on his jade tie-tack with the back of her heel. Choking and flailing, he fell, losing his grip on the weapon as it blasted noisily toward the ceiling.

Annja bounced to her feet, darted around the squat mechanism and onto the main floor as somebody else hopped out behind, spraying the oil-spotted place she'd been an instant before with bullets. Men with guns were running toward her. She summoned the sword again and charged.

She slashed left, right, left. Two men fell, screaming and spurting blood. A third stood staring in mute horror at the blood flowing freely from his numerous wounds.

Bullets snapped past her ears and cracked against the concrete by her flashing feet. She dived over a table laden with rusty parts, tucked her shoulder, rolled. She still hit hard enough to hurt and make her fear for a moment she had dislocated her left shoulder when she landed on it.

She pressed against the pedestal of a grinder. Reversing at once, she rolled back against the table she had cleared. She tried to squirm beneath the bottom shelf. A hand appeared over the table's edge, holding a Heckler & Koch MP-5K, a little stubby machine pistol with a sort of piano-leg foregrip. The gun yammered, spraying bullets at a downward angle.

The stream was directed away from her—but right against the gray-painted cast-iron pedestal of the grinder. Annja cringed and cried out as ricochets buzzed about her like angry hornets, stinging her arms and face with concrete particles as they spanged off the floor and punched holes through cans above and to either side of her.

The bullet storm stopped. Almost reluctantly she lowered her hands from her head, which she had covered in a futile attempt to protect herself from the ricochets. The compact but heavy German machine pistol bounced once on the floor next to her with a ringing sound.

She looked up. The hand lay draped over the table edge like an abandoned sock puppet. Its skin looked almost bluish white in the half light; she could see blue veins through it. She raised the sword.

Rising slightly, she found herself staring into a pair

of surprised gray eyes. They showed no sign of seeing her. Nor were they likely to—they stared out from beneath an irregular hole right in the center of a high forehead, where one of the shooter's own bullets had came tumbling back and struck him.

Annja sprang to a hunched-over posture. Guns blared at her. Bent low she darted this way and that like a fox pursued by hounds, trying to throw off the aim of her multiple enemies by speed and sheer unpredictability. She knew that since few if any of them bothered to actually aim, whether or not she took a hit would pretty much be a matter of luck anyway. But moving made her *feel* better, somehow.

A pair of Malkuth goons appeared before her as she darted toward the rear of the smelter, where the furnace roared, oblivious to the doings of mere flesh. She darted right, bowling over two more men closing in from that direction, sprinted across seven yards of open floor, threw herself into a forward roll.

Another Malkuth man jumped out from behind a machine and into her path, firing a Glock. But he anticipated a target running at him upright. Annja skidded forward on her butt with bullets cracking right over her head. She thrust upward at an angle and skewered him right beneath the rib cage as she slid past to his left. He fell, sword still transfixing him, momentarily pinning her right hand to the floor.

As her feet hit the wall something made her look up and left. Sir Martin Highsmith stood at the top of the stairs with the yellow glow of the still liquid metal in the hanging crucible illuminating the right side of his body and underlighting his craggy face and mane of white hair with deceptive sunset gold. He held a 9 mm Beretta out before him like his own sword of vengeance.

"You are dead, interloper!" he declared. "You cannot reach me with that sword of yours."

He was right. As he began to trigger shots and bullets cracked around her, Annja willed the sword away. Then she yanked the Glock from the dead Malkuthian's nerveless fingers, rolled onto her back, pushing the blocky handgun out before her in a two-handed isosceles grip.

The white dot of the front sight lined up on the center of Highsmith's chest, its black post contrasting nicely with his old-ivory waistcoat. She squeezed the trigger, hoping the Glock's characteristic long pull wouldn't throw her aim off too badly. The weapon roared and bucked in her hand.

SIR MARTIN CAMDESSUS Highsmith felt a piledriver impact to the center of his chest. Instantly his gun hand ceased obeying instructions and began to drift downward. His weapon no longer fired.

He couldn't breathe. His vision blurred. He teetered. *Spirit of wild nature, who have guided me so long,* he prayed, *help me now so that I might yet bring our shared vision to pass.*

But the voice in his head, which had always been so warm and honeyed, now dripped with scorn.

Useless fool, it sneered. *I have no use for failure. Die.*

Sir Martin reeled and fell backward over the rail.

He screamed as he felt the heat growing on his back like a rising sun. Screamed louder as his hair and the backs of his coat and trouser legs took fire with a huff.

And then the molten metal caught him, enfolded him and drew him into infinite agony. His shriek achieved a steam-whistle pitch and volume as intolerable agony was augmented by the moisture in his lungs boiling in an instant, searing throat, palate and tongue.

The scream died.

"WAIT," ANNJA HEARD Mark Peter Stern command. "Take the woman alive. She may know where the jar is."

Transferring the Glock to her left hand and summoning the sword back into her right, Annja leaped to her feet. With their leader gone the White Tree survivors seemed as inclined to obey the Malkuth guru as his own followers were. Annja was surrounded, a dozen men closing in on her, faces grim or gleeful over leveled weapons.

"Ah, yes," Stern said, tipping his head to one side. "That's a nifty sword you have there, Ms. Creed. If you hand it over, we might be persuaded to let you live."

Her eyes darted left and right. To surrender the sword was unthinkable. She wondered fleetingly if she willed it gone before they killed her, whether it would remain eternally sealed in its pocket universe. Probably not, she decided.

There was no possible escape for her. Even using gun and sword simultaneously she could never get through before someone put a bullet in her, or she was dragged down by sheer weight of male muscle and bone. If I go down, she thought, I go down fighting. But winded, exhausted, disoriented by the relentless attacks of the swarming demons, she hesitated for the space of half a breath.

That was all it took. Strong hands gripped her arms from right and left as two men closed with her. In despair she felt her strength and will drain from her. She was trapped.

The man to her right said, "Be a love and give us the sword, then." He was a tall, young Englishman in a dark green pin-striped suit, no tie, with curly chestnut hair. He smiled and reached for the hilt of her sword.

Then his eyes went wide and his head snapped to the side.

27

Annja's eyes widened as a cloud of pink mist and dark shreds puffed out above the left ear of the handsome young Englishman. He dropped as if he were a suit of clothes slipped from the rack.

The burly Malkuth man who had her left arm grunted. His meaty hand went slack on her arm. Turning toward him, she saw his eyes standing unnaturally out from their sockets, the skin of his face sagging.

The right side of his head was bloody ruin.

From the front of the foundry a sound erupted as if a decade's worth of hailstones were being unloaded on the corrugated metal roof at once. Out on the floor men closing in on Annja began to spin and fall with little red sprays jetting from bodies and limbs and heads.

Her head snapped toward the entrance. She gasped.

A line of men marched shoulder to shoulder into the smelter, dark forms silhouetted against the tropical morning sun. Most were firing machine-pistol-sized Kalashnikovs from the hip. They stepped aside only to walk around machines in their path. Interspersed with them was a quartet of what Annja recognized with a shock as Orthodox priests, in flowing vestments with basket-shaped hats on their heads and magnificent beards. They intoned prayers and swung smoking censers on chains before them.

In the middle of the line a smaller man was dwarfed by the burly gunners. He walked with a bandy-legged swagger of total self-assurance. He looked oddly familiar.

The man raised his hand. Flame bloomed from it— right toward Annja's face. She set her jaw and waited for the fatal impact.

Instead the bullet cracked past her head. She heard a sound similar to a bat hitting a ball. She turned back to see a Malkuth cultist toppling backward with a yard-long fixed wrench falling from his hands to ring on the concrete.

The invaders mowed down Malkuth and White Tree men with a fine lack of discrimination. Several of the well-dressed Englishmen threw down their weapons and raised their hands.

Then died.

"The Babylonians come again!" Annja heard Mark

Peter Stern shout from the back of the foundry. "But I will not be taken into captivity."

All the rest of the cultists lay on the floor, dead or dying. The diminutive man with the Glock held up a hand. The shooting stopped. He halted near Annja. His men stopped at the same time, lowering their weapons but staying alert.

He was a very trim man, with receding hair cropped close to a narrow skull and piercing eyes. He wore a dark suit over a dark pullover of some sort, very well tailored to his athletic form.

It took Annja a moment to regain some composure. She looked at the man with surprise. He was the leader of the group of *mafiya* goons who had surprised her and Aidan in Amsterdam.

Mark Peter Stern's tall form suddenly appeared silhouetted against the furnace's blinding yellow maw. Blue flames jetted in like fangs from the periphery.

"I am protected by the power of the Lord of Hosts," Stern said, "'Yea, though I walk through the Valley of the Shadow of Death, I will fear no evil—'" he turned and walked into the furnace "'—for thou art with me; thy rod and thy staff, they comfort me.'"

His outline blurred as his suit took flame. He stopped. Then he turned and staggered back toward the entrance, a figure of darker flame against the furnace's brilliant fire, waving wings of fire. His hands burned like white torches.

His screaming cut through the furnace roar like a razor.

He made it three steps, then fell to his knees. A moment later and he slumped into a shapeless mound, like a wax figurine melting.

An especially tall *mafiya* man with a head like a shaved bear's and hair in his ears said something to his small and dapper leader. The smaller man shrugged.

"What's going on?" Annja asked, devastated by the carnage around her.

"We are restoring peace," the small man said. "Did you never hear 'Blessed are the peacemakers'?"

It seemed to Annja a useful distinction might be drawn between peacemaking and mass murder. However, it did not seem that it would be useful to bandy words just now.

"Why haven't you killed me yet?" she demanded.

He looked at her. No one seemed to be paying particular attention to her despite the fact she stood there with an archaic broadsword in one hand and a thoroughly modern semiautomatic pistol in the other.

"I forget my manners," the small man said. "Please forgive me. I am Valeriy Korolin, formerly captain of special-designation soldiers in armed forces of USSR. Now I work in private sector. You are Ms. Annja Creed."

She lowered her sword, which Korolin had started to examine. The big man at his shoulder crossed himself in the Orthodox manner. The constant murmur of the priests' prayer spiked briefly.

"You haven't answered my question," she said.

"You are a very courageous young woman," Korolin said, "if maybe not so prudent. But we knew that." He suddenly grinned. "We haven't killed you because you have not gotten in our way, if you will forgive my speaking candidly."

"You tried hard enough before," she said.

"Those were mistakes. In Amsterdam my men misconstrued my orders under misapprehension you might be the killers of that poor old lady shopkeeper. In Jaffa our attempt was to incinerate Dr. Stern—who seems to have escaped our efforts only to carry out our intentions by himself." He shook his head, still marveling at Stern's walking voluntarily into the blazing furnace.

"And now," Korolin said, "since it is obvious you do not have the jar, if you will excuse us—"

"She doesn't have it," a voice called from above. "But I do."

Everyone looked up. Aidan Pascoe stood on the catwalk perilously close to the crucible of still molten metal into which Highsmith had fallen. Above his head he brandished a gleaming metal jar, in the shape of a globe with a funnel thrust into it, and two oddly slender, scrolled handles.

Annja drew in a sharp breath. She could feel it. It was Solomon's Jar.

With a guilty start she realized Korolin was looking

at her closely. He nodded sharply. Then he turned to look up at Pascoe.

"Mr. Pascoe," he said, "please throw down to us the jar."

"I won't," he said. "And if you shoot me, or try to take it from me by force, I'll throw it in the melt. Then no one will get it."

"What do you want it for, Mr. Pascoe?" the Russian asked.

"Tell him, Annja," Pascoe said, his voice strained.

Anna was concerned. He seemed to be standing in the midst of a dark whirlwind. She wasn't sure if she was literally seeing it with her eyes, or some other sense. But she knew what she was seeing. Aidan Pascoe was struggling with temptation.

"Why don't you tell them, Aidan," she said, trying to keep her voice neutral.

"The power to make the world a better place," he said. "That's what I've dreamed of since I was a child. What do you want it for?"

"Very simple," Korolin said. "A wealthy and well-connected collector in St. Petersburg offers a substantial sum of money for authenticated jar of King Solomon. He desires this object solely for its value as artifact of the ancient world. He is an atheist. He is merely obsessed with history."

"He wants to display it?" Annja asked.

"He wants to be able to admire it, and to show it off

to favored guests, or so I presume. He is prepared to preserve it using the best modern techniques."

"What about you?" Annja asked Korolin. "What do you think about the jar?"

"I think I will receive a munificent reward for success," he said, "rather than getting shot in the back of the neck for failure, maybe."

"But the demons—"

"I myself am also atheist. I do not believe in demons," he stated with a shrug.

"Why did you bring the priests?" Annja asked.

"I do not believe in demons, but I do believe in hedging my bets, Ms. Creed. After all, if there are no demons, I have only subjected myself to smelling some incense and listening to some mumbo jumbo. And if there are demons…"

Aidan shook his head. "Selfishness. Pure selfishness. The root of all evil."

"How do you plan to make the world better, Aidan?" Annja asked.

He frowned at her. "Whose side are you on?"

"You know which side, Aidan. Ask yourself that question. Please," she said trying to quell her fear.

He looked at her, suspicion narrowing his blue eyes.

"Very well. I will put an end to human suffering— to evil, if you will—by confining the demons that were released through the selfish greed of the treasure hunters who breached the seal."

"Aidan," Annja said, as gently as she could with any hope of being heard above the furnace roar, "are you sure that would even work?"

His eyes narrowed in suspicion. "What do you mean? Of course it would do."

"Do you think all the evil went out of the world when Solomon sealed the demons in that jar, Aidan? The demons may personify human evil, abet it, but they don't cause it. Humans do that themselves. Don't they?"

Aidan was frowning. But he was also listening. Annja sensed his struggle. He had experienced so much horror. He had heard her story. He simply didn't know what to believe.

"Treasure hunters sought out the jar and released the demons back into the world because of greed. Wasn't that evil? But obviously they did it when the demons were trapped in the jar. Right?" She hoped she could reach him.

"And after you've trapped all the demons, and you find out evil hasn't left the world—what then, Aidan? When you start to feel frustrated in your very praiseworthy desire to do ultimate good—and the demons start to whisper from their captivity that they can give you the power to do the good you so want to do—what will you do then?"

He shook his head. "I don't know. But—" He raised his head. "I hear them now. Whispering to me. They're telling me not to listen to you, Annja."

She caught a breath in her throat.

He smiled. "We know what *their* advice is worth, now, don't we, Annja love? What about you? Do you want it, then?"

"No." She hoped she wasn't answering too quickly, perhaps making him think she was trying to cover uncertainty with emphasis. She wasn't. She had no interest in the relic other than to keep it from causing more harm. "It isn't for me, Aidan," she said plainly.

He glared around him as if at a flock of gnats buzzing about his head. "Should I destroy it, then?"

He held it out over the crucible. Orange light glowed on its rounded belly. The Russians raised their guns again. Korolin shouted them down.

"Do you really want to destroy such an artifact, such a part of history?" Annja called out.

He sighed and looked at Korolin. "Your principal will hire professional archaeologists to see to the jar's preservation?"

"He has already done so, Mr. Pascoe."

"And if we give you the jar, what then? What becomes of us?"

Korolin shrugged. "We walk out of here. You get on with your young lives."

"Do you trust him, Annja?"

She shrugged. "They could have shot me," she said. "I don't see we have any choice but to trust them."

He drew in a deep breath. When he sighed it out

he seemed to lose an inch or two of height. "Very well," he said.

He tossed the jar to Korolin. The Russian fielded it deftly.

He gestured briskly. A man with his AKS hanging from a waist-length sling by his side brought a bulky satchel. When he opened it Annja noticed the sides were unusually thick, as if insulated. She was reminded incongruously of the packs pizza delivery stores used to keep their pies warm on their way to customers.

A man even shorter and skinnier than Korolin whom Annja had not noticed previously, in a rumpled brown suit, came forward and frowned at it through thick-rimmed and thick-lensed glasses. He nodded abruptly.

At a nod from Korolin the priest with the most grandly decorated hat and the grandest beard came up and blessed jar, satchel or both with sweeping gestures. Then Korolin carefully placed the jar in the satchel, closed it up and handed it to the bearlike man.

Korolin turned to look at Annja. "My patron, Mr. Garin Braden, thanks you," he said with a smile. Annja's blood ran cold.

He nodded and smiled. "Good day, Ms. Creed, Mr. Pascoe." And he walked with his bantam-rooster walk out the side door into the sunlight.

His men followed without a backward glance.

EPILOGUE

Annja and Aidan sat at the feet of Jesus.

"You know, if there is a God, He must have a mighty sense of humor," Aidan said. "He made us, after all."

"Are you still a doubter? After what you've experienced?" Annja asked.

He angled his head to the side. "Just because I've seen some unbelievable things," he said in a quiet voice, "doesn't necessarily imply the existence of an all-powerful Creator. Nor does the existence of a living embodiment of good, actually."

She sighed. "Good point. And thanks so much for being so helpful with my own crisis of faith."

He looked at her, alarmed. Until she smiled enough to let him off the hook.

They sat at the base of the giant statue of Christ the Redeemer that gazed down upon Rio de Janeiro with arms outstretched. They watched tourists appear at the far end of the walk that led across the flattened hilltop to the statue, hot and sweaty from trudging up the 222 steps embossed in the side of the thumb-shaped granite dome called Corcovado Mountain from the road. Behind them the sun was sinking.

"Did we do the right thing, do you think?" he asked.

She didn't need to ask what thing that was. "I think that's the sort of thing that has to get left to the verdict of history," she said. "What do you think?"

He thought for a moment, then drew in a deep breath. "I think we did. Hope we did."

"I suspect that's about as much confirmation as we're ever going to get." After a pause she added, "For anything, really."

"I'm afraid you're right." He shook his head. "And I thought I could solve all the world's problems by trapping some surly spirits inside a tin pot. You must think me a right git," he said with a hapless grin.

Annja took him by the chin, turned his face to hers and kissed him. "I think you're a wonderful man, Aidan," she said when they finally broke apart.

They looked in different directions, suddenly self-conscious.

"So what's next?" he asked.

"What do you mean?" she replied, already knowing the answer.

He waved a hand. "Us—"

"What does your heart tell you?" Annja asked.

His brows lowered over his eyes, which were lighter than the tropical late-afternoon sky. "Do you answer every question with a question?"

"Do you?" she said, laughing.

"All right, then, Do you have to answer my bloody question either like Dr. Phil or a fortune cookie?"

She laughed again. "I guess it goes with the job. Or maybe I'm just rationalizing a secret desire to pontificate."

It was his turn to laugh. As always she admired his laughter in its surrender to joy.

"Hard to think of you as pontificating. Although if the church were ever to get its hooks in you, I think you'd make a smashing first female pope," Aidan said.

"Don't go there," she said, mock-serious. "There supposedly was a female pope, and she was called Joan. Controversial women of the Catholic Church by that name are something of a sore subject for me."

"I can see why."

For a moment he gazed off at Sugarloaf peak, jutting up out of the bay. He sighed again. "In my hands, just for a moment, I held—"

"Damnation," she said.

He looked sheepish. "I suppose you're right. Thank

you for helping me make the right choice. Especially counterintuitive as it was."

"Don't thank me. The choice was all yours. Otherwise it wouldn't have counted."

He smiled a bit wanly. "It hurts a bit to be coming home doubly empty-handed. I don't get the girl, and I don't get the relic. Whatever am I going to tell my uncle?"

"He was expecting you to come home with a girl?" Annja said, feigning outrage.

"You know what I mean," he said.

"But you're not going back to him with nothing to show," she said. "Not unless he's so old-fashioned he doesn't watch television."

"Whatever do you mean?" Aidan asked.

"I've gotten in touch with some friends of mine who work for the Discovery channel," she said. "They'll be getting in touch to interview you. I believe they intend to devote a large part of a one-hour feature to you. And your uncle, of course, as your patron."

"To me? Because I found a jar I don't bloody *have* anymore? What am I supposed to tell them, that I handed it over to the Russian *mafiya?* Good God, woman! You'll be the ruination of me."

"No, silly. They want to make you an archaeologist superstar for your part in busting a major international relic-forgery ring that branched into multinational murder. Even if the old gent isn't satisfied with your results, you'll still have your reputation made."

He stared at her. "Whatever am I supposed to tell them?"

"Not the truth, certainly." He stared at her for a moment. Then they both laughed.

They laughed, perhaps, louder and longer than was strictly necessary. Some Japanese tourists passing by glanced at them, then quickly away. It was impolite to stare at crazy people.

"What about you?" he asked. "Did you get what you were looking for?"

She thought for a moment. "Yes," she said. "I saw a very powerful relic into safe hands."

He grinned. "I pity the zealot who tries to pry the jar out of the fortified dacha of a former KGB muckety-muck," he said. "I do believe I'd pay to see them try."

She smiled. It was in part to cover her real thoughts. She had fulfilled her true role when he made the choice to turn away from the temptation of near ultimate power the jar may have offered. She knew Garin Braden was worried about what power he might derive from the relic. She'd worry about that another time. She felt certain Garin did not present an immediate threat.

By mutual accord they stood. He held out his hands.

"It's goodbye, I suppose," he said, "and not *au revoir*."

"It's better that way," she said. "We both know it is. What we came together to do, we've done."

"And a right lot of fun it was, too," he said, with a cockeyed leer and music-hall Cockney accent.

She smiled and kissed him. "Yes," she said quietly. "A lot of fun." She blinked her eyes rapidly to clear them of sudden moisture.

"Right, then," he said. "Goodbye, Annja love. And thanks for everything."

"Goodbye, Aidan," she said from low in her throat.

He turned and walked jauntily down the steps toward the vast and teeming city, leaving Annja standing alone in the shadow of Christ the Redeemer with his arms outstretched to the world.

James Axler
Outlanders

**An ancient Chinese emperor
stakes his own dark claim to Earth…**

HYDRA'S RING

A sacred pyramid in China is invaded by what appears to be a ruthless
Tong crime lord and his army. But a stunning artifact and a desperate
summons for the Cerberus exiles put the true nature of the looming battle
into horrifying perspective. Kane and his rebels must confront a four-
thousand-year-old emperor, an evil entity as powerful as any nightmare
now threatening humankind's future….

Available November 2006 wherever you buy books.

JAMES AXLER

DEATH LANDS®

Shatter Zone

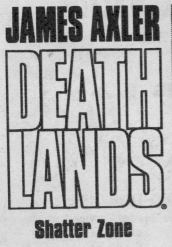

In this raw, brutal world ruled by the strongest and the most vicious, an unseen player is manipulating Ryan and his band, luring him across an unseen battle line drawn in the dust outside Tucson, Arizona. Here a local barony becomes the staging ground for a battle unlike any other, against a foe whose ties to preDark society present a new and incalculable threat to a fragile world. Ryan Cawdor is the only man living who stands between this adversary's glory...and the prize he seeks.

Available September 2006 wherever you buy books.

A drug lord attempts to exploit North America's appetite for oil... and cocaine

Don Pendleton's Mack Bolan

Ultimate Stakes

A double political kidnapping in Ecuador is cause for concern in the U.S. when the deed threatens a new and vital petroleum distribution agreement between the two countries. The question of who is behind the conspiracy and why turns grim when the trail leads to one of the biggest narcotraffickers in South America, a kingpin ruthlessly exploiting the demand for oil—and narcotics.

Available September 2006 wherever you buy books.

AleX Archer
THE SPIDER STONE

In the crumbling remains of a tunnel that was part of the
Underground Railroad, a mysterious artifact reveals one
of the darkest secrets of Africa's ancient past. Intrigued by
the strange, encrypted stone, archaeologist Annja Creed
opens a door to a world—and a legend—bound by a
fierce and terrible force. She is not alone in her pursuit
of the impossible, and her
odyssey deep into the
primeval jungles of Senegal
becomes a desperate race
to stop those eager to
unleash the virulence of
the Spider God....

**Available November 2006,
wherever books are sold.**

GOLD
EAGLE ®

GRA3